THE MIDNIGHT HUNTRESS

THE MIDNIGHT HUNTRESS

BOOK 1 IN THE CAPTRIX CHRONICLES

SHELBY MCCRALEY

ISBN-13: 978-1-7378242-0-6 (paperback)
            978-1-7378242-1-3 (Ebook)
ASIN: B09FFHYCPF (Kindle)

Edited by Whitney Morisello at Whitney's Book Works
Cover Design by Stone Ridge Books

www.shelbymccraley.com

First edition

CHAPTER ONE

She pulled the bloody, silver knife from her chest and grinned.

"Was that supposed to hurt?" The creature stood in front of me examining the useless blade.

Little spots of blood dribbled onto the floor from the knife. The witch creature stood in front of me with red blood oozing onto her white flour-sack dress. The blood spread through the fabric like a dye, giving it a sickly brown-red starburst like a morbid tie-dye. I wasn't sure where to place this dress. It didn't feel like it was a part of any particular time period, but it didn't belong here, either. Why did she choose this outfit? Maybe for the way it allowed her to move? But I also didn't know enough about witch creatures to judge their wardrobe choices. However, I knew her choice to wear white made this encounter even more terrifying.

Her thick, black, wavy hair was a tangled heap framing her pale face. Without a few more brushes, this witch would have a head of nothing but filthy knots she could never get through. I had a feeling her haircare wasn't a top priority by the way she was looking at me. Her black eyes stared deep into my soul as if they were judging its contents. Even though she had no visible pupils or irises, it still felt like she was smiling at me with hungry eyes. The fear I squashed down upon entering the warehouse to face her for my first hunt crept up to the surface.

"You have got to be kidding me," I groaned, realizing I had made a life-threatening mistake. This broad wasn't the witch creature I thought she was, and now, I was about to end up as some type of weird human soup in an abandoned warehouse for my mother to find.

"I mean, silver was a great choice if I was a Brujadan." Her grin grew larger, showing yellowed teeth, as she dangled the silver chef knife in front of her.

More blood dripped off the tip of the knife, making splatters on the concrete. As it dried on the floor, the red blood faded into a mucky brown color. It appeared so human, but I knew this creature in front of me was not human. She was a predator, and I was her prey, even though I was meant to be hunting her down.

Only four feet separated me from her, and I was running out of options. My brain rushed through my limited knowledge, trying to remember all the various witch creature derivatives I studied earlier today. There wasn't much to ponder since I had only skimmed the book entries until I decided what she was. I could have sworn she was a Brujadan. She had the cackle and a taste for babies according to the research I read out of my mother's hunt notes. This description fit what I saw in Mom's encyclopedia perfectly. Obviously, in this case, I was wrong.

Otherwise, when I stabbed her with a silver knife, she would have screamed from the metal burning her skin and died after a few more jabs. On my way to the warehouse, I imagined her death being like when Dorothy poured the bucket of water over the wicked witch and the witch dissolved into a puddle. Not like this.

She dropped the knife causing it to land on the floor with a loud clang and glide across the concrete further away from me. I backed up a few steps, patting myself down to see if I remembered any other types of weapons. She sauntered toward me, licking her lips, knowing this would be fun. Her confidence oozed out of her skin so much that it began to turn the ends of her black hair white.

Oh no. There was only one type of witch creature whose hair turned when they were preparing to slaughter their prey. I clearly remembered this from my quick skim. This broad was a Venefica, way older than a Brujadan and way harder to kill. The worst part was I barely read the entry before I moved on. I had no idea how to actually stop her.

"Enough playing with my food. I'll suck your soul out quickly, so it won't hurt," said the Venefica.

The Venefica ran at me, chanting Latin words I didn't understand. It seemed like the Latin words hung in the air, casting a spell. I looked around, trying to see if her words affected anything, but noticed nothing. Then, I saw my veins pulse beneath my skin and bubble. The heat in my entire body was overwhelming, and I felt like my blood was going to boil out of my skin. Red blotches appeared all over my arms, and I knew I had to be right. The pain was excruciating, and it was getting harder for me to focus. My blood leaked out of the pores on my body and began making its own bright crimson red droplets on the floor. I didn't have much time.

I reached into my pocket and found my copper 1943 dated penny my grandfather gave to me before he died. I kept it around for good luck, but it did me no favors tonight. I knew certain metals harmed witches in different ways, so I could only hope the Venefica was sensitive to copper since she didn't react to silver.

The Venefica continued advancing as more red blood leaked out of my facial pores, staining my medium-length blonde hair. My entire face felt sticky and tugged with an uncomfortable crust made from blood. It felt like I was doing a clay mask, but not as relaxing and a thousand times more painful. The Venefica finally reached me, her yellow teeth fully exposed with her grin. She opened her mouth and attempted to remove my soul.

I had no idea if this would work, but I had nothing else with me to try. I said a quick goodbye in my head to my penny and shoved it in her mouth, forcing her to swallow it. The Venefica chomped down on my wrist, causing more searing pain and rehydrating the small bit of dried blood. I pulled my hand out of her mouth and glanced down at the half-moon teeth marks that now lined my bloody right wrist. I got woozy as more blood forced its way out of my skin. The Venefica blurred in front of me.

"Really? A penny? That won't actually kill—" The Venefica fell to her knees, vomiting red bile with black swirls onto the concrete.

"It won't kill you, but it's a start," I said, feeling hot blood running down my arms. If I didn't stop her soon, I would pass out.

The Venefica vomited again, sending my lucky penny into the pile of blood and previously digested soul. I looked around the room for another weapon and saw nothing in my blurred vision except the outline of the useless silver knife. I decided that if I was going to die, I wanted to die fighting. She grabbed my ankle as I ran for the knife and yanked me back. I fell to the ground, hitting my head on the concrete. A throbbing pain invaded the side of my head, already forming a swollen bump. My blurry vision began turning red as my eyes filled with blood. I kicked my leg, attempting to break her grip, but she only clasped my ankle tighter. She dragged me toward her, smearing crimson on the concrete. I thrashed, still trying to break free, but she flipped me over and pinned me down. The Venefica made me look at her and take in her black, hungry eyes.

"I'm so sorry," I whispered to my ancestors and my mother, who weren't there. I prayed they would forgive me for my ignorance when I reached the other side, wherever that was.

She forced my jaw open and inhaled deeply through her mouth. I tried to not stare at the saliva strings coming off of the roof of her mouth, but I didn't want to watch her eyes anymore. The Venefica took another deep breath. This time, I felt something come alive inside myself and begin stirring, adding to my discomfort. Turning my bloody eyes away from her face, I watched a piece of my soul float out of my mouth into the air.

My soul took the form of a small rabbit, resembling the rabbit featured on my family crest. This rabbit wasn't opaque, like the way I had seen it my entire life on the crest. Instead, the rabbit was a transparent white that looked similar to a wisp. The soul rabbit peered around the room, panicked at its arrival. Its eyes bulged, recognizing it didn't belong out in the open. Then, it jumped through the air, trying to escape the warehouse, not knowing where it needed to run. Every time the rabbit tried to scamper away, a gravity coming from the Venefica's mouth pulled it to her.

When the translucent rabbit was close enough, the Venefica let go of my shoulders and bit at the air, devouring the rabbit as it struggled to hop away. I felt a deep pain in my heart, as if it had been stabbed and crumbled into a ball to ease it. Another wispy rabbit exited my mouth as I closed my eyes. My soul rabbit's terrified face as it endured its last moments was too much for me to bear. I couldn't watch her eat my entire soul.

The Venefica let out a chilling scream, and the rabbit ran back into my mouth. I gasped as the fragment resettled itself back into my soul. I forced open my sticky blood eyes and saw the witch laying on her side with a copper spear run through her, writhing in agony. Through blurred eyes, I noticed a tall woman with cropped blonde hair standing behind the witch. She wore a look of disapproval, as if she knew me. The Venefica stopped twitching, and the copper spear caused her to dissolve as I had originally imagined. She became a sizzling heap of dust next to her pile of vomit and rivers of my blood. As the dust settled, the blood stopped dripping out of my skin and the pain in my chest eased.

"Mom," I said in disbelief, realizing who the woman was.

Mom walked over to me, content with the Venefica's demise, and started pulling me up to my feet. I felt faint, and the entire concrete floor was slick, so it wasn't a simple task. Finally, after a moment of struggle, I stood up and commanded myself to stay upright. I observed the ground, realizing it looked similar to a murder scene. My smeared blood created an abstract painting on the floor I never wanted to see again. The useless knife remained in the corner, a few feet away from the witch's vomit. My stomach turned, as I considered adding to her pile.

My entire body felt bruised and exhausted. Wounds of defeat covered me, and I seemed to belong in a crypt rather than standing before my overachieving mother. She observed me, noting all the wounds that encompassed me. Most mothers would shower their daughters with kisses, thanking a higher power that their child was safe. Mine was immune to those feelings, as far as I could tell. All she saw when she looked at me was a blood-crusted disappointment.

"What are you doing here?" I asked.

Her arrival annoyed me, but my gratitude for being alive overshadowed it, even if I didn't reveal it. If she hadn't shown up, I would be soulless and probably dead. I had no idea how she realized I was here unless she followed me to the hunt. Maybe she went off of her Captrix intuition? All I knew was that she was here now and I would never recover from this mistake.

"Atalanta! The better question is why you're here," said Mom, not having my tone. I pissed her off, and I dreaded the consequences of living through this.

Mom let go of me and I fought to stay vertical, rather than laying back down. She reached down to grab the copper spear from the pile of witch dust. Mom pressed a button on the side of the spear, and it retracted into a smaller spear the length of her forearm. With the spear in one hand, she wrapped her arm around me to help me stagger out of the warehouse.

"Wait! My penny!" I turned around to see my penny shining bright even though puke covered it.

I let go of Mom and went back for my lucky penny. It took everything in me, but I reached down into the witch's vomit to pull out my penny. I wiped the black substance off it on my blood-soaked pants and slipped it back into my pocket. The penny wasn't really clean, but a dirty penny was better than having soul on it.

With Mom's help, I hobbled my way out of the warehouse. As I got into her truck, I winced as I realized my blood would stain the leather seats. It was another thing to add to the list of transgressions I committed this evening. I looked back at the warehouse one last time, remembering how I failed. I, Atalanta Capp, the daughter of the greatest witch creature huntress ever, had just failed my first witch hunt and almost died. Now, I would be trapped forever in my mother's house.

CHAPTER TWO

My bathwater resembled a murder scene when I exited the tub. It had taken me over an hour to scrub off all the dried blood that encompassed my entire body. Every time I loaded my rag up with antibacterial soap and scrubbed, it never seemed like I was getting any cleaner. I could never view my skin or bathwater the same again without seeing the crimson blood making a disgusting pool. My skin ached from expelling blood out of its pores and felt raw from my scrubbing. The goose egg at the side of my head continued to throb and requested an ice pack. I sighed. My body felt weaker than a healthy eighteen-year-old's should. I didn't know how much blood the witch had boiled out of my skin, but I knew it wasn't good.

After drying off, I walked to the medicine cabinet with my towel wrapped around me to find some ointment for my wrist. The plan was to treat it like a rabid dog bite rather than acknowledging the half moon, human teeth marks that remained. Before opening the cabinet, I caught a glimpse of myself in the cabinet's mirror and shuddered at my appearance.

I looked like a reanimated corpse. Popped blood vessels appeared in both of my blue eyes, creating a spotted display on the whites of my eyeballs. The ocean blue color of my irises seemed clouded, as if something had diluted the color. My dark under-eye circles and snow-white face completed the look. I shook my head, trying to bounce the image from my mind, and opened the cabinet. On the middle shelf, I found a triple antibiotic ointment and bandage wrap. I went to work treating my "rabid dog bite" and wrapped the injury.

My clothes laid in a pile in the corner of the bathroom, creating a stain on the tile, but I was too faint to worry about them. I would have to throw them away anyway, since there was no way those stains were coming out. It saddened me to lose those jeans, though. They were the only ones that looked good on my slender, athletic frame. They gave me the curves I desperately wanted. But I was built to kill witch creatures, not attract male attention, so those curves had eluded me my entire life. I exited the bathroom and put on some pajamas from my bedroom before descending the stairs to the kitchen.

The smell of steak overwhelmed me. Mom must have been making me her typical "you lost too much blood" meal of steak and orange juice. She created this meal for herself after her witch hunts to bring herself back up to strength. Most of the time she didn't need it. I couldn't remember the last time she came back injured like I was. Personally, I thought she enjoyed the meal instead of consuming it for the health benefits. It wasn't the worst meal to eat after almost dying, but the idea of red meat juices mixed with orange juice caused me to gag. A large meal also didn't sound appetizing to me, but it was something I needed to endure to get an ice pack for my head.

I walked down the stairs carefully, counting each step as I went. The last thing I wanted was a fall in my condition. When I reached the kitchen, my steak and orange juice was already waiting for me at the dinner table, along with a disapproving mother. I considered going to the freezer first to search for an ice pack, but angry brows and a tense jaw on Mom's face told me that was a bad idea.

"I can explain," I said, sliding my chair out from the table. I sat down and inhaled the scent of cooked steak.

"I sure hope so." Mom took the seat across from me, putting us on opposite sides of the table.

I recognized it was a power move, but it was still intimidating all the same. If there was one thing Artemis Capp knew how to do, it was how to scare people into submission. She sat there like a regal queen, looking down upon an unloyal subject. Mom pulled off her blonde pixie cut and slender frame with grace I didn't possess. Her blue eyes revealed the huntress beneath the grace. If you peered at them too long, you could see her calculated mind weigh the best options to kill creatures. Evidently, I stared too long because she raised her eyebrows, looked down at my plate, and back up to me.

Understanding the message, I cut the steak into tiny bites and took a sip of orange juice. I gave a sigh of relief when I saw she cooked the steak well-done so I wouldn't have to see or taste any more blood. I pushed a few bites around on my plate to postpone the inevitable. The orange juice was supposed to help with iron absorption from the steak, but the tangy flavor made my nose wrinkle. Mom cleared her throat and looked down at my plate. To my dismay, I took a few bites of the steak to satisfy her. The tension in the room thickened as I realized Mom was waiting for an explanation.

"I found your finished notes. I thought I would save you some time and take care of my first hunt," I said, mentally preparing myself for the yelling response to come.

To determine if they were ready to face the world alone, at eighteen, a rising Captrix would complete their first hunt. Before then, they were forced to live in their mother's home, hidden from the world, until they completed this hunt. It was customary for the first hunt of a Captrix to be observed so their mother could acknowledge they were ready to fight alone. The fact that I did it by myself and failed was a spit in the face of tradition. But I was so tired of being trapped in this house.

"Apparently, you didn't read them well, otherwise you wouldn't have brought this!" Mom slammed the chef knife on the table.

She had cleaned it after the hunt, but it still had a faint murky brown spot she hadn't gotten out. I struggled to remember when she went back to get it and drew a blank. I must have been really out of it when we got to the truck. My body tensed, but I tried to keep up a confident facade.

"I made a mistake." I gulped down a swallow of orange juice.

I drank more to lengthen the silence between us. The fewer words I said, the quicker this lecture could be over. My mind returned to the aching bump on my head, and I begged it to hold on a little longer. A few more gulps of orange juice passed until I almost finished the glass. I gazed at Mom's face, wishing she would say something. Her face was a mixture of fury and worry. I had seen these emotions on her separately before, but now that they were together, I wasn't sure how to react.

"A deadly one!" Mom banged her fist on the table, causing it to shake.

Her fury was winning over her worry. Every ounce of concern on her face drained, replaced only with anger. I slid my chair back a bit from the dinner table as my orange juice sloshed to create some distance. The closer I was to the table, the harder it would be for me to leave when I needed to. I took another bite of steak, trying to think of what to say.

"I just wanted to complete my first hunt," I said, breaking eye contact.

I couldn't look into her eyes anymore as they were seething in anger. I hadn't seen her this angry since I told her I didn't want to be a Captrix.

"If you were ready to complete your first hunt, then you would have realized that it was a Venefica, not a Brujadan quickly." Mom slid me her notes I didn't read closely before.

I moved my plate and glass to the side to see. There was still half a steak there, but I figured her proving I was inadequate was more important than my iron levels. I studied her note, searching for what I missed before.

Babies are dying in the hospital unexpectedly. Hearts are always missing. The rest of innards remain. No medical diagnosis can be given. Definitely a witch creature present.

I looked up from the note, still confused. Studying it again, I read the sentences for the third time. I came to the same conclusion as earlier.

"She should have been a Brujadan. She was eating babies. Venefica don't eat babies like that," I said.

I was desperate to be right, so I could go upstairs to get some rest. I gave up on getting an ice pack. My lack of energy was becoming a problem, and I was ready for this conversation to be over.

"The babies' innards were still there. Brujadan always eats all the organs. Venefica eat hearts when they suck your soul out of your body," said Mom matter-of-factly, like we were having an angry science lesson. "You would have known that if you actually cared about this."

"Well, I'm sorry I got it wrong. Big deal." I rolled my eyes and stood up from the table.

I didn't want to be a witch huntress and didn't care what witch ate hearts versus organs. I just wanted to be done with my first hunt, so I could live a life out of these four walls.

Mom's nostrils flared. I knew I said the wrong thing, but she didn't understand how closed off I was. I was never allowed to go outside and leave this house. Instead, I spent the last eighteen years stuck in this prison, forced to live by her rules. She expected me to rise and be the next greatest Captrix to ever live, but I didn't want that for myself. I wanted to be free to live my own life and make my own choices.

"It is a big freaking deal, Atalanta! That Venefica almost killed you! You were almost soulless!"

"Well, maybe if you spent the time teaching me different witch creatures before I was eighteen, I would know the difference. Or hell, if you would spend any time with me at all that didn't involve talking about witches, I would want this."

I needed to escape her now. If only I could distract her like a Venefica by putting a penny down her throat.

"I was out there saving innocents from these creatures! I'm sorry I didn't have time to baby you into doing your Captrix readings." Mom moved in front of me, blocking my path.

"I'm getting better. I just need to take more time to study. Then, I can do my hunt again."

"Exactly. Which is why you're not going on any other hunts until I think you're ready."

"But that's not fair! I'm eighteen. You can't keep me here anymore!"

"I can keep you here until I believe you are ready." Mom stepped to the side calmly, trying to simmer down her fury, and pointed upstairs. "Now, go get some rest."

I had waited for years to go on my first hunt for freedom, and I blew it for not reading enough.

"You're refusing me the right to my heritage, so you can keep me here." The anger left my body, turning into sadness. "It's a stupid tradition. I want to see the world. Maybe even go to college."

"Being a Captrix is a responsibility, not a choice. We don't leave our posts because we feel like it. People need us." Mom's lip quivered. "You understand nothing."

"I didn't choose this. Why am I not allowed to have a life?"

"Because you are a Captrix. Your life is to protect humanity from witch creatures." Mom motioned upstairs again. "Go to bed. We will ramp up your training tomorrow."

"I don't want to train any—"

"Atalanta, go to bed."

I wanted to fight her some more, but ever since I left the warehouse, I felt awful. Apart from the blood loss and random battle wounds, something inside me felt empty. I thought about the soul rabbit again and wondered if the Venefica did something to me. Blood I could regenerate, but it seemed like a piece of me was missing in a way steak could never fix.

I walked upstairs back to the bathroom to deal with my clothes before going to bed. The clothes remained in a gross heap in the corner of the bathroom. I reached down to check the pockets and the smell of iron and stomach acid smacked me in the face. Gagging, I continued my mission. I fiddled through the pocket to find my lucky penny. Vomit stained the penny, so I took it over to the sink to wash it clean.

This penny was too special to stay covered in blood and witch bile. My grandfather, who had lived with us, gave me it as a gift before he passed away. He knew that copper was a powerful tool against certain witch creatures from my grandmother, who was also a Captrix. When he found a 1943 penny, he kept the penny for me. The penny had a high concentration of copper at 95%. It was more useful than today's zinc pennies, which did nothing against witches. I cherished the penny, not only because it kept me safe, but because of the sentimentality.

After cleaning the penny, I rested it on the sink, so I could put my clothes in a black trash bag. Mom kept contractor trash bags under the sink for these instances. I held my breath, placed the clothes in the sack, and shoved them back in the bathroom's corner. Normally, Mom would have forced me to take it to the backyard and burn it, in order to make sure the surroundings were clear of Venefica magic. I was so physically exhausted that the idea of taking these clothes back down the stairs felt impossible. Mom hadn't mentioned it before she sent me up here, so I assumed the clothes would be fine until the morning.

I walked to my bedroom and plopped down on my bed. Reaching over the nightstand, I flicked on the string lights behind my bed to fill the room with a soft yellow glow. I knew I should go to bed, but I wanted to look at my secret scrapbook, so I would dream about something else other than the Venefica's black eyes.

I reached in the tiny gap between my bed and the nightstand and pulled out a purple hardcover scrapbook. When I bought the scrapbook, I tore out all the contents and filled it with beige cardstock coated in magazine clippings and photos from the internet. I ran my fingers over the decoupaged pictures, taking in the beautiful pictures of California. I loved looking at the beaches and seeing the thick redwood forests. If I tired of nature, I could flip the page and look at images of lofts in downtown Los Angeles. Everything seemed like it was a fantastical dream, and I wanted to be in it more than anything. I dreamed of being able to go to college and actually make friends. Hell, I would live in a van down by the river if that meant I could get out of New Meadows, Georgia.

A Capp family member hadn't escaped New Meadows in at least three generations as far as I knew. It wasn't normal for Captrix to have roots in a territory for too long. We were supposed to be nomads, but this area had been a hotspot for witch creatures since it was founded after the inquisition when the witches fled Europe.

We always ended up here, one way or another. The witch creatures liked it when all the elements were close together, and New Meadows was a perfect landscape for that. We had a swamp, plenty of trees, and the earth was hot, yet damp at the same time. Especially now, during the summer where humidity hung in the atmosphere like a steamy blanket.

I hated it. I wanted somewhere where I would have a temperature or season that wasn't never-ending wet heat. California might not be the answer, but I thought it may be a start. Flipping the page, I touched a picture of people gathering in an outdoor mall. It could be an opportunity to at least make friends. I turned to another page to view a collage of emo boys and girls holding hands with cliche love sayings on them. I smiled, trying to imagine what that would feel like. Maybe California would be a chance to find romance too.

In the very back of the scrapbook, I created a flap envelope. I opened the worn cardstock and pulled out the cash I had stuck in it. The random bills equaled two hundred dollars. I saved the ones, fives, and twenties from various birthdays and tucked them away into this envelope. The money was just enough to buy me one bus ticket to Los Angeles, and I was determined to purchase it after I successfully completed my hunt.

I inserted the money back into the pocket and closed the scrapbook. A giant yawn overtook my body, letting me know it was time to rest. I put the scrapbook back into its hiding place and turned off the string lights. Tomorrow had to be a better day.

CHAPTER THREE

The sound of water woke me from my deep sleep. Grogginess overwhelmed me at first, but annoyance quickly replaced it. I managed to avoid any nightmares, but now I didn't want to risk going back to sleep. The Venefica's grin and black eyes were drilled into my brain. Sometimes when I closed my eyes, I would see her there, opening her mouth to suck out my soul. It was only a matter of time before my subconscious betrayed me and I dreamed about her since my exhaustion had passed.

I looked toward the window and noticed the subtle glow of the streetlamp shining into my window. What time was it? Rolling away from the window, I felt around on my nightstand and picked up my cell phone. I clicked the power button to show the time. With squinted eyes, I saw three AM glowing on the screen. I had woken up right at the beginning of the witching hour. I thought it was a weird coincidence, but I set my phone back on the nightstand and contemplated going back to sleep.

A crash echoed through the house. The sound of water overran my ears again, and I realized the noise that woke me wasn't a sleepy hallucination. I threw off my covers, ignoring the chill bumps on my legs that appeared from wearing only an oversized t-shirt to bed. I grabbed the doorknob, ready to check and determine what was going on, but stepped backwards as the sound of water came closer.

The water sounded like crashing ocean waves as the noise came closer to my door. Something in my mind gave me the feeling of danger as if it already knew what was going on. I wondered if it was my Captrix instincts kicking in. I knew we all had them, and they were never wrong, but I had never felt or heard mine until now. If they were showing up now, it may be a good time to listen. I tiptoed to my accordion style slatted closet door and opened it. With my fingers in the slats, I pulled it closed. Through the slatted door, I saw a distorted view of my room. The noise grew louder until it stopped at my bedroom.

Water leaked under my bedroom door as the door creaked open. A woman with long turquoise hair walked into the room. Her feet were bare as far as I could tell, but were covered in tiny, shiny scales to her ankles. She was sort of beautiful as her scales shimmered in the light pouring through the window, but her beauty paled in comparison to the pit forming in my stomach. This feeling inside my head was terrified of her and the water being in this room. I kept trying to shut the sense off by pressing my hand against my temples, but it refused to be silenced.

She stepped in further, motioning with her hands, causing

water to rush through my entire room as if it was searching for something. I looked behind me for something to stand on before the water could touch my feet. I wasn't sure what I was dealing with, but I knew her water couldn't be great news for me based on my current mental response. Looking around the closet, I found a cardboard shoebox and reached for it. The water continued coming closer to my closet, seeking me. I had seconds before it would flow under the closet door and cover my feet.

I stepped onto the shoebox. This wouldn't hold me for long, so I tried to think light thoughts like it would somehow help. I distributed my weight onto the edges, trying to prevent the box from collapsing, and held my breath. Water flowed under the doorway and surrounded my shoebox. As if it sensed my presence, the water began forming small white-capped waves that licked the top of the box. I released panicked air. It was going to find me. Another tall wave crashed near my big toe, and I felt the mist coming off of it. I swore the water touched me, but I wasn't sure.

A crash sounded from the other side of the house and all the water drew away back to the scaled woman. My cardboard shoebox collapsed under my weight, and I balled my fists, preparing for the worst. As I was waiting for the scaled witch to burst into the closet, I heard stomping coming up the staircase.

"What are you doing in here?" The voice sounded female, but it cracked through every word.

When the voice arrived at my door, my room filled with warmth like a fire had been roaring in here for hours. The room became unbearably hot, and I stifled the urge to fan my face. I couldn't make out the new woman through the door.

All I saw was red.

"I'm looking for the girl," said the scaled witch, each word falling beautifully out of her mouth like a flowing stream.

"She's not important right now."

Had I ever been important? None of these witch creatures were supposed to know that I existed. To keep me safe was the entire purpose of being trapped in this house.

"She murdered one of us."

"That Venefica is none of our concern. Let's go," said the red blob that I assumed was a witch.

The distorted red body began walking out of the door. I didn't know how they thought I killed the Venefica. The news of my botched hunt couldn't have spread that fast.

"What about Artemis?" The figure of the scaled witch creature shifted and pulsed with energy. Drops of water dripped off her fingers as she stopped focusing on keeping her powers contained.

I flinched at the sound of my mother's name. I had to warn her about the witches in the house, but my phone was still on my nightstand. It was impossible to reach as long as the two witch creatures were in here. But I also had a feeling that would do nothing. Knowing my mom, she already realized they were here. If they made it to my bedroom, something was clearly wrong.

"I've secured her. Now let's go." The red witch exited the room, and the air cooled.

The scaled woman took one more look into the room and stared at my closet door. Then, she shook her head and followed behind the other woman. I heard them move down the stairs and exited my closet. Immediately, I grabbed my phone from the nightstand and ran toward my mother's bedroom to find her. Her bedroom door hung open, and black ash covered the entry. I entered the room to see everything singed, like a fire exploded and disappeared. How had a witch set this place on fire without a smoke detector going off? I was way out of my league.

"Mom," I whispered, already knowing she wasn't here, but I was holding on to what small shard of hope I had.

Her metal dagger sat on the floor, untainted by black ash. I couldn't believe she had left it. The dagger was special because the forger swirled the blade with six types of metal—gold, silver, copper, iron, tin, and lead. This made it incredibly lethal to all different types of witches, so Mom never left it behind. I picked the dagger up, held it in my hand, and examined it. No blood dotted the blade. She didn't use it against the creatures, or Mom didn't have the chance. I hunted for the sheath of the dagger, but I didn't find it. I assumed the sheath was still on Mom's side since she wore the dagger to bed sometimes in case of emergencies. Then, I scanned the room for any signs of a struggle, finding nothing but the black ash coating everything.

I tightened my grip on the knife, preparing to stab anything that caught me by surprise. The house was quiet now, but I had to find Mom before the witch creatures changed their minds and came back for me. I rushed down the stairs, and my eyes widened. They tore the kitchen and living room to shreds. Damp saltwater and burn marks covered the rooms, showing a visible struggle. I peered into the rooms, but Mom was nowhere to be found.

No, no, no. Panic rose in my chest. I fought the urge to run around the house screaming for her. I checked the kitchen, but saw nothing but flipped over furniture and burned spots.

Giving up, I walked into the damp living room and scanned it for signs of witch creatures or Mom. They broke nothing except for the side lamp laying on the floor. Surprisingly, everything in this room wasn't scorched, just soaked.

The bookcase in the living room was soaking wet, like a gigantic ocean wave hit it. The witches failed to get into Mom's study. This explained why she left her dagger behind in her bedroom. You needed it to pry open the secret bookcase door to enter the study. Nothing else would work because there was a special place between the bookcase and the wall that the dagger fit into. She didn't want them to get inside. How did the witches know the entrance to the study was there? My mind rolled with unanswered questions.

A truck door slammed outside, separating me from my thoughts. I ran to the window and stared outside. In the back of our family truck, wrapped in chains with a mouth gag on, was my mother. She wore her pajamas, but fire singed the fabric on the edges. On her leg, I saw the missing holster halfway hanging off like someone had pulled it. Her hair looked soggy, but she was still thrashing in the truck bed, trying to free herself. Mom glanced at the window and found my eyes. Before I made a plan to go save her, a giant ball of fire burst through the window. I ducked and the fireball narrowly missed my head. It landed in the corner of the room and began burning even though everything was damp. There shouldn't have been anything to catch fire, but the inferno roared on anyway, burning up the walls and spreading across the floor.

I heard the truck door slam again and tires screeched away on the pavement.

"You need to leave," said a clear voice in my mind.

My eyes bulged out of my head at the sound of my intuition. I wasn't sure what it was meant to sound like, but mine sounded like a mixture of a robot and my grandmother's voice. Her voice was soothing and melodic with a cheery ring to it. Based on her career as a huntress, it made no sense for her to have such a pleasant voice. However, in my mind, it now sounded mechanical, taking away the cheer I grew up with.

I didn't like it, but I didn't know how to force it to change, either. This was all becoming too much. My intuition coming in, my mother being kidnapped, witches trying to kill me. I could feel a mental breakdown coming on as my intuition tried to tell me what to do, but I couldn't listen to what it had to say with all the noise in my mind.

The fire spread from the room's corner into a perfect trail toward me. Smoke filled my lungs as the fire circled around, trying to trap me. Coughing, I ran to the bookshelf and slipped the dagger into the special place and pried. The flames touched my ankles, making me wince in pain. I pried at the door again, but it wouldn't come loose. The flames climbed up my legs, and I screamed in agony. Adrenaline took over my body, and I used all my strength to pry at the door again. Finally, it popped open as the flames reached the tail of my oversized t-shirt.

I ran into the concrete hallway and pulled the bookcase closed behind me. An ordinary fire wouldn't be able to go past the secret door. This entire study was witch proof, including fire prevention, but I had a feeling this wasn't a typical fire since it came sailing through the living room window. I limped down the hall with my burned legs to the study and patted out the small flame, trying to ignite on my t-shirt. I had to find the book and get out of here.

Since the Roman empire, when Captrixes became necessary to control witch activity, Captrixes have kept a hand-written encyclopedia that detailed every witch creature they came across. Adding to the book was the job of every Captrix generation. It was their duty to detail new species and mixed-creatures, but to also add in new tactics on hunting them. I couldn't leave the house without this book. Even if I didn't want to partake in adding to it, it would be a disservice to all of my ancestors to let all of their hard work go to waste. It had to be in here since the witches didn't make it into the study before escaping.

Tons of books sat in bookcases that lined the walls of the office. Colored spines and bound leather peeked out the most with embossed titles about the written history of the famous Captrixes, individual guidebooks on each witch creature, and potion books to help Captrixes prep their weapons for battle. This was all meant to be mine if I chose this lifestyle, and now I had to leave behind this wealth of knowledge. Finding the encyclopedia was all that mattered at this point.

I limped over to Mom's desk where all of her recent hunt notes laid waiting, ready for filing or transcription into the appropriate book. Sitting in the middle of the desk was the brown leather encyclopedia, tied shut with a cord for protection. On top of the encyclopedia was a note written in Mom's sloppy handwriting, as if she didn't have enough time to make it look elegant. I read the note and tried not to dwell on the "how did she know to write this" questions that filled my mind.

Put the book in the backpack and find Bridgette. 250 BeeBrush Drive.

I had no idea who Bridgette was or where BeeBrush Drive was, but I felt like I had no other choice if my mom wanted me to do this. She hadn't told me this was coming, but she evidently set up a contingency plan. It was my responsibility to follow it if I wanted to have any chance to find her. I tried to weigh my options, but the sound of crackling fire echoed in the hallway.

The warmth of the growing fire came to me from the hallway. The flames broke through the bookcase door, and it was following me as if there wasn't an entire house to burn instead. Smoke filled the ceiling, so I knew it was time to go. I searched around the desk until I found the black backpack left for me. Inside there was water, a few snacks, and pain medicine. I shoved the encyclopedia and dagger into the main compartment and placed my cell phone in the front pocket. Clutching the note in my hand, I put the bag on my back.

The fire roared, building a wall at the opening of the study. There was no way I was going to be able to go back into the main house. I hobbled my way to the exit door in the back of the study and opened my escape. Then, I stepped into the night air and shut the door behind me as the siren of a firetruck got closer to the house. Staggering my way through the backyard, I found the back street, so I could avoid the first responders before they saw me. I turned around to look at the house one more time, only to regret it. Orange and yellow-white flames covered the entire structure. All of my bus ticket money was being burnt up now, along with the tactile memories of my grandparents and my mother. I now had nowhere else to go and no idea where Mom was. So, with a black backpack, wearing an oversized t-shirt and burnt legs, I began my journey to BeeBrush Drive to find the mysterious Bridgette.

CHAPTER FOUR

I LIMPED DOWN THE street for thirty minutes before my phone GPS found BeeBrush Drive. As I walked down the sidewalks, I felt naked in the evening light. It was pitch-black dark except when I ran across a streetlight. For the first time in my life, I didn't want to be seen, yet I was visible, and not for the right reason. I was a teenager with severe burns and half of her butt hanging out of a t-shirt. How would I explain my wounds or outfit choice? Even though no one crossed my path, I still couldn't shake the devastating thought of being hunted. I constantly looked over my shoulder, expecting some sort of witch creature to be there. They released me into the world with little protection and absolutely no idea what I was doing. It only made sense for them to take advantage of me while I was vulnerable.

A dirt road was not what I was picturing when I found BeeBrush Drive, but I wasn't sure what I was expecting. Then again, I didn't have much of a reference since I had never been on this side of town. Goosebumps covered my body along with the throbbing of my legs, so the idea of hobbling down a dirt road with no end in sight didn't appeal to me. My burns had blistered, and the exhaustion of losing blood and being severely burned took its toll. I had never had so many attempts on my life, but these witches tried to make up for lost time.

These years of hiding kept me safe from personal witch attacks, but also kept me from being captured and used against Mom. The fact Mom had been kidnapped instead of me was irony not wasted. It seemed ridiculous. Of course, I worried, but the best Captrix known to be alive was in the back of a vehicle to who knew where. It should have been me inside that truck according to everything I learned. Not her.

I hobbled down the dirt road for another ten minutes, and the pain along with the emotions became too much. I wanted to give up and throw myself into the ditch on the side. Chanting some witch hating language would cause at least one of them to find me. Especially since I was the new V.I.P. it seemed. It would be over quickly. Maybe a Venefica would come and suck out the rest of my soul, so I could die in peace. Burning would suck, but that would be okay too. At this moment, I just wanted to die or for things to return to what they were before my hunt.

Tears crowded my eyes and escaped down my face. Mom was depending on me, though. I'm not sure why because I barely knew any witch creature lore. I had proven myself incompetent on my first hunt. Not to mention, she anticipated a crazy witch creature plot to come to the house, since she left me the dagger and note, but didn't tell me. To add to my list of inadequacies, I never did my reading out of spite, figuring I would have sand between my toes by now, but also because the threat of witch creatures seemed too far away. I was a useless Captrix, and I didn't even want to be one. I laughed maniacally through my tears at how ridiculous this whole situation seemed.

In the middle of my mental breakdown, a gold glitter-like substance rained down from the trees on the right side of the road. The glitter was so beautiful that I stood there mesmerized until the last flake fell to the ground. I wiped the tears off my face and turned to study an ornate sign reading 250 BeeBrush Drive. Behind the sign was a short stone path leading to a cottage. The path had green grass peeking through the cobblestones. A gravel driveway was to the left of the cottage, but the ending of it faded into the trees. I looked down the road again to see if I could find the end of a driveway, but it was too dark. I glanced back at the cottage and took in its quaint appearance.

It was a small cottage with a light grey stone on the outside and a brown-colored roof. Accenting the windows were brown wooden shutters with flower boxes underneath them. If I didn't know any better, I would have thought that Snow White lived here with the seven dwarfs. It was lovely and unlike anything I had ever seen. I needed to learn what the inside looked like.

I dismissed the glitter as a side-effect of my mental breakdown and ambled down the cobblestone path. Glancing down at my phone, I read the time. Five AM. I hoped I wouldn't be disturbing the Bridgette written on the note, but I didn't see any other way around it. I couldn't wait outside for the time to become appropriate. It amazed me I hadn't been spotted thus far. I reached the door, drew in a deep breath, and gave a soft knock.

Immediately, I picked up movement within the cottage. A light came on inside and shone a sliver of white onto the grass beside me. I could make out more flowers, but some plants in the flower beds appeared to be cooking herbs as well. It interested me that they weren't contained in a particular garden. They grew and roamed as they pleased. I heard footsteps inside the cottage and returned my focus to the door. It only took a few seconds for the brown wooden door to crack open. Barely half of a face revealed itself in the dark.

"Can I help you," said the female voice behind the door. Her voice was as smooth as honey, but concerned. It had a tinge of sleepiness, and she was stifling a yawn.

"Umm, my mom left me a note to find Bridgette. She wrote this address under her name," I said.

She reached her hand through the opening, not allowing the door to crack anymore. Her fingers were long, and her nails were a natural almond shape, left bare. I handed her Mom's note, and the hand slipped back behind the door. A moment passed while I assumed she scanned the note.

"Artemis," she whispered, clutching the note harder. The paper crinkled in her hand.

"My mom." Relief flooded my body. She knew who Mom was.

"And you are?"

My excitement drained. I remembered no one would recognize me. This would actually be one of the first people I had met apart from my mom and grandparents, unless you counted random cashiers at the shoppes in town.

"Atalanta."

"Bridgette."

Bridgette opened the door, and I got a good look at her in the hallway light. She was taller than me. I estimated around 5'7 and lanky, since I was around 5'5. Bridgette's long wavy brown hair was lined with a few grey strands that glimmered in the light. Her eyes were brown pools of honey with small silver flecks in them. They were unlike anything I had ever seen. Beautiful, even though sleep crust crowded in the corners. The beginning of lines on her pale forehead and around the eyes creased her face, but her glowy skin overshadowed them. If my skin looked like that, I would never want to cover it in the long-sleeved blue satin pajama set she was wearing. Based on her appearance, I assumed Bridgette was close to Mom's age, early forties. I wondered how long they had known each other. Mom had never spoken about her before.

Bridgette gasped when she took in my appearance. I realized how awful I must appear and immediately crossed my arms in front of my chest. Her eyes looked me up and down in shock. I was so embarrassed I probably could have died right there. I stared at my feet, not wanting to make any more eye contact, but avoiding eye contact forced me to look at my legs, which also looked horrific. Blisters and pus pockets covered my aching legs. A few of the blisters had busted when I was walking here and grew more painful. I was on a road straight to an infection if I didn't get those treated. Looking back at Bridgette, I tried to hold back tears. I wanted to appear strong, but I felt so weak.

Bridgette looked at me with pity that I wasn't sure that

I wanted, but needed. Her nervous demeanor dissolved into caring and motherly. She gave me a soft smile that I took as everything would be okay. In her presence, I encountered calm, something that eluded me the past few hours.

"Let's see if I can fix you up." Bridgette motioned me to follow her down the hallway.

She led me to her living room and forced me to sit on a huge brown leather couch while she went to gather supplies. I laid my backpack on the ground, sank into the comfy sofa, and took the room in. The room was smaller than my living room at home, but it made up for it with coziness. All the furniture was dark wood with little knick-knacks and books lining the built-ins around the stone fireplace. A large window sat to one side of the den where a leather recliner faced the outdoors. A basket next to the recliner held quilting fabric, knitting needles, yarn, and various embroidery hoops. There wasn't a TV anywhere, but it seemed Bridgette had plenty of crafts to keep her occupied. I assumed she lived alone without many guests.

I found a homemade quilt at the end of the leather couch and pulled it close to me. I intended to cover my legs with it to hide their ugliness, but once the fabric touched my blisters, I winced. These burns were going to make grotesque scars. I feared I would never look the same again.

Bridgette returned with gauze in hand and a homemade salve in a mason jar. The purple color was unlike any other salve I have ever seen. Little pieces of flowers and herbs swirled throughout the purple balm. I thought it'd make a lovely candle, but something to put on burn wounds? I wasn't really sure.

"What is in the jar," I said. The strange color and texture

made me nervous, but my new intuition wasn't alarmed.

"It's a homemade burn salve. Some different herbs mixed with butters and aloe vera. The butters and aloe vera will keep everything moist, so you don't dry out while the herbs will make sure you don't get an infection," said Bridgette.

Bridgette unscrewed the lid of the purple salve and a woodsy floral scent smacked me in the face. There was nothing medicinal about this salve at all. I had no hope that this concoction was going to help my burnt legs or prevent scarring. If I didn't end up with an infection from it, I would be lucky. Bridgette seemed confident about it, though, and I didn't want to hurt her feelings after her kindness to me.

"Now I'm warning you, this is going to hurt. Just try to remain as still as possible." Bridgette scooped the salve onto her fingers. It shined in the low living room light.

I raised my eyebrows. A herbal salve was going to hurt me? I shrugged it off and peered around the room, not paying attention. When she touched me with the balm, I screamed. Thousands of tiny needles ripped my skin apart on top of the burns. The cooling sensation from the aloe vera didn't make it any better. My legs twitched away from Bridgette's hands, but she grabbed them to hold them steady.

"I'm so sorry. I promise it will be better in the morning." Sadness filled her eyes like she hated putting me in such pain.

I struggled to believe a woman I barely knew was invested in my well-being, even though she just met me. It touched me. I started to realize why Mom sent me here, but questions plagued my mind. Why did Mom never tell me about Bridgette? Why would she want to keep such a kind woman from me?

Bridgette continued spreading the salve on my legs, and I endured the pain. When she finished distributing the salve, she wrapped my legs tightly in gauze. I kicked my legs to determine if I could still move them. The wound dressing constricted my legs, but moving my knees was still possible. I tried not to compare myself to a mummy, but the longer I glanced at the bandages, the more I felt like one. However, I preferred being a mummy over having this gauze peel off before it needed to.

"I'll see if I have some pajamas you can wear. I don't have a spare bedroom, so you'll need to sleep on the couch," said Bridgette.

I patted the leather sofa and delighted in the fact it was soft. It was long, so I figured I would fit on it perfectly. This option beat sleeping on the street, so I nodded. Then, I realized how stupid I was. Focusing on something other than my leg burns, I remembered the reason I had come here.

"Wait, I need to tell you about Mom," I said.

"It can wait until after you've had some rest." Concerned passed over Bridgette's face, but melted away like she had her own suspicion about what happened.

"But you don't understand. Witches kidnapped her. Our house is burning to the ground!"

"I know." Bridgette placed her hand over mine. "She wouldn't have sent you here unless something bad happened."

It was meant to be a calming gesture, but being calm right now was insane.

"We have to do something." My voice came out frantic, and I snatched my hand away.

"Atalanta, what time is it?"

The motherly tone Bridgette let out caught me off guard. She sounded like my mom during my last lecture.

"It's after five."

"Exactly. Witch creatures don't move in the daylight very often. The sun is rising. What do you want us to do?" Bridgette gave me a serious look, waiting on my response, but it seemed like nothing I said would be right.

"I don't know," I said.

"The best thing we can do for Artemis right now is to get some rest and to take care of you. We can work out saving details in a few hours. Okay?"

I felt she wouldn't take no for an answer, so I stayed silent. Bridgette took this as her cue to get up.

She rose from the couch and went to her bedroom. From the room, she returned with a cotton tank top and pajama pant set with a black cat and moon pattern on them and an unopened packet of underwear. I decided not to question why she had underwear laying around like this and took the clothing with no protest. Bridgette pointed me toward her small bathroom, so I could change. It took a minute to change my clothes because I was avoiding messing up the gauze and my legs felt sore. Getting out of my old ratty t-shirt made me appear more human and less mummy, since I didn't realize how strong the smell of smoke and sweat had become until it was off of my body. I looked around the room for a black trash bag to put my clothes in like home, but I didn't find one. I thought about calling out to Bridgette and asking, but I threw the t-shirt and my underwear in the trash can next to the toilet. Clasping the leftover underwear in their plastic package, I brought the rest of the intimates back with me to put into my backpack.

When I returned to the living room, Bridgette laid me out a pillow and fixed the quilt into a small bed. She also left me a medium-sized decorative box that was empty for my things. I decided to put the rest of the clean underwear in this box, so it wouldn't be so close to the encyclopedia in my backpack. Something about sitting underwear on top of it seemed dishonorable.

It had to be close to six AM, but I was too exhausted to care about sleeping through the morning. I hoped wherever Mom was that she was okay until I could get to her. Stretching the quilt delicately over my legs, I sank into the couch. Under the quilt, the final wave of sleep hit me, and I fell into a deep sleep.

CHAPTER FIVE

Instead of water, this time, I woke to blinding sunshine coming through the window in the cottage living room. I squinted at the light coming in as my eyes attempted to adjust to the new light. After falling asleep, I sank into a deep, dreamless sleep. My exhaustion once again saved me from any nightmares. There was a slight pain in my back from sleeping on the couch, but it was nothing I couldn't rub out in a moment. I blinked my eyes a few times until I could stand the light and looked out the window. The sun was high, so I estimated it had to be early afternoon. I pulled my cell phone out of my backpack and clicked the power button to power the screen, but it remained black. My phone was now useless without the charger from my bedroom—the one I didn't have anymore. All the problems that led me to Bridgette's cottage came rushing back in.

My mother. Was she alive? Was she dead? Where was she sleeping? Had the witches taken her soul? The thoughts poured into my mind like a burst pipe. I tried to take deep breaths, but the questions overwhelmed me. My heartbeat quickened, and I knew if I didn't make myself calm down, I would have a panic attack. I searched my mind through all the questions for a solution.

My grandpa told me once that Captrixes always knew when someone close to them died. He said grandma claimed it had something to do with the deep intuition we possessed. Grandma told him we could ask our intuition questions, but I had never tried to ask my intuition anything. Now, with it coming in full force, I hoped I could use it for something useful other than an alarm system. I relied on general feelings since my intuition started making itself known, but now, if ever, was the perfect time to ask my intuition questions. I wasn't sure if I needed to have a ceremony or what, so I decided to take a simple approach.

I leaned up on the couch and crossed my legs to enter a meditative stance. I flipped my palms up to accept information and closed my eyes. Before now, my intuition hadn't required such pomp and circumstance, but this time, I wanted to control it. If I was forced to have an all-knowing voice in my head, I desired it to work with me, not against me. I sat in silence for a moment, staring into a black abyss until I got the courage to ask.

Is Mom alive, I thought.

I continued to sit in the quiet, staring into the black. It felt like hours had passed with no response. Was I doing this right? I begged my intuition for an answer. Ages passed until I heard the voice in my head.

"*Yes*," whispered my intuition.

The clang of china in the kitchen scared me and broke my trance. My eyes snapped open, and I found myself in awe. I did something where my intuition responded like I meant it to. Maybe I was getting the hang of it after all. Another clang sounded from the kitchen, so I stood up to follow the sound.

I stumbled along the hallway, trying to keep my gauze wrap secure. Luckily, Bridgette's cottage was small, so it didn't take me long to find my destination. When I reached the kitchen, Bridgette sizzled bacon on a white stove. The bacon smelled delightful, and my stomach rumbled in response. I'd ignored my hunger until now, but with fresh bacon cooking on the stove, there was no denying it anymore. Bridgette laid bread, lettuce, and tomatoes on the counter. I watched her work for a moment in the doorway and wondered why she wore long sleeves in the Georgia heat. She was wearing a thin, long sleeve navy t-shirt tucked into a long cream-colored maxi skirt. It looked suffocating to me, even though I wore long pajama pants.

I took a seat at the round wooden table in one of the four chairs. The kitchen was smaller than the living room, but somehow the window over the sink made it feel spacious. Bridgette had herb bunches hanging in the window along with some rainbow sun catchers. The sun catchers made beautiful rainbow designs on the plank flooring. On the opposite side of the kitchen, away from the appliances, a large open shelving unit sat full of potted herbs, salves, and liquids in vials. It was like Bridgette had her own apothecary shop in her kitchen.

Bridgette continued cooking at the stove and flipped the bacon when it was perfectly cooked—not too crunchy, but also not too chewy. Her long sleeve shirt pulled up on the sleeves as she removed the bacon from the pan, and I could see her forearms. They seemed to sparkle in the light like she covered them in fine glitter. I stared at them for a moment longer, but figured it was light coming off of the sun catcher, making her skin shine.

"Oh, good. You're awake," said Bridgette, turning to face me. "Is BLTs okay?"

I nodded in reply. She sliced the tomato into thick slices. Reaching across the counter, she opened the bread and took out a few slices, then she spread something white onto the bread that I guessed was mayonnaise.

"You need to check your gauze to see if it needs to be changed." Bridgette looked over her shoulder at me.

I raised my eyebrows at her. There was no way with how bad my burns were that the gauze would be ready to be changed. My burns were second-degree burns for crying out loud. A purple salve couldn't heal them in a few hours. Bridgette hadn't been wrong yet and helped me the night before, so I felt like I owed it to her to follow her medical advice. I unwrapped the gauze with no pain at all. Miraculously, when I finished unwrapping the bandages, my legs had healed except for a few small scars. Both legs looked moisturized and healthy, as if I had just shaved them and applied a thick lotion. This was impossible. I looked at Bridgette with my jaw dropped. My eyes kept glancing from my legs to her.

"I was afraid they wouldn't heal up this soon. They were pretty nasty burns," Bridgette said, amazed at her own skill.

"But how?" I said, completely perplexed.

Bridgette placed a BLT in front of me and sat in the chair across from me. She ate bites of her sandwich, ignoring my question.

I ate a few bites of my sandwich, wondering if Bridgette was going to ask me about what happened last night. I didn't know if she wasn't curious or if she was being gentle with my feelings. I wondered if she grasped everything about Captrixes or if she didn't realize the gravity of this situation. I didn't understand how she could be so calm with her friend kidnapped by witch creatures. Bridgette ate half of her sandwich and took a deep breath.

"Okay. Start from the beginning. What happened yesterday?" Bridgette reached for a notebook and pen on the far side of the table and opened a fresh page to take notes.

"How much do you really know about Captrixes?"

"Everything. I thought that was obvious."

"I just don't understand how you can be so calm about this," I set down the last fourth of my sandwich on the plate.

"It's a part of my nature. I have to stay calm. Please tell me what happened yesterday."

I thought Bridgette was sweet and kind. She had been a blessing to me, but the longer I stayed with her, the more mysterious she became.

"I had my first hunt yesterday. I guessed I was hunting a Brujadan, but it turned out to be a Venefica." I searched for disappointment in her eyes.

Bridgette raised her brows at me as if she was surprised that I mixed those two creatures up. I wondered if it disappointed her that Artemis's daughter would make such a dumb mistake. She remained silent and nodded at me to continue.

"I obviously wasn't prepared, so Mom came in at the last minute and saved me." I wasn't ready to mention the fact that my soul left my body and I almost died.

Bridgette scribbled down a few words in her notebook. She chewed on the edge of the pen clip, deep in thought.

"Did the Venefica curse you in any way?" Bridgette looked up from her notepad.

"Some sort of blood spell, maybe? I'm new at this, so I don't recognize a lot of Latin like I should. But whatever she said made my blood boil out of my skin," I said, trying not to conjure the image of blood coming out of my pores again.

Bridgette's eyes widened. Whatever the Venefica did to me must have been a nasty curse. She wrote down a few more notes.

"After that, Mom and I went home. We had dinner and went to bed. Around three AM, a strange noise woke me up."

I relayed the information about the sea witch creature searching for me in my bedroom and the red witch creature telling her to leave me for another time.

"By the time I got downstairs, I saw they had Mom tied up in the truck. She was fighting them. But when the red witch caught me looking, she started the fire that burned my legs."

I continued the story about my journey to BeeBrush Drive to find Bridgette and concluded the events of last night. Bridgette reread her notes and tried to make sense of it all. She reminded me of how Mom would always pour over her notes when she was hunting. Definitely a skill I needed to pick up on if I was going to moonlight as a Captrix until I got Mom back.

"That's not a normal bunch of witch creatures to be working together." Bridgette chewed on the end of her pen again.

"What makes you think the Venefica was involved?"

"They wanted to avenge her, one. Second, a Mare and

Ignis don't work together normally. They are opposite elements. But, also, the curse could have allowed them to track you."

I mulled the terms Mare and Ignis around in my mind. These terms must be the official names of the witches I saw in the house. I tried to remember seeing them in the encyclopedia, but nothing came to me.

"What did you do with your clothes that night," said Bridgette.

"I put them in a trash bag to burn the next day."

"Bingo. They could track the Venefica's magic through your clothes."

"That still doesn't explain why they wanted Mom, rather than kill her."

"I'm not sure about that one, either. Nothing about this makes sense."

Bridgette closed her notebook and looked lost in thought. She rose from the table and cleared the lunch plates. It was obvious we wouldn't be finishing our sandwiches.

I wondered how Bridgette knew so much about witch creatures. She didn't look like any Captrix I had ever seen in the books. We all tended to have straight blonde hair and blue eyes. It was a part of the whole family lineage thing.

"Are you a Captrix too?"

"Not exactly," said Bridgette.

As soon as the words left her mouth, Bridgette knocked a glass off of the counter. Instead of it crashing on the floor, she held her hands out and the glass suspended in the air. Her eyes widened as she realized what she revealed.

"No, no, no. You're a witch."

I began looking for exit points. It all made sense now. The glitter before I found the house must have been a hidden protection spell. The special burn salve that magically cured my legs in six hours. The unlimited witch knowledge. The fact that her arms glittered in the sunlight. Mom wouldn't lead me here. She would never put me in danger with a witch creature. It must have been a trap set by one of last night's witch creatures to capture me. The line of thinking made little sense, but I was so confused.

I stood up from my chair and broke out into a run. I asked my intuition for answers, but it only kept saying 'safe.' This made no sense to me, either, unless it was referring to the book I left in the living room. I knew now that I had to make it to the living room to grab my bag before I could leave. The encyclopedia couldn't be left for a witch creature to steal. I ran to the living room and reached for my backpack.

Bridgette let the glass crash and chased after me.

CHAPTER SIX

"W‍ait, I'm not like that!" Bridgette continued closing the gap on my head start.

I found my backpack next to the couch and unzipped it, pulling out my dagger. Zipping it back up, I threw it on, holding the weight of the encyclopedia on my shoulders. I heard Bridgette advancing to the living room, so I knew I had to make my big break now, or she would trap me. I raced to the front door, but she was already there, blocking me from leaving.

Bridgette held her hands out, motioning me to stop. I tightened my grip on the dagger, feeling terrible that I would have to kill someone that had been so kind to me. But Bridgette was a witch creature, no matter how she acted. I already experienced what they could do to me, and I didn't want to be the victim this time.

"Please, Atalanta. I'm not going to hurt you," said Bridgette.

"I don't know what you are, but I promise this dagger will kill you." I brought the dagger up higher on my body, preparing to attack.

Bridgette took a step toward me, and I stabbed the dagger at her. She dodged it and plastered herself to the door. In her quick movement, a piece of floral artwork hanging on the wall crashed to the floor, breaking the frame. The crash made me jump back a little, but I held the dagger steady. Bridgette glanced down at the broken frame and looked back at me. She continued to hold her hand out in a stopping motion and took a deep breath.

"Listen to me. I'm not like them. I'm a Domum. A house witch."

"I don't even know what that is."

I stabbed at Bridgette again, but she blocked it with her hand. A slight cut, the size of a paper cut, began bleeding on her palm. A small line of smoke erupted from the tiny cut, and Bridgette screamed in pain. She grunted, pressing a thumb from her other hand on top of it. Across her arms and face, a sheen of glitter sparkled on her skin like a disco ball. It was incredibly beautiful, but scared me to the core. I had no idea what I was dealing with.

"Your mother wouldn't have sent you here if she didn't trust me." Bridgette winced in pain.

"I don't know anything about who she trusted or didn't trust. I do know that in the past twenty-four hours three witch creatures tried to kill me."

"I know that. But I swear, I'm not trying to hurt you."

"Prove it then." I held the dagger, ready to strike again.

Even through her pain, Bridgette remained miraculously calm. If she really wanted to hurt me, wouldn't her true nature come out by now? This is one of those times I wished my intuition would give me a sign, but so far it had been silent.

"Look in the book," said Bridgette.

"Why? So, you can steal it?"

I was going to give her a speech about how I wasn't a fool, but my intuition finally joined the party.

"*Listen*," said my intuition. I was getting used to the mechanical tone of my grandma, but I still didn't enjoy it.

I turned my head to the side like a dog listening to its master. Out of all the things it could have said, my intuition came up with listen. Bridgette didn't seem surprised at my expression change. She was used to this happening.

She continued pressing her thumb tightly against the cut. Finally, Bridgette's palm stopped smoking. She removed her thumb gingerly, and I saw a huge red welt over the small paper cut. I looked down at the dagger, amazed at what it had done with a small cut.

"Look Domum up in the book. Please," said Bridgette.

"Stay here." I lowered the dagger back to my side.

I walked to the living room alone and peeked behind to make sure Bridgette didn't follow. She remained at the door, guarding it and picking up the pieces of the broken frame. I sat my backpack on the couch and the dagger right next to my leg in case I needed to grab it again. I reached for the witch creature encyclopedia inside of my backpack and set it on the coffee table. Untying the leather strap on the book, I opened up crinkled yellow pages. I only looked in here once yesterday, but I had an idea of how it worked.

In the encyclopedia, Captrixes listed all the witch creatures in alphabetical order. On each page, the header was the Latin name of a witch creature written in a huge cursive script. Below the witch's title, they wrote her plain name. Along with the witch's name and title, they listed characteristics, powers, and weaknesses. It was like looking at lab entries by scientists of natural creatures. If a witch creature was particularly hard to kill, a Captrix would write their hunt experience, hoping it would help another not make similar mistakes. I flipped to the Domum page and began to read.

Domum

A House Witch

Domums are docile witch creatures that have more in common with humans than any other witch creature. Generally, a Domum is more human than witch. They take part in the day-to-day life like humans, but know a few spells to help them along their way. Domums specialize in the healing arts and protecting others. They are also extremely talented with gardening. So far, Captrixes have not had any issues with Domums unless they are working with other witches.

You can recognize a Domum by seeing a light glitter sheen on their skin. Apart from their skill in potions, Domums possess the power of telekensis. They do not

*use this power often because bad transformations
tend to happen.*

I expected there to be more about their transformation, but the initial entry stopped there. I didn't understand why the writer would make someone search in a different book when they could write about it right there. My annoyance faded when I looked further down the page. At the bottom of the page, a passage was written in the same fancy script Mom used to write in the encyclopedia when she had information to add.

I heard Bridgette's footsteps walking back to the living room. I glanced up from the book and saw she stopped at the opening. She clenched her hand to her side now, covering the wound while the other held the floral artwork and two large frame pieces. I grabbed the dagger and held it toward her, prepared to strike at any moment. Now that I knew how powerful it was against her, I had more confidence in my abilities.

"Don't come any closer." My fingers tensed about the handle.

"Just read Artemis's story," said Bridgette in a soft voice.

She didn't move from the door frame. Bridgette rested her body on the wood and appeared drained. You would have thought she hadn't slept in days. A ping of sympathy wracked my body. Had I done this to her? I lowered the dagger but kept it pointed in her direction. I dropped my eyes to Mom's story.

*I met my first Domum at the grocery store today. I
wasn't actively hunting, but I could tell what she was
by the way her skin glittered in fluorescent light. It
wasn't a strong glitter that regular humans could*

notice, just a slight sheen that made her skin look healthy and dewy.

I rolled my eyes to myself and felt stupid. Even Mom knew the sheen on Bridgette's skin was a sign of a witch creature. I spent the entire time assuming my eyes were playing tricks on me.

The Domum pulled down the sleeves of her sweater to hide more skin, but we made eye contact, and she realized I knew what she was. After paying for my groceries, I followed her home until her car disappeared down a dirt road. I stopped the car and continued on foot, but I couldn't find her house. There were rows of thick forest on the side of the road with no driveway. I began searching for a secret entrance. Before I realized, I was being chased by a rabid dog sent by a witch's curse. The dog bit me in the calf, making it impossible for me to reach my leg sheath. Before I could consult my intuition for guidance, the Domum came through the trees and sent the dog away with a spell. She showed me her home and healed my leg with a special salve. We talked for a few minutes until I knew it was time to go home.

The pen blotted at the end of home, showing Mom had spent a long moment contemplating her next words. The pen skipped for a second as she started the next sentence, then the ink flowed again.

I truly believe Captrixes and Domums can work together to keep the world safe from other witch creatures. There is no reason to actively hunt Domums.

"You want me to believe that you're the Domum in that story?" I lifted my head to look Bridgette in the eye.

"Yes. After I helped Artemis that night, we built a friendship. She mentioned having a daughter but never told me your name." Bridgette pointed at the built-ins next to her fireplace with her wounded hand. "May I?"

I let go of the dagger next to my leg and nodded. After sitting the frame pieces and artwork in the leather recliner, she walked to her built-in bookshelves and grabbed a small wooden box off a shelf filled with fake flowers, wooden trinkets, and a Polaroid camera. Bridgette opened the box and fished through some photos until she found the one she was looking for. She laid it face up on the table, not wanting to invade my space, and backed up to the fireplace. I kept my eyes on her as I grabbed the photo off of the coffee table and looked at it. It was a Polaroid of my mom and Bridgette, taken selfie style in the cottage's kitchen. Bridgette was grinning ear to ear with her arm wrapped around Mom's shoulder. Mom was laughing in the photo. I stroked the photo for a moment and looked at the bottom to see that it was dated six months earlier. Mom looked so happy.

I closed my eyes and asked my intuition for the truth. In a moment, a small voice inside said, *"Good."* I sighed and hoped I could really trust her. I sat the photo back down on the coffee table and looked at Bridgette. The guilt of what I had done to a woman who had only been kind to me settled in.

"I'm sorry about your hand. Can I help you fix it?"

Bridgette gave me a weak smile and nodded. We entered the kitchen with the floor covered in glass from the broken cup. On the side of the fridge a tilted broom rested, so I grabbed it and swept the glass into a pile to pick up. I walked to Bridgette's medicinal shelf and grabbed a bandaid. Bridgette had lined the shelf with a rainbow of different salves, but I didn't know which one to pick.

"The yellow one." Bridgette pointed to a group of small jars with a texture pattern, reading my mind.

I grabbed the jar of yellow salve and unscrewed the lid. Bridgette took her seat back at the table. She revealed her palm to me, and the minor cut had swollen to a large red welt. I scooped some salve onto my finger and rubbed it onto the cut. Bridgette swore and turned her head away. I placed the bandaid on as fast as I could manage and closed the jar. Bridgette massaged the bandaid to rub out some of the soreness, and I went to the sink to wash my hands. I returned to the table and sat down.

"If you're really my mom's friend, then you have to help me find her. I don't know this stuff like I should. I can't even hunt right yet," I said embarrassed.

"If you really want to find Artemis, you need to know how to be a Captrix. You need to do your reading, so you understand what you're up against. There is so much to catch up on."

"I know. I never—" I stopped myself. This wasn't a time to share my woes about having to become a Captrix.

"We also need to go back to your house to search for clues about these witches. We know what they are, but I want to take a second look."

"Give me a few hours to study. Around sunset, I'll take you to my house," I said.

I knew exactly the first witch creature I wanted to read about. First up was the one I had a bone to pick with. I flipped to the page "Ignis" to read about the red witch.

CHAPTER SEVEN

Bridgette backed out of her driveway in her blue sedan. When we got to the end of the driveway, trees lined the end, so I prepared for impact. Before we hit the first tree, though, a glitter substance rained down, and we were on the dirt road. The glimmer mesmerized me. I couldn't believe I hadn't noticed how beautiful, yet strange it was before.

The sun was beginning to set, so we had at least an hour before nature would paint the sky in orange and yellow. I spent the last couple of hours reading about the Ignis, the red witch creature, and the Mare, the sea witch creature. In the encyclopedia, there were hundreds of different entries talking about the different hunts Captrixes had done to kill these creatures, but I never found a single instance of them being found together. Their elements were complete opposites. I assumed they wouldn't even want to be near each other to avoid discomfort.

Bridgette turned off BeeBrush Drive and onto the pavement. She looked at me, waiting for directions, so I gave them to her. This helped solidify my trust in her more. If she didn't even know where our house was, how would she send a group of witches to it? If I was going to work with her, I needed to trust her. This didn't stop me from giving her directions that took the long way to get to my house. I thought I should desire to get there quickly, but I didn't want to see the lonely sidewalks I walked the night before. I didn't want to relive those memories and see my entire world burnt to the ground. It was the only place I'd ever known.

Bridgette continued driving with her hands firmly on the wheel, scanning the landscape for my burnt house. I gave her more directions. Bridgette glanced at me for a second, then back to the road.

"So, what is an Ignis?" Bridgette slowed the car and turned on another street.

It felt like I was being given a spelling test, but the stakes were much higher than getting a word wrong. Bridgette was trying to teach me as fast as possible, and I wanted so badly to impress her. I needed her to think I could be as good as Mom.

"An Ignis is a fire witch creature." The words came out slowly as I tried recalling my reading from earlier. "They are one of the strongest elemental witches because they can set anything on fire with a touch."

"Correct. What kinds of spells do they cast?"

"Generally, they use touch or their bodies to create fires.

Their nastiest spell is a fireball that tracks their target until they are burnt alive." I swallowed hard. I knew that this was the spell the Ignis had thrown at me. She had no intention of setting my house on fire.

"What kills them?"

"A vial of blessed water."

"What is a Mare?" Bridgette made another turn, and we were minutes away from my house.

I had stretched out a five-minute drive into fifteen minutes.

"A Mare is a water witch creature. They are another strong elemental witch. Mare's bend water to their will."

"Good. What kind of spells do they cast?"

"Anything that has to do with water. Since they bend it to their will, they can track you or drown you with it. They can pull water from anywhere, but stay near the ocean."

"What kills them?" Bridgette's voice sounded exactly like a teacher's voice. She was taking this persona seriously.

"Fire." I tried to hide my uncertainty, but I couldn't precisely remember what the encyclopedia said.

"Firebombs to be exact. I believe you can also stab them with the mixed metal dagger since it was forged specially. Firebombs are quicker, though, because of their range and heat." Bridgette made the last turn onto my street.

I gasped when my house came into view. The house barely stood with all of its blue siding gone or covered in black ash. All the windows were broken with curtains and blinds disintegrated. You saw completely through the structure into more black and darkness. I peered at the second story to look at my bedroom. The dormer was still somewhat there, but the fire charred it like the rest of the house. As I looked at it, the dormer walls crumbled and the remaining second floor collapsed into the lower part of the house. My entire bedroom was gone, along with my scrapbook that contained all the money I saved and my lucky penny. A sob welled in my throat, and I swallowed hard, trying to keep it from coming to the surface. This wasn't the time to play the pity card.

Bridgette parked on the street in front of the house and got out of the car. I slammed the car door and walked to where my front door used to be. The hole for the door remained, but the fire had consumed the wooden door that used to be there. Bridgette followed close behind and took out a small notepad to take notes. As we walked up to the house, the plaster continued to crumble from the remaining walls on the first floor. Bridgette immediately placed her notebook back into her pocket, realizing this was going to be a venture that required all hands on deck. This house was a ticking time bomb, ready to finish collapsing.

I entered the house and covered my nose to clog my nostrils. The smell of mildew and char dominated my senses. The firefighters' hose water soaked everything, and it wasn't drying. More plaster tumbled from where the kitchen used to be, so I made an immediate left to go into the living room area where the fire started. The flames had turned all of our furniture into ash, including the bookcase door to the study. The TV had melted into a blob of plastic on the opposite side of the room. I looked down at what was left of the hall to the study to determine if any books survived, but the fire had devoured all the papers. There was no reason to risk my life to go down to the study to see if anything was salvageable because of the deteriorating structure.

I glanced at the floor and observed a perfectly round circle where the tracker fireball landed before consuming the house as it followed me. Fear rose inside of me as I tried not to remember what it felt like to be chased by fire. I peered at the marking, hoping it would give me a clue, and noticed a round black circle beside the impact and kneeled down to check it out. When I touched the circle, I felt texture ridges on the side like a coin. I picked at the black coating with my fingernail to reveal an orange color underneath. My heart leaped, and I clutched the forgotten coin in my hand. My lucky penny made it through a witchy house fire after saving my life. The best gift my grandpa gave me was coming with me now. The penny didn't replace everything I lost in the house fire, but it was enough of a start to give me some hope. I slipped the dirty black coin in my borrowed jean's pocket and stood up.

When I looked back into the living room, I noticed an intact wall between the living room and the staircase. The wall was perfect, as if it wasn't even in this house when the fire raged. I walked over to the wall and touched it. It was a little damp, but still strong with barely any black soot on it. It was as if someone had just splashed the wall with a bowl of water instead of dousing it with a fire hose.

Bridgette entered the living room from the kitchen, looking around on the ground like something could be there other than black ash.

"Is that normal? I thought the fireball consumed everything," I said, glancing back at Bridgette and pointing at the intact wall.

She wore a puzzled look on her face and came closer to inspect the wall.

"It normally does."

Bridgette knocked on the wall gently to avoid sending chunks of drywall on our heads. I pushed my ear against the wall and listened closely. It didn't sound hollow like an empty wall should.

I pulled the dagger out of my back pocket and began cutting into the plaster. It was dangerous for me to be carrying this special item like this, but I had nothing else to put it in. Bridgette promised to search for a sheath for me when we returned to the cottage, but for right now, this would have to suffice.

After a few minutes, I cut a rectangle in the plaster big enough to remove, dulling the dagger blade. I lifted the chunk of plaster off the wall to see what was inside. Suddenly, piles of small burlap bags spilled out of the wall. Bridgette and I jumped back, looking at each other in disbelief. When the bags stopped pouring out, I grabbed one off the ground and sniffed it.

"It smells earthy. Like herbs." I passed the bag to Bridgette.

I closed my eyes. The scent seemed so familiar, like I should recognize it. Then, it donned on me.

"These are flame retardant bags. My grandpa used to spread them all over the house whenever we had candles or a fire going. I didn't realize he stuffed them in this wall."

Bridgette smelled the bag. She grinned, knowing I had given her the right answer.

"Makes sense. This blend of herbs would repel a fireball. I'm surprised he did this, though. It's Domum type magic," said Bridgette.

I shrugged my shoulders and decided that would have to be a question for Mom. I reached in the hole in the wall and moved the remaining flame retardant bags out of the way, allowing them to rest on the floor by my feet. My fingers touched a huge piece of metal before feeling the back of the wall. I wrapped my fingers around it and pulled the front end of an old-fashioned crossbow out of the wall.

"Is that a crossbow?" Bridgette's jaw dropped.

"Apparently so." I dragged out a quiver of bolts and a book the crossbow rested on.

Stunned, I took a few moments to twirl the unloaded crossbow to look at every aspect of it. It was a light brown colored wood with silver metal trim. There was a place for me to pull back on to load the crossbow and a silver trigger. It didn't look like a modern crossbow, but I wasn't sure how old it could be.

I sat it on the floor and turned my attention to the book that came out with it. The book was a bound leaflet whose title was *Captrix Weapons and How to Use Them*. I flipped to the inside cover and saw a note.

Atalanta, when you need this, you will know what to do. Love, Grandma & Grandpa.

A wave of emotions came over me. Sadness mixed with joy racked my body, as I tried to keep it together. They had left this here for me before they passed. This was the last gift I would ever get from them, even though I thought this moment had come a long time ago. As I was lost in thought, the ceiling began to crumble over my head. I decided it was best to go then.

I put the dagger back in my back pocket and pulled the crossbow and quiver over my shoulder using their leather straps.

We ran out of the house as the ceiling over the living room collapsed. I stared at the house, trying to figure out a way to tell it goodbye. Bridgette scribbled a few notes down in her notebook and huffed in frustration.

"Mare's usually leave some sort of water trail on land since they pull their water from the earth, but I'm not seeing any here at all." Bridgette slammed her notebook closed.

"Could the Ignis's fire evaporate the trail," I said.

"I guess so if she was intentional about it."

Bridgette walked closer to the house and crouched. She squatted at the stoop for a few seconds and walked back to me, shaking her head.

"Normally, I can sense when magic has been somewhere, but I'm not even getting a read. It's like they weren't even here." Bridgette tucked a brown curl out of her face and stared at the house.

"There has to be a clue here somewhere." I grew desperate for answers. This entire trip seemed to lead to dead ends.

I was going to suggest getting back into the car, but my inner intuition alarm went off screaming. The inner voice yelled about being watched. It was one of the strongest feelings I had felt so far and came through crystal clear. I was getting used to the voice, and it wasn't as jarring when it made itself known.

"Someone's watching us," I whispered to Bridgette.

She didn't flinch or seem confused. Mom must have told her how strong our intuition could be.

"Look around and see if you can figure out who it is."

She walked away from me like she was checking for something near the exterior of the house again. I turned around and scanned the street, looking for anything amiss. At first, nothing stuck out to me. Cars lined the street curbs or were in their driveway. Finally, I found something interesting. A little off to the left was a tree in a neighbor's yard with a man wearing a black hoodie with the hood up and jeans propped against the tree. He was the only person on the street other than us and seemed interested in our direction, so it made sense.

"The man on the street corner by the tree," I said, as she returned beside me.

"I see him." Bridgette looked in his direction.

The man noticed us staring at him and began taking his leave from the tree. Bridgette panned the street and flexed her fingers. She seemed to question herself but held her hand out in his direction. The man broke out into a full sprint.

"Retardo," said Bridgette with force behind her voice.

Glitter specks left her fingertips and floated toward the man. I watched as they encompassed him and laid themselves gently on his clothes. Little sparkles danced off of the hoodie like a disco ball.

"Come on, we don't have much time." Bridgette broke out into a run.

I started running behind her, trying to get used to the weight of the crossbow on my back. The man began running on the street in slow motion. It was comical how he only took one step compared to the yards we were covering. We were a car length away from him when the spell wore off. Suddenly, the turtle speed dissipated, and he was running like a track star leading us to New Meadow's downtown area.

"Crap," I said in frustration, quickening my speed. The crossbow slowed me down, and my panting proved to me I was not in the best shape.

I pulled ahead of Bridgette and chased after the man. After a block of running, he entered the town's business shoppes area, and I knew I was running out of time. The chance of being seen by people running around town with a crossbow on my back was becoming highly likely. Deciding to take a risk, I took a bolt from the quiver and loaded it into the crossbow. I had never used one before, but I hoped it was in my blood. The man ran down an alley between an herb shop and an abandoned building. This was my chance.

"Stop! Or I will put this bolt in your back." I aimed the loaded crossbow at the center of the hoodie.

The man turned around and flipped his hood down, revealing choppy layered, chin-length black hair with a shaggy bang that resembled a scene kid from the 2000s. He wore a grin that flashed almost perfect teeth as his brown eyes looked me up and down. His face was boyish and slightly pale, so I assumed he had to be around my age. I resisted the urge to give him a once over and moved the crossbow to point at his heart.

"Why are you watching me?" I kept my body steady and bore into him with my eyes. I wanted to come across as confident.

"Because I can," he said. His voice was raspy, like he had smoked too many cigarettes.

I wasn't sure if he was trying to be sexy, but the voice came across as fake. It was like he was trying to use a voice changer, but failed miserably.

"I'm not going to ask again," I said, fingering the trigger of the crossbow.

"I believe you will." His more natural deep-toned voice came out this time. Dare I say it, it was sexy. I noticed a shiver make its way down my spine.

Before I could consider pulling the trigger, energy threw me against the wall of a building. I dropped the crossbow on the ground as my hands plastered against the brick wall. A woman with long black wavy hair came out of the herb shop's backdoor and balled her hands into fists. When she tightened her fists, I felt my bones trying not to crunch. Bridgette made it into the alley and threw her hand up to defend me with magic without hesitation. She did a sideways motion with her hand, and the boy was slung onto the same wall as me. We were so close together our fingers almost touched.

"Let her go, or I will crush his bones too," said Bridgette, making direct eye contact with the woman.

Bridgette balled her fist tighter, and I saw the boy cringe in the same pain I was in. The bone-crushing pain intensified in my hand that was holding the crossbow before. Every second that passed, I felt my finger bones cracking. I bit my lip, trying to control my scream. Bridgette balled her fist, and I heard the boy cry out in agony. He clutched his knee like she had broken his kneecap.

"Stop," said the woman, seeing the boy in pain. "We will be civilized about this."

She dropped her hands, and I fell to the ground. I hit my knees on the concrete and sensed a bruise forming. The concrete tore into my hands, but nothing too terrible. I grabbed the crossbow I dropped, prepared to use it. Bridgette dropped her hands too, making the boy fall down on his knees as well. He grabbed his knee and cursed.

"We need to get off the street." The woman opened the

back door.

I looked to Bridgette to see if she had any objections, but she gave me a nod to tell me it was okay. I noticed both of the women's hands glowed with a light sheen from performing telekinesis. Now, I was in the presence of two Domums.

I flexed my hand to know if any of my bones had broken. Luckily, I seemed all intact. The man stood up and winced when he put weight on his leg. He limped toward the door, no questions asked. I wasn't so sure about how I felt about walking into a place with a woman who just tried to break my hands, so I stood still. The woman coughed to get my attention. I looked at her and then to Bridgette again. Bridgette began walking to the door as my intuition murmured that something was off here. I wanted to listen to it, but it didn't seem like I had much of a choice if I wanted to figure out how these two fit into my mom's kidnapping.

CHAPTER EIGHT

I FILED INTO THE back of the tea and herb shop behind the strange man and woman. Bridgette followed me to cover my back. We walked through a dusty backroom where shelves were filled with mysterious-looking jars and vials filled with substances I had never seen. The wood-paneled hallway covered in various business awards narrowed past the storeroom. I forced myself to stay straight and not knock anything down with the crossbow on my back. After what felt like forever, we all passed through an opening into the main store.

The main store was bright and open with windows at the front letting in natural light. Behind the register, a special stock of eclectic herbs sat on open wooden shelving that served as a focal point for the shop. I glanced at the labels and had a hunch these weren't all for cooking when I saw a jar labeled death powder. Past the white counter that held the cash register were shelves filled with various spices, herbs, and teas. A few I recognized, but a lot of them seemed driven to the exotic cook.

The woman led us to the middle of the store where an empty space opened in front of the cash register. She took a stool from behind the counter and moved it to the store side for the man to sit on. He happily obliged to rest his aching knee. She then pulled another stool away from the counter to rummage through storage below the cash register. She retrieved two glasses from under the counter and a jug of foggy white liquid and placed it next to the register. Bridgette and I took our spots in front of the counter and waited. When the woman stopped fiddling with her glasses, her eyes darted at me.

"Why did you have a crossbow pointed at my son?" She filled the glasses with the foggy white liquid and sat the jug onto the counter.

"Why was your son watching me," I said. I wanted to come across as fearless, so I kept my tone aggressive.

She handed a glass to the man. They both chugged the concoction and sat empty glasses back on the counter. My brain felt a little fuzzy, like it had turned my intuition off. I looked at Bridgette in alarm, but she remained steady. I wiped the worry off my face and returned my gaze to the woman.

"Because I told him to go keep an eye on the burnt house," she said.

I reached my hand behind me, trying for my dagger. Cutting into the plaster at home made it dull, but it would still do its job.

"Why?" I curled my fingers around the dagger's holt.

I knew I was dealing with a witch, who I assumed was a Domum like Bridgette. Her skin glowed after doing magic in the alley, but now she hid her skin under a black long-sleeve shirt. The rest of her outfit was simple—dark wash jeans and black flats. She looked a few years younger than Bridgette, but the crow's feet near her eyes gave her away. The rest of her porcelain skin was smooth and exuded youth.

"That's none of your business." The woman stashed the jug back under the cabinet.

"I believe it is her business," said Bridgette. "It was her house."

Recognition flashed across her face. She squinted her eyes at me, waiting for my response. I stared at her harder, trying to let my intuition tell me what I needed to know. My intuition became clouded and empty, still turned off. I felt naked, like the power I had grown to accept had been stripped away from me. I wanted to give a snarky response because I realized it was something she did, but the man popped up from his stool and hobbled closer toward us.

"Look, two witches came in a week ago asking for special ingredients for a potion they needed," said the man.

The woman snapped her attention toward him and mouthed hush. I pulled the dagger out of my back pocket.

"One way or another, you're going to tell me." I aimed the dagger at the woman.

"I wouldn't test her." Bridgette examined them both, sizing them up.

The woman brushed her wavy black hair back, unfazed by the weapon's arrival, making me angrier. I knew this would hurt her. I experienced what it could do, and the witch acted like I whipped out a butter knife. She mulled over the idea of revealing information in her head and then spoke.

"Fine. Two witches came in and requested some ingredients from my private collection. It didn't look off for a regular ritual, so I sold the ingredients to them. It wasn't until the fire broke out that I thought something was amiss."

"She sent me to monitor the house to see if anything weird was going on. And you were there, so I stayed and watched. End of story," said the man.

"What did you sell them?" Bridgette pulled out her trusty pen and pad.

"I can't remember. I'll have to look through my sales records." The woman motioned to an old-fashioned ledger next to the cash register.

I thought what she was saying had to be lies, but I couldn't sniff it out like normal. Bridgette walked behind the counter to watch the woman flip through the records. The man moved over to me, and I hesitantly put my dagger back into my back pocket.

"I'm Tristan, by the way." Tristan extended his hand for a handshake and flashed a row of bright teeth.

I took the hand and shook it. When our fingers touched, an electric shock pulsed through my fingers. I snatched my hand back and looked down at my fingers, confused. Why did he shock me? Static electricity, maybe? It wasn't like anything I had ever felt, but he didn't seem upset. Maybe it was just a me thing. Of course, my intuition was currently unhelpful for sniffing out whatever was going on.

"I'm Atalanta," I said halfheartedly.

He looked cute in an alternative sort of way. A lot like all the guys I had seen on the internet when I cozied up in the living room surfing the web, rather than reading the Captrix books I needed to read. He gave me a smirk, and I noticed the dimples in his cheeks. In any other situation, I would have thought he was handsome. But now that he didn't pose a complete threat, I didn't know how to talk to him.

"That's an interesting name. Where does it come from?" Tristan broke my train of thought.

"I'm named after the Greek goddess. She was a huntress."

Bridgette remained behind the counter with Tristan's mother. The longer I looked at her, the more I realized they had the same brown eyes and the same dimples on their cheeks. Tristan caught my eyes and then looked at where I was staring.

"That's my mom, Morgana. She's a Domum, like your friend." Tristan gestured toward Morgana who flipped another page in the sales log.

At least now I knew I was right about her witch species. I was getting better at this after all.

"She's a bit intense, huh," I said.

"She can be sometimes. She's just protective."

"And you are?" He looked completely human to me, but I had to be sure. I understood it was rare for men to be witch creatures, but I wasn't well versed in witch creature genetics.

"Completely human, but I'm good at making medicine. Salves and stuff," Tristan said.

I nodded and eyeballed any exposed skin. It didn't have any glittery sheen at all, so I took his word at face value. He must have taken it as a once over and raised his eyebrows. He returned the gesture, looking me up and down like he was undressing me with his eyes. It made me uncomfortable, but I also didn't want him to stop. I'd never experienced this type of male attention before, so I wanted to bask in it before it went away.

"And I'm assuming you're a—."

"Captrix," I cut him off.

The word felt weird rolling off of my tongue. It was the first time I used the moniker to identify myself. I didn't know what I thought about it, causing an icky feeling. He swallowed hard and looked at his mother. He tried to hide his concern, but I could tell he thought I planned to put a bolt in her head or, better yet, stab her with the dagger she didn't take seriously.

"They bought nightshade, phoenix feather dust, and essence of water lily," said Morgana to Bridgette.

Tristan and I both turned to watch them. I never heard an ingredient list like that before, but I knew it sounded off. Morgana slammed the sales book shut as Bridgette scribbled down the ingredients.

"You and I both know those don't go together." Bridgette eyed Morgana suspiciously.

Bridgette walked back to me, changing positions with Tristan. He moved next to Morgana, taking a protective position.

"On a surface level, yes, but with the right tinkering they can make a house combust," said Morgana.

Bridgette didn't look convinced, and I wasn't, either. My house didn't combust because of a potion. I saw the Ignis heave that fireball straight at me. But I didn't want to reveal that piece of knowledge to Morgana, knowing I couldn't trust her. Especially with my intuition being so cloudy.

"Was there anything about these witches that stood out to

you," I said.

"Well, it was an Ignis and a Mare. They normally don't work together." Morgana shrugged.

I nodded. It had been my mom's kidnappers that bought ingredients here. No question there. It still didn't explain why they bought those ingredients.

"But the Mare smelled funny. It wasn't normal ocean-salty like they usually smell," said Tristan.

Morgana cut her eyes at him like he was revealing too much, but he seemed eager to help. She murmured something about protecting customers to him, but I couldn't quite catch what was being said.

"What did she smell like?" Bridgette brought back out her notebook.

"More like a swamp. Like she had been hanging out there instead of the ocean." Tristan shook his head at Morgana.

"I thought it was odd, but not a lot of oceans around here." Morgana gave an uncomfortable smile.

Bridgette's eyes brightened. I had a feeling she figured out a clue but didn't want to say everything in front of them. I took another scan around the room, but nothing else seemed suspicious. A pink vial glowing on the shelf behind the counter caught my eye. I thought about asking about it, but once Morgana saw me looking at it, she conveniently positioned herself to remove it from my view. Our warm welcome had worn off. To get any more help from Morgana would be like pulling teeth, and the sun was setting. I wanted to be back at Bridgette's cottage by nightfall, so we could make a plan.

"Well, thank you for your help. We'll be on our way then."

I turned to leave out of the front door.

"Anytime." Morgana plastered on another fake smile.

Tristan came up behind me and whispered in my ear.

"Maybe I can help," Tristan said, keeping his voice low.

"I think we've got it, but thanks." I shivered at his breath, touching the sensitive part of my neck.

I was still so unsure about Morgana, but I realized she wasn't telling me the whole truth about what was going on at her shop. I couldn't consult my intuition for help because her drink was preventing me from getting a read on her. On the other hand, Tristan seemed fine. I wished I got a read on him.

Bridgette shook Morgana's hand and thanked her for her help. I gave Tristan's hand a courtesy shake and said a mental goodbye. I knew I would never see him again, so I took a mental picture to remember a first crush by. Then, Bridgette and I walked out of the front of the store, exiting onto the street to walk back to the car.

CHAPTER NINE

Bridgette and I walked for a block in silence. We kept a quick pace because of the crossbow on my back. It wasn't something someone would normally see in New Meadows, and we didn't have an appropriate answer if townsfolk questioned us. Bridgette seemed to be thoughtfully mulling over things, so I didn't want to break her train of thought. I figured she didn't want to make a statement until we had plenty of distance between us and the herb shop. Since she didn't want to speak, I chose to get lost in my own thoughts.

Nothing we had been thrown into made any sense. Witch creatures buying random things from a supply shop where the owner became curious? She became so curious she sent a scout to check out my house, yet when we tried to ask questions, she became increasingly unhelpful. What little help Morgana gave bothered me. She hid from my intuition, so I wasn't sure what to actually believe from her. I did know I didn't like her special interest in my situation.

But then there was Tristan. He was dreamy in a lead-singer-of-an-emo-boy-band sort of way. I loved his dimples and his hair. I felt this pull to get to know him more, even if I only met him for a few minutes. He genuinely seemed like he wanted to help me, even if he drank the strange liquid. He didn't request it; his mother forced it upon him. In that situation, I would have drank it too. Or at least, this was what I was telling myself because I couldn't get him out of my head.

The way our fingertips shocked each other when we touched refused to leave my brain. I wondered if he felt it too, but he never acted like he did. I wanted to write the experience off as static electricity, but it seemed like something more.

Bridgette looked at me, as I let out a depressed sigh. I didn't fill the space with words, though, because the sadness of never seeing him again weighed on me. I considered it a lost connection. No matter how excited I was to meet a man my age, I needed to focus on finding my mother. Mom needed me more than my love life needed a boyfriend with a sketchy mother.

We were almost halfway to the car, and I couldn't take the silence anymore. It made me ponder too much.

"What do you think about Morgana?" I kicked a rock, sending it tumbling off the sidewalk.

"I can tell you she knows more than what she's letting on," said Bridgette.

"That thing she drank made my intuition not work."

"I thought so. I've never made it, but it looked like a

variation of a mind fogging drink."

"She's hiding something that she doesn't want me to know. But Tristan…I believe he's honest."

Bridgette looked at me like I lost my mind.

"The boy is going to do whatever she says. You saw the way he drank that stuff immediately. No questions asked," said Bridgette.

I realized she was right, but I didn't want to give her the satisfaction.

"Don't you think it's odd for a Mare to smell like a swamp?" It seemed like a better idea to steer the conversation back to the witches.

I learned earlier Mares sourced their magic from ocean water, not swamps. Swamp hags, surprisingly, weren't a real thing. The witch was choosing to be weaker just to have a water source.

"It's odd alright. If she camped out there, her magic would be significantly weaker." Bridgette thumbed through her notes, searching for a missed connection. "But I know what swamp she's in. There is a large one on the edge of town. It's the closest one to the herb store and your house."

I read earlier the Ignis worked better in hot climates, or at least one's with regular heat and low wind. An ocean is going to be damp and breezy past the sand. However, a Mare couldn't work anywhere too warm because the heat would dry them out. It would make sense for them to camp at the swamp together.

"They are there together. The swamp would even their powers out like a neutral ground," I said.

"And the Ignis wouldn't smell because it would just evaporate off of her."

"We're going to have to go there tonight before the

witching hour to catch them in action. I still want to know what they are doing with those ingredients since they weren't used to burn my house."

Bridgette began to reply, but we heard footsteps running down the sidewalk behind us. I flipped my head to see Tristan running toward us, wearing a black backpack.

"Wait," said Tristan, gasping for air. "I want to come with you!"

Bridgette and I stopped. She looked at me, and we both turned around. We both looked at him like he was completely insane. My heart skipped a beat, excited at the opportunity to speak to him again. It would be so nice to have someone around my age.

"Look. I know it sounds insane, but I want to help." Tristan gathered himself together as he reached us.

He had shed the black hoodie he was wearing earlier and wore a grey t-shirt and jeans, ripped at the knee from the alley's concrete. His knee was no longer broken or sprained based on the type of run I just witnessed. Either Bridgette didn't break it like I thought she did, or Morgana quickly healed it after we left.

"Absolutely not," said Bridgette, appalled at the suggestion.

I knew this was a terrible idea, so I played along with Bridgette for now.

"I mean really, what skills do you have," I said, following Bridgette's lead.

"I can recognize them for you." Tristan readjusted his backpack to let it slide onto one shoulder.

"So can I?" I shrugged.

"Uh, they won't feel threatened by a human they've never

seen. They know who you are. No element of surprise.”

He was grasping at straws, but he did have a slight point, now that I thought about it. Depending on what the Ignis and Mare were doing with Mom, he could make a great distraction, or at least be bait. What I really wanted to learn was how Morgana and he fit into this situation. This could be our shot to possess an inside man.

“Again, absolutely not.” Bridgette pulled me toward the car we had finally reached.

I thought she would shove me in it like a mother, but instead, she pulled me to the driver’s side, leaving Tristan frozen on the sidewalk. I realized Bridgette was being smart, but all I focused on was the electric shock I felt with him. This might be my only opportunity to figure out what was brewing between us while also getting more clues.

“Bridgette, he could be useful,” I whispered.

“How, Atalanta? He’s a human with little skill.” She looked at me sternly and made no attempt to lower her voice.

“Hey, I heard that,” said Tristan. “I know a lot more than you think. I’ve worked in that herb shop with my mom my whole life.”

I peered around the hood of the car and waved at Tristan. He gave me a huge grin with those perfect teeth. I ducked back around, so he couldn’t read my lips. I put my finger over my lips and gave Bridgette a shush.

“If we want to figure out if Morgana is in this, we need to let him come.” I continued to keep my voice low.

“That’s a stupid idea, and you know it.”

“Come on, Bridgette. Please?”

I looked back over the car at Tristan and pleaded with my intuition to give me a sign. For a moment, everything in my brain was blank, like nothing was able to respond. I wanted to punch something. That stupid drink was still affecting my mindset. I focused hard, trying to get some sort of an answer. Finally, one word came into my brain. "Unsure."

"I don't think it's a good idea. But if we must—" said Bridgette.

"He could be a good distraction," I said, extra loud so Tristan could listen.

Bridgette rolled her eyes. She hated this, but I had too many questions about him I needed answered.

"The moment I walk in there, they are going to know who I am."

"You're going to get him killed," said Bridgette.

"I can handle myself." Tristan readjusted the strap on his backpack again.

The initial confidence he ran up with was waning. He rocked back and forth on his feet, waiting for an answer.

"You can come as long as you take care of yourself. I can't have your back and Bridgette's." I circled to the front of the car to the passenger side.

Bridgette coughed and rolled her eyes. She was right. The odds of me protecting them both were slim. So far, Bridgette and my mom protected me. Now, I was just telling jokes. Embarrassment overwhelmed me, and I prayed Tristan didn't hear her reaction.

I looked at Bridgette with pleading eyes, needing her permission to bring him along. She gave me a death stare, begging me to change my mind. I shook my head to tell her I was sure in my decision. She unlocked the doors to the car, and Tristan came galloping from the sidewalk. Bridgette huffed in frustration and got into the driver's seat. She cranked the car and gave me an annoyed "let's go" face. I didn't regret my decision to bring Tristan with us yet, but I knew Bridgette would be pissed off at me for a while.

It was selfish to bring him on our hunt, but I couldn't help myself. I wondered for a moment what Mom would say about this. Nothing good would have come from that discussion. She would have reacted more harshly than Bridgette. Then again, she wasn't here right now to tell me what to do. I could run this hunt how I saw fit, even if I screwed it up.

I grabbed the car door handle to get in the car before Bridgette left out of frustration as Tristan grabbed it to open the door for me. Our hands touched for a moment on the door handle. His hands weren't rough like they worked very hard, but they weren't soft, either. Their roughness came from lack of moisture and never wearing gloves when working with things. Butterflies churned in my stomach. I thought I would faint.

This time his fingers didn't shock mine. An unexplainable warmth came from them that was soothing and comforting. Tristan's hand felt like home. The feeling caught me off guard. I'd never felt this sense of home, and he gave it to me with one touch. It was intoxicating.

I pulled my hand away while Tristan left it on the car latch. Blushing, I turned away as he opened the car door for me. I wanted to ask my intuition what any of this meant, but my brain seemed too scattered. Tristan gave me a small grin, like he knew the feelings I had churning inside.

I slinked into the passenger seat, and he closed the door. Bridgette rolled her eyes at me again as Tristan opened the door to the backseat. He threw his backpack in, and it rolled across the seat. Then, Tristan leaned up between Bridgette and me, sporting his boyish grin.

"So, where are we going," said Tristan.

Bridgette shook her head and pulled away from the curb, not answering his question. Tristan leaned back into the backseat, unfazed by Bridgette's cold shoulder, and watched the landscape pass by out the window. Reaching into my pocket, I pulled out the tarnished penny. I frowned at the black coating and tried to scratch more of it off, but it didn't budge. I sighed, accepting I would never see the beautiful copper again. Bridgette glanced over at me, before returning her eyes to the road.

"What is that," asked Bridgette.

"It's a real copper penny my grandpa gave to me before he died. I left it in the house during the attack." I turned the penny over to determine if the fire ruined the back like the front. The back of the penny wasn't quite as black as the front, but still had a coating of oxidation.

"I think I can get the black off. I'll try when we get home." Bridgette looked over at the penny, then back to the road.

I smiled, feeling a sense of hope restored, and tucked the penny back into my pocket. The longer I spent with Bridgette, the more I understood why my mom wanted to be friends with her.

CHAPTER TEN

Bridgette drove us back to her house to gather supplies and to plan our strategy for the swamp hunt. We understood who we were looking for, but many unknown answers weighed heavily on my mind. I wished I knew everything about what we would face, or be completely ignorant. This in-between didn't settle well.

It turned out to be strange going from doing a hunt alone and failing to having a team to hunt with. Mom had always hunted alone as far as I noticed, but I needed all the help I could get because the stakes were so much higher now. I was not only responsible for myself, but I also had to save Mom while making sure Bridgette and Tristan didn't die in the process.

The idea of it all was making me anxious, so I distracted myself with preparation. I learned what killed these witches, but things needed to be crafted by hand. At home, I was sure Mom kept these supplies around, but Bridgette wasn't running out to kill witch creatures every day. Therefore, I had to craft my own weapons. I'd never crafted weapons before, but I was sure this was something in my blood.

First, I started the blessed water bolts for the Ignis. Bridgette had found me a small bottle of blessed water in her stores, so I had to be extra careful to not spill a drop. We didn't have enough time to find a priest to have water blessed, and none of us were pure enough to do it ourselves.

I removed the blades of the broadhead off to reveal a reservoir that I could add liquids into. In action, the water would leak out the end of the bolt when it pierced the witch creature's skin, allowing the liquid to take effect. I knew these bolts had to be special, so I took a mental count of them. I had no idea where I would buy these ever again. To add more pressure to my crafting, I couldn't mess up adding in the liquid, or I would be down a bolt.

Bridgette gave me a small funnel, so I placed it on the top of the opening and tried to grab the water. My hands started to shake as my anxiety consumed me.

"Let me help you with that." Tristan came from the hall, breaking my thoughts.

I looked over my shoulder to see Tristan standing in the living room doorway. He walked over toward me and kneeled down next to the coffee table. I tried to decide if I wanted to let him help or not. Crafting the weapons felt like it was supposed to be my responsibility since it was my crossbow and bolts. I was also attempting to appear better at this than I really was. I bit my lower lip.

"I'm not saying you can't do it on your own. I thought you could use some help, so you wouldn't spill anything," said Tristan.

Gratitude washed over me as he didn't point out my shaky hands. I handed him the vial of water, being careful not to touch his hands. I needed to focus right now, and I was already struggling enough. Every time I touched him, my mind wandered to a place that wasn't here.

I held the bolt in one hand, careful to avoid the rest of the blade that wouldn't be removed. With my other hand, I held the tiny silicone funnel for Tristan. Tristan poured the blessed water carefully into the bolt. We filled two bolts in comfortable silence. When we began the third one, I decided it was time for some conversation to get to know him better.

"So, how was your talk with Bridgette," I said.

Bridgette had him in the kitchen for the past thirty minutes since we got back to the cottage. She was still not happy with the idea of dragging Tristan along on the hunt, so I could only imagine what type of lecture he was getting in there. If it came to be like any of the ones I had received from my mom, I perceived it was no fun. So far, I had avoided any long lectures, but I had a feeling my time was coming.

"She gave me some guidelines to follow," said Tristan, avoiding the conversation.

"Oh, okay." I screwed the lid back onto the bolt and prepared another to be filled.

"That's really it." He caught my disappointed tone. "She's freaked out about me getting in the way."

To be honest, I was too. I realized it was my idea to let him come along, but I was feeling selfish then and not thinking of the consequences. I mean really, what skill did Tristan have? We knew he made medicine and potions, but those skills didn't translate into combat with witch creatures. This could really be a mess if stuff hit the fan.

"I understand where she's coming from. We have a lot at stake here." I forced my gaze on the funnel.

"I promise not to mess this up." Tristan took the funnel and a filled bolt from my hand.

His eyes widened when our fingers grazed each other this time, but he still managed to screw the blade back on the broadhead and set it down onto the table. He had to feel the mind-boggling warmth and spark between us because he blushed instead of maintaining a poker face. I sensed a warm tingle run down my spine to my feet, then back up to my core. The tingle nestled itself there, begging to be stroked and held. I tried to keep my face steady and pretend like I felt nothing, but the more I tried to ignore it, the more lust filled me. I didn't know how I could be so attracted to someone I just met. It was unnatural. We had barely said more than three words to each other, and I was ready to jump his bones.

I glanced down at his lips and noticed they were slightly parted, ready for a kiss. I thought about closing the distance and making his mouth mine. We leaned in slightly, but I shook my head to come to my senses. No matter how much I wanted it, locking lips with someone you'd known less than three hours seemed ridiculous to me. I refocused my attention on the remaining broadheads.

We finished filling the bolts as quickly as possible. An

awkward tension permeated the air between us as we carefully avoided touching anymore. With the last bolt filled, we laid them all out on the coffee table.

When we finished, Bridgette came in with the herb firebombs she crafted in the kitchen. The Mare was going to be complicated to kill because of her weakness. I read we could kill them with extremely hot fire that caused them to evaporate or by being stabbed with iron. We didn't own a pottery kiln to bring along, so Bridgette improvised. She crafted a blend of herbs and spices that were highly flammable and would react with each other when lit on fire or with extreme impact. However, impact wouldn't cause these to light on the Mare because of the moisture on her skin. They needed to be ignited in order to begin the burn. She placed them in small clay jars, so they would crumble easily without becoming a hazard for ourselves.

"Now for these, we will have to throw them at the Mare to throw her off balance," said Bridgette, placing the clay jars alongside the bolts. "Once she's covered in the blend, we have to figure out a way to ignite it to burn her."

She took a seat in her recliner next to the window, sitting up straight like she wasn't planning on staying there for long.

I nodded, understanding that the Mare was going to require a lot of creativity to get rid of. If I brought a lighter, I would need to be extremely close in order to properly use it. This seemed to be the only option since the likelihood of me winning hand-to-hand combat to stab her with the dagger seemed slim.

"Are we just going to bring a lighter?" Tristan echoed my thoughts.

Bridgette sat pondering for a moment. She pursed her lips

in deep thought before coming up with an answer.

"I guess so. I could use telekinesis to bring the flame closer to her as long as we have a source."

I caught a worried edge to her tone I didn't know what to make of. Was she worried about everything not going to plan? I made a mental note to ask her if we got a moment alone before the hunt. I considered making a comment, but Bridgette stood up from her chair.

"Atalanta, there's one more thing I need to give to you." Bridgette walked around the furniture toward her bedroom.

I looked at her, confused. What else did she have? We had already made up all the weapons that I knew of.

Bridgette entered her bedroom and dragged out a small black trunk, struggling against its weight. Tristan took his cue to rise and got up to help her bring it to me. He grabbed the other weathered black leather strap, and they carried it to the side of the coffee table. I moved the weapons to one side of the coffee table and took in the chest.

The chest was a dark black wood littered with scuff marks and dents. It looked well-traveled, but I couldn't tell exactly how old it was. The lock was made of ironed hardware along with the bolts that dotted the front. They had turned bronze over the years, but still seemed to be in great condition. I leaned in and studied it closer, taking in the rows of initials carved on the top. Rows and rows of initials were carved and crossed out, but they all ended with a C. One set of initials remained uncrossed. A.R.C., for Artemis Renee Capp, sat there fresh and barely weathered.

"This is my mom's." I touched the black wood. The chest was rough against my fingers, but I managed to not get any splinters.

"She dropped it off a few weeks ago for safekeeping. You were supposed to get this after you rose, but I think you need it now." Bridgette handed me an iron key.

I took the key from her, admiring it in my hand. It was about the length of my palm and had a small rabbit forged into the handle. The rabbit made the key awkward to hold, but I realized whoever made the lock did it special for the Capps since the key featured our family animal. The fact Mom left me this chest here bothered me, though. This seemed like too much of a coincidence. Did my mom know witch creatures were coming for her? Why else would she leave this chest here for me? The more I learned, the less I felt like I knew.

I put the iron key into the lock and heard it click into place as I turned it. I opened the chest and peered inside. My mouth dropped open as I took in how beautiful the chest was. The top of the chest was painted with our family crest. The outside of the crest was a beautiful teal color, and the inside was a bright yellow. In the center of the crest, a brown rabbit stood on its hind legs, smelling the air. I rubbed it with my fingers, touching the acrylic paint. It wasn't weathered like the rest of the chest, so my ancestors must have chosen to upkeep the paint over the years. I touched the iron chains that kept the lid from falling all the way to the back, amazed at the craftsmanship.

There was an array of knives and sheaths in the bottom of the chest. I recognized some of them but wasn't sure about a lot of them. There were also a few books about weapons and witch creatures I was grateful for since I didn't have access to a Captrix library. Pulling out book after book, I set them on the coffee table. I shuffled through the holsters until I found a black leather hip holster that would fit my dagger perfectly. I placed the holster on the table along with the books and moved the rest of the remaining weapons to the side to find a Captrix huntress outfit at the bottom.

Lifting the outfit to get a better look, I realized this was the outfit that had been passed down for generations. Magically, it was still intact, even though I knew Mom had worn this along with my grandma and other ancestors. Most Captrixes would wear this outfit for a year until they created their own. Then, it would be passed down to the next generation. There was no telling how many countless other Captrixes in my family had worn this. Captrix women were overjoyed to wear this and carry on their family legacy. My stomach churned, as I didn't feel the same way. I was an impostor, holding a sacred Captrix tradition. If I held it long enough, I was afraid the outfit would realize that I never wanted to put it on in the first place. Holding the leather outfit in my hand, I looked up to see Tristan and Bridgette looking at me with bated breath. I knew they wanted me to try it on, but it still seemed wrong to hold in my hands. The anticipation wafting off all of them became too much, so I gathered the complete outfit and scurried to the bathroom to try it on.

I entered the bathroom and shut the door behind me. I plastered my back against the door and slid down it. The anticipation left the air in here, so I could breathe for a moment. I sat on the floor, caressing the leather in my hands. It was soft and supple from being worn in, yet as structurally sound as the day they made it. I stroked the seams, admiring the craftsmanship, and a lump formed in my throat. I didn't deserve to wear this. I wasn't sure I wanted to put it on, but I knew it was what Bridgette and Tristan were expecting. It was what my mother expected. I had spent over a year trying to bust these expectations, but here I was, fated once again to do the thing I tried to avoid. I wondered if fate would have ever allowed me out of this.

The clock in the bathroom ticked, and a few minutes passed. If I didn't put on this outfit soon, Bridgette would be in here to check on me. I sighed heavily and stood up. Putting on each piece carefully, I imagined I was putting on the armor of my ancestors. It shocked me when each piece fit perfectly, like someone had made it for me all along. When I finished lacing the corset, I took a deep breath to face the mirror.

In the mirror, I teared up when I saw the whole look come together. The outfit began with a thin white undershirt and black leather pants with multiple pockets built in. It would be easy to slip all the firebombs and extra water vials into my pockets. I buckled on the sheath for my mixed metals dagger, so it would lie at my hip for an easy grab.

I felt the most badass in the final piece. A black leather corset hugged my waist and protected my entire midsection. The stiffness was taking some getting used to, but it supported my body in a way I never experienced before. The corset held everything in the right place, so I could move freely without worrying about my body getting in the way. I completed the outfit with a fresh pair of black lace-up boots in my size left in the chest. All of this leather made me feel sexy, but I also understood it would protect me from claws and blades up to a point. Even though I still felt guilty for putting it on, I knew I would have to show Bridgette and Tristan the completed ensemble eventually.

I exited the bathroom and walked out into the living room to show them my outfit.

CHAPTER ELEVEN

"So, what do we think?" I twirled around to show the entire outfit. Tristan did a double-take, and his mouth dropped open.

"You look, uh, prepared," said Tristan, searching for more words to say.

"Your mother would be so proud to see you like this." Bridgette beamed with how happy she was.

Walking over to the coffee table, I looked at how I would load my pockets with the weapons I needed. Bridgette's comment made me emotional, even if I tried to ignore it. I really did feel close to my mother in this outfit, closer than I'd ever felt before. I needed to find her to show her me looking like this, so she could be proud of me for a moment, even if I wasn't sure this was what I wanted.

"I have one more thing for you." Bridgette walked to the

fireplace mantle and grabbed something off it.

She returned to the group and reached out an open palm to me. In her hand my lucky penny glimmered with a dull shine. I picked it up from her hand and marveled at it. The penny had been returned to its former glory apart from the black stuck in the raised edges.

"How did you fix it?" I flipped the penny over to look at the back and saw it was as clean as the front.

"Lemon juice, baking soda, and a bit of elbow grease. It's not perfect, but it looks better than before."

"Thank you so much. This penny really means the world to me."

"You're welcome." Bridgette smiled as she stifled a big yawn. "Let's take a couple hours to nap and we'll head out."

She left us with the slim furniture selection of the living room and shut her bedroom door. Tristan came and sat with me on the couch since there was only a wooden chair or Bridgette's recliner to choose from. I wouldn't be comfortable sitting in either of those places as well. We ended up right next to each other on the leather couch, alone. I laid my cleaned penny on the coffee table and handed Tristan a blanket from a basket Bridgette kept next to the couch. I considered trying to lie down to shut my eyes and get some sleep, but my curiosity took over me.

"How in the world did you convince Morgana to let you go on this hunt?" I unlaced my boots and corset. The boots found a place next to the couch, while I laid the corset on the coffee table.

"I just told her it was something I needed to do. I mean, I'm not a kid anymore, so she doesn't get a lot of say," said Tristan.

I wasn't sure I believed that after seeing their dynamic in the herb shop, but I didn't want to accuse him of lying. I, of all people, understood how complicated mother-child relationships were. Tristan inched his way closer to me on the couch as I formed my next comment. He was so warm I could feel the heat radiating off of his skin. I wanted to fall into his arms and have his warmth on my skin.

"She has to be worried, though." I stripped off my socks, placed them into my boots, and returned to Tristan's gaze.

"Yeah, she is, but she knows I can handle myself. It was kinda her idea for me to come."

That struck me as odd. What Domum would purposely send her son on a hunt with two people she barely knew? This solidified my reason to invite him even more.

"It was her idea?" I tried to keep my suspicion out of my voice.

"Yeah. She really wanted me to see if these witches were really working together and using her stuff to do it."

"She's really curious."

Tristan sat silent, looking at his feet, so I took it as my chance to learn more about him. I figured if there was a good time to pry, it would be now.

"Tell me about you," I said.

Tristan looked back up to me with a bit of a sparkle in his eye.

"What do you want to know?"

I thought for a second. What did I really want to know?

"Everything." I gave him my biggest smile.

He chuckled at me. "Well, that's a long story."

"I've got the time."

"I grew up with my mom. My dad left before I was born. She's been my whole life. I started helping at the shop as soon as I could. Other than that, I've just gone to school and lived my life."

I nodded, empathizing with him. I understood what it was like to have no father.

"That's a lot like me. My dad left before I was born too. Except I've been trapped in a house for eighteen years to do what I'm doing now," I said.

Tristan's eyes widened like I figured they would. I wasn't sure what reaction I was expecting. I recognized it was weird that I had hardly been out of the house, but I wanted to be honest. He tried to come up with a response, but it fell flat.

"You sound really close to your mom. Has she always been this curious or protective?"

"Pretty much how she's always been. She does a lot to not go evil, so she doesn't want witch creatures using her potions for evil. She's afraid it will come back to her, so she likes to keep tabs on things she sells," said Tristan.

I noticed he didn't answer the protective question, but I decided to avoid asking it again. I was more intrigued about what he said about Domums going evil.

"What do you mean 'go evil?'"

"You know, Domums that do too much evil begin to morph into Veneficas. Them staying good keeps them more human like," said Tristan.

His pinky finger grazed mine. A smart girl would have immediately snatched her hand away, but I left it there. He seemed pleased that I hadn't moved my hand, but I didn't care about that in this moment.

All I could imagine was Bridgette turning evil and sucking out a piece of my soul and devouring it. The night in the warehouse came flashing through my mind. The pain. The blood. My soul exiting out of my mouth in the shape of a rabbit. The rabbit floating around, looking for escape. The Venefica eating it and smiling. Me losing a piece of myself and still not knowing if there would be any consequences.

I snatched my hand away from Tristan and prepared to stand up. He touched my arm in concern.

"Wait, what's wrong," said Tristan, perplexed by my mood change.

"Nothing." I shook my head. "Just brought up a bad memory."

"You can tell me. I won't judge."

"I don't know. It might make you think I'm stupid."

The last thing I wanted was for him to think I was too incompetent to complete this hunt. I didn't need the judgment in his eyes that I faced from Mom for my ignorance. He already saw me as the weird girl, but did I really want to add more?

"Please, Atalanta, tell me."

Listening to my name come off of his tongue was like listening to music. For a moment, I wanted him to keep saying my name over and over. I didn't hunderstand what was coming over me, but the longer I was in Tristan's presence, the more I wanted him to never leave. It was almost like I was under a spell.

"I had a run-in with a Venefica a few nights ago for my first hunt. I mistook her for a Brujadan, so I was unprepared. She got the better of me, and my mom had to save me." I avoided his eyes.

I knew she ate a piece of my soul. I felt it leave my body that night, but I wasn't ready to admit that out loud yet.

"I'm so sorry," said Tristan.

"But I've learned more now, so I've gotten everything under control."

Tristan nodded. It shocked me that he didn't immediately pull away. He seemed genuinely concerned for my well-being. I just didn't understand why. I waited for him to question how I mixed them up, or why I didn't have a back-up plan. But we remained there, sitting in gentle, understanding silence.

"We should get some sleep. It will be the witching hour soon." I shimmied down on the couch and laid on my back.

I poked Tristan with my feet, and he laughed at me. Slumping down to mirror my position, he laid on his back also. He stroked my bare feet, sending chills down my spine. My entire body relaxed, and I felt the sleep creep into me. I pulled the quilt up higher for warmth and prayed I would be able to rest. I needed to be at full capacity to deal with two elemental witch creatures.

"Goodnight," Tristan whispered, still rubbing my feet.

I smiled. "Goodnight," I whispered back.

§

I sat across the table from Mom and Grandpa. It had been over a year since Grandma passed, and I still ached for her inside. She was never there to answer my questions, and I constantly looked for her and wanted to ask her things. I completely stopped my studies when she died. I couldn't page through books anymore and read about all the things that hurt her over the years. All the things that came for Mom and would one day come for me. I only dared to go into the history of Captrix and witch creatures.

Now, I was supposed to be learning how to actually kill them. I didn't have it in me.

"Now, sweetheart, you can't stop learning about your heritage because Grandma is gone," said Grandpa.

He was trying to be gentle. The good cop in this situation, like he always was. The women in this family were the loud and aggressive ones. This left Mom to be the bad cop.

"Look, your eighteenth birthday is in six months. You have to be ready." Mom slid the Captrix encyclopedia across the table.

Grandpa nodded, agreeing with her. Looking at the book made me nauseated. Grandma dying made everything clear now. I even started looking at a place to travel to after I turned eighteen. Being a Captrix was something I didn't want anymore. I wasn't sure if I ever wanted it.

"I don't have to be ready for anything. I'm not doing this anymore." I slid the book back to them.

Grandma didn't die technically of Captrix injuries, but we all knew she did. Ruling a natural cause of death at sixty-five wasn't normal for regular healthy people, but it was for our family. All the Captrix related wounds did this to her. The bruises, the internal bleeding, the curses, the cuts, the war to enslave humankind had done this to her. Premature death came with the Captrix responsibilities.

"This is your duty," said Mom. She tried to put off the tension building in her throat, but she did a poor job.

She was getting angry, but I had my mind made up.

"So, our duty is to die without one thank you from our fellow humans? If we don't die from being cursed, we die because we won the fights." I matched her angry tone. "Why aren't we allowed to be something more?"

"Our duty is to keep our people free, not to be given thank yous. We don't get a choice. It is our birthright." Mom looked at Grandpa for backup. "This is not how your grandmother would want you to act."

He stayed silent, making Mom more irritated. I looked at him, pleading with my eyes. All I needed was for him to turn to my side. I was his favorite grandchild. His only one. I needed one ally in this conversation. My stare turned him into Switzerland, and I could visibly see the shift to neutrality on his face. It pissed me off, and I felt all the loneliness wash over me. If he wasn't going to help me, I was truly alone.

"Well, she's not here to tell me different because of them," I said. My scream startled me, but I kept pouring out my anger. "She is gone because of this duty. I refuse to end up like her."

I rose from my seat at the dinner table and slammed my chair into the table. Storming out of the room crying, I raced up the stairs. Before I made it to the top, I paused to listen to what they were saying.

"It's not up to us to force her into this. She will learn if she wants to learn," said Grandpa to Mom.

"By the time she learns, I'm afraid it will be too late."

I almost thought I heard her choking back tears herself, but I dismissed it and continued stomping up the stairs. I slammed the door on both of them and began to make a plan for what I was going to do after I turned eighteen.

CHAPTER TWELVE

Bridgette woke me up out of my memories.

"Atalanta. It's time to go," said Bridgette gently, realizing she had awoken me from something tragic.

The impact of what I dreamed settled within me. I didn't expect an old memory to still come across so fresh. I told myself I couldn't even say if it was an accurate memory since I dreamed it, but I knew that was exactly how it happened. Tears filled my eyes, but I dabbed them away using the quilt. I had to be fine. This wasn't the time to crumble.

I looked at the other end of the couch where Tristan slept when we went to bed, but it was empty. There was barely an indentation where he had been. I circled the living room with my eyes, finally spotting him entering from the bathroom. I realized I was the last one asleep.

Atalanta, get it together, I thought. I whipped the quilt off of me and sprang to action. Disrupted sleep migrated to the corners of my eyes, but I wiped it away with my fingers as I reached for my boots. After putting on my shoes and lacing up the corset, I loaded my belt with vials of blessed water and a firebomb. The rest of the firebombs that belonged to me, I loaded into my backpack along with a few extra knives. I grabbed my penny off the table and slipped it into my pocket for good luck. After packing all my supplies, I felt ready.

I picked up my backpack, and we all loaded into Bridgette's car. We placed the supplies into the trunk and took our places in the car. Bridgette was in the driver's seat, and I sat in the passenger seat. Tristan took his place in the back behind me. Bridgette reversed into the black night where there was hardly any light due to the moon hiding behind a cloudy sky.

The drive to the swamp was long and silent. I didn't think it was over thirty minutes out of town, but it still seemed like it took days to get there. Bridgette refused to turn on the radio, and I didn't want to mess with trying to find a station. The only sounds heard were the wheels rolling across the pavement and the whooshing of the wind.

I believe we were all sleep drunk and didn't know what to say. At least, I was still tired, even though I hadn't gotten over my dream. I kept trying to shake it off, but I could listen to the argument in the back of my head playing on a loop. I considered chatting to see if it would shut off that part of my brain, but making small talk on the way to kill witch creatures didn't seem right.

Since I felt weird talking, I decided to try doing more prep to turn the voices off. I checked my backpack three times to make sure the crossbow and all of my bolts were safe. I looked at my belt again and murmured numbers as I counted all the supplies twice. Chill bumps rose on my arms and legs as the jitters came in. I was about to start shaking when Tristan reached up to touch my shoulder. He did it in a calming way, and I took it as his way of saying that everything would be okay. Before I had the chance to return any gesture, we reached the edge of the swamp.

The swamp was gross. The humid air that surrounded it was sticky and warm. Every time I tried to breathe, it tasted like I was sucking air through a damp washcloth. I was from Georgia. I knew what the weather tended to be like. This place, however, was on a different level. It felt ominous and wet.

The moss that hung from the trees made a thick curtain around the place which made it impossible to see in the three AM light, especially with the obscured moonlight. The worst feature turned out to be the never-ending fog that wouldn't dissipate. It added to the ominous tone by keeping a healthy haze over the trees. If I hadn't known any better, I would have expected a werewolf to hop out of the trees to howl at the moon.

I shuddered.

If I was a witch creature searching for a hideout, this would be the last place I would pick, but then again, no one wanted to come here. Apparently, they were on to something.

"Okay, here's the plan," I said. "We're going to stay together and circle the swamp until we see signs of them. If we find them, then we'll split up and surround them."

My plan felt dumb when I said it aloud. This swamp was massive and covered with fog. The odds of us stumbling upon the witches were slim, but no one else offered another idea.

"Be careful of stepping into any water. This may not be ocean, but the Mare will still have some control." Bridgette pointed at the large puddles connected to the deeper body of water.

"So be quiet and stay out of the water. Got it." Tristan fumbled with some vials as he stuffed them deeper into his pockets.

Bridgette rolled her eyes. She definitely still wasn't happy with our extra hunting partner. The awkwardness hung in the air, and I realized they were waiting for me to move. I tiptoed with my hunting partners following close behind. Bridgette was silent like she had done this a few times, or at least possessed stealth capability. On the other hand, Tristan was crunching almost every stick he walked near.

"Dude, seriously," whispered Bridgette.

I held back a laugh from her saying dude. It sounded foreign on her tongue. She was getting annoyed fast, but I couldn't blame her. He ruined our element of surprise, if we had any. With Tristan's noise level, we sounded like a herd of elephants in a swamp. I took a deep breath to calm my nerves, then switched to the middle to give Bridgette and Tristan some space.

We walked some more until I caught the smell of smoke and paused. There had to be a fire burning nearby. There was no mistaking that scent for me. I found my clue to the witches' location. Bridgette and Tristan sniffed the smoke too and nodded for me to keep going. I returned to the front position, hoping they would focus now that we had an obvious clue. I listened for the sound of a crackling fire and followed it.

The smell led us to the edge of the swamp bank next to the water. I squinted my eyes to look through the fog and saw the faint yellow orange glow of fire. The fire burned on a small island not too far from the shore. I thought I saw some figures dancing around the fire, but I couldn't be too sure because the fog distorted my vision. The water between the island and us was black, dark, and covered in the fog. There wasn't any other land close by, but this water didn't seem too deep. I figured we were further inland since we hadn't been walking too long. We could wade through the water, but the Mare would be a problem.

"She will definitely know we are coming once we touch that water," said Bridgette.

"She'll drown us before we even get there." I massaged my temples to stop an anxiety headache. "Or worse."

Tristan's eyes widened. He didn't seem too keen on being drowned. I didn't blame him. It wasn't super high on my list of things, either. There had to be a way to get over there safely.

I searched for something we might float on, but nothing was around but old trees and moss. Frustration rose in my chest. I had a feeling Mom was on that island. I wasn't sure why, but my intuition just knew without a doubt. I took another scan of the ground but still came up empty.

I needed to figure out a way there. I took a deep breath and listened to my intuition. It was quiet for a moment, but eventually it uttered, "*Distraction*," softly. My brows furrowed.

"We will have to draw the Mare out somehow. That's the only way we get over there alive," I said to Bridgette.

"And what do you suggest we do?" Tristan peered at us both with horror.

Bridgette and I looked at each other and then back to Tristan. The thought of using him as a distraction crossed both our minds.

"Negative. The last thing I want to do is drown." Tristan crossed his arms in front of his chest.

Bridgette shrugged. I gave her a look, and she softened. It was a solid plan to send him in to draw the Mare out, but I didn't want him to drown, either. I didn't know what she would actually do to him, but it wouldn't be good. He would be dead one way or another, and I wouldn't be able to deal with it. Especially when we hadn't even kissed yet. I couldn't keep going with the what ifs if he got hurt.

"I'll go then," I said.

Once they realized who I was, there was no telling what the witches would do. I sensed they wouldn't kill me on sight, though, like the others. They hated my kind and desired to draw out death as long as possible for revenge. I was the one with the highest chance of survival simply because of who I was. Bridgette clearly didn't agree with me, though, because anger clouded her face. Tristan's face also showed a combination of mixed emotions I wasn't able to read.

"No, I'll go," said Bridgette, her voice taut with anger.

Bridgette slipped off her shoes and began walking to the water.

"Bridgette, wait! I can't lose you too!" I chased after her until the water almost reached my feet.

Even though I had only been with her for a few days, in this moment, I realized I needed Bridgette. I didn't have anyone else to cling to. Everyone else I loved had died or been kidnapped. She seemed to be consistent, safe, and I felt like she cared about my well-being. Bridgette turned around and grabbed my hand, anger fading from her body at my plea. She smiled and gave my hand a gentle squeeze.

"I'll be alright. I'm a witch." Bridgette winked at me.

She turned around and began wading into the shallow water. Tristan and I crept behind a tree, hiding ourselves among the fog. I handed him two of the firebombs from my belt and sat my backpack on the ground. I figured he would be closer to the Mare than me. He held them in his hands, having nowhere else to put them. I unzipped my backpack, took out my crossbow and bolts, and slung them onto my back.

Immediately, there was activity on the small island. I saw the shadows on the island move, and the Mare came into view in the moonlight. She ran into the water, knowing her hiding spot had been disturbed, and began moving her hands wildly.

The Mare split the water in half, creating a direct path to Bridgette. Shallow swamp water became two massive walls on either side of Bridgette. She sucked all the water into her walls, leaving the ground under my feet crusty. The fog thinned out in the air as the moisture in the swamp became concentrated within the witch's powers. The water wall remained still, holding the wall, even though water still seemed to flow normally. Bridgette took more steps across the barren ground, not caring about the water next to her head. The Mare made another motion with her hands and a small river flowed out of one of the walls to encircle Bridgette's neck.

The Mare walked barefooted slowly down the line as she continued commanding the water. She appeared even more beautiful than when I looked at her through my closet the other night. The witch's skin was pale like she never went out into the sun, but it complemented the long blue wavy hair that ran all the way to her butt. She dressed her hourglass-shaped body with a loose-fitting sheet tied into a dress. Her eyes emitted a blue glow through the night that I found intoxicating. She wasn't a horrific looking witch, and that made her even more dangerous. I could see past her siren spell, but she enthralled Tristan, leaving him with a mouth dropped open and moving toward her.

"Snap out of it." I grabbed the back of his t-shirt and pulled.

The last thing I needed was for him to reveal our location. I shook him to bring him back to reality. Tristan shook his head and remembered what we were here fighting. He licked his lips to give me a response, but I held my finger up to my mouth to shush him. I worried he wouldn't be able to focus. I was also a little jealous he found the witch so mesmerizing.

Even though the water shouldn't have been painful around Bridgette's neck, the Mare caused it to have a magical pressure, and I saw it closing on Bridgette's windpipe. She gasped for air. Tingles erupted over my entire body as I attempted to control myself. I began moving toward the water.

Bridgette held her hand around her back to give the okay symbol. I froze, trying to decide if I believed her or not. I refused to go back behind the tree when she was this close to danger. The Mare finally reached Bridgette and, with a wave of her hand, sent the choking water away. Bridgette gulped the air and composed herself. I let out a sigh of relief, but maintained my position.

"What are you doing here?" The Mare twirled her fingers, sending bursts of mist out of the water wall.

"I was out here collecting some plants, and I saw your fire. I thought I would say hello to a fellow sister." Bridgette massaged her neck.

"Really? Where's your basket?"

Bridgette's fingers searched for the invisible basket. It was a terrible lie, but I couldn't judge her too hard. The Mare moved her fingers, and water from the wall flowed around Bridgette's ankles, up to her kneecaps. With a quick fist, the Mare froze the water, leaving Bridgette's legs in a frozen prison.

"Try again, Domum," said the Mare. It came out like a hiss, and the irritation showed on her face.

"Fine, you got me." Bridgette looked down at the rising water level. "I wanted to meet the witches that took down a Captrix. Everyone is talking about it."

"Interesting. Doesn't seem very Domum of you to be curious about the dark arts."

"I've actually been reconsidering that. I think I'm ready to begin my transformation."

The Mare reached a damp hand out to touch Bridgette's face. I expected it to be webbed or scaly, but it was a delicate hand with long fingers. She stroked the side of Bridgette's face and wrapped her hand around Bridgette's throat.

"You seem awfully pure for that." The Mare tightened her grip on Bridgette's throat.

I wasn't taking any chances now that the Mare was so close. I motioned at Tristan, and he tossed me a firebomb. The delicate clay cracked in my hand and some herbs spilled onto my fingers, but the bomb was still mostly intact. I ran toward the water walls and threw the firebomb at the Mare.

She coughed as some of the herbs and spices coated her wet skin. Bridgette held her hand out behind her and I tossed her the lighter I had in my pocket. I ran down the open path past the Mare through the swamp water she had created, determined to make it to the island. Bridgette broke the witch's grip on her throat and clicked the lighter. The flame glowed hot, and she held it on some spices that landed from the bomb. Immediately, the area caught on fire, but there wasn't enough of the herbs there to engulf her in flames like we planned. The Mare screamed in pain and surprise.

Even though she was burning, the Mare turned around to discover I was halfway to the island. She threw her hands up in the air to close the walkway and called some water to her to extinguish the flames on her arms. I sprinted as hard as possible until all the water the Mare used to build the walls began crashing into turbulent waves.

Water licked at my heels, and the Mare screamed behind me. I wanted to turn back to check on Bridgette, but I knew that was a terrible idea. The water was coming in too fast, and if I turned back, I would never reach the island. All I could do was run and escape the waves. I tripped onto the island right as water grabbed my ankle.

The water tightened around my ankle like a hand and pulled me back. I thrashed around like a beached dolphin to get loose and crawled up further on the bank. It was almost like I disappointed the water by escaping because it drew back from the island. Sand coated my hands from my fall, and I felt it getting into my clothes. I began the laboring process of standing up out of wet sand, but it wasn't fast enough.

My intuition screamed, *"GET UP!"*

I rose from the sand, as a fireball flew behind my back, singeing the top of my undershirt beneath the leather corset.

The scent of my burnt hair invaded my nose as I turned to see the Ignis, running toward me. Her skin was an entire fire engulfing a human body like a pulsing, red bodysuit. I couldn't make out her face because of the sheer brightness and heat she produced. Terror filled me as the raging ball of fire ran closer to me.

"I see you came to pick up Mommy." The Ignis threw another fireball straight toward me.

I ran, swerving to the side, praying the ball would hit water and not track me. The last thing I needed was burnt legs again. I sensed the heat as the fireball whizzed past me and crashed into the water the Mare had released.

The ball hissed in the water, and the tension in the air between us grew stronger. I turned to face the Ignis as she prepared another fireball. Pulling the crossbow off of my back, I thanked myself for preloading a blessed water bolt during my car panic. I aimed at the heart of the Ignis and smiled as I pulled the trigger.

The bolt sailed in the air right toward her heart, but suddenly, a gust of wind blew and pushed it to the side, making the bolt pierce the Ignis's shoulder. I couldn't believe I missed when she was that close.

She howled in pain as her flamed shoulder turned to tan skin. The water spread, running down her arm, extinguishing her fire everywhere it touched. Her body hissed like putting a hot pan in a sink. I was awestruck that she transformed in front of me. The water worked. I could do this. I shook myself out of my trance and reached into my quiver for another bolt.

As I loaded it into the crossbow, I overheard a noise over the Ignis's painful wails. I looked toward the campfire and saw Mom tied up next to it. The witches had her perched on a log with her hands tied with rope behind her back. They placed a gag over her mouth, and I heard screeching through it as she tried to force it away with her mouth. To my relief, she didn't appear badly beaten and hardly had any marks on her from fighting. If I untied her, it would be like nothing ever happened.

"I'm coming, Mom. Give me a minute," I said to her, assuming she yelled at me to come untie her.

Another fireball whizzed toward me. I dodged it again, but this time I heard no hissing. I turned around and saw the fireball coming back toward me, tracking my every step. Even with a quarter of her body extinguished, this Ignis was going to kill me. I finished loading the bolt and threw the crossbow onto my back.

I ran across the beach, away from the Ignis and the fire, trying to think of a solution. I overheard the Ignis laughing in the background, as her pain from the blessed water subsided. She wasn't able to reignite the part of her body that was extinguished, but I knew it was only a matter of time before she regained her strength. I needed to get the blessed water into her heart.

The heat of the fireball was on the back of my legs, getting closer to engulfing me with flames, when I saw a dead log on the bank. My intuition drew me to it, and I hoped it was right.

I ran to the log, picked it up, and turned to play ball. It seemed like a terrible idea, but it was the only solution my intuition desired to give me in my time of need. The fireball came toward me, and I swung the log, praying it would make contact. The fireball hit the log, engulfed it in flames, and burnt my hands before ricocheting off of the log into the water. I held my hands out and squealed from the pain. Anger bubbled up inside me. It was time for this witch to die.

I fought through the pain rushing through my hands as I grabbed my crossbow off my back again. When the wood touched them, I wanted to scream at the tenderness. I wasn't sure how badly my hands were burnt, but it felt to be on par with how she had burned my legs. I cursed my intuition. That couldn't have been the right move. How was I supposed to save Mom with no hands?

Adrenaline pulsed through my body to dull the pain as I pointed the crossbow at her heart again, determined not to miss this time. The bolt sailed out of the bow, straight for the Ignis's heart. Again, a gust of wind came and knocked it off course. I cursed as the bolt exploded in the middle of her chest. The Ignis fell back as the water extinguished her fire in the center of her body. She coughed, screamed in pain, and seized a bit on the ground. There were only a few flames left on her legs. I could finish her now, but I didn't think she would be able to generate another fireball. I ran over to Mom instead of finishing her off.

"I got you, Mom." I untied her gag.

She looked haggard, but still in better health than I expected. It looked like they had been keeping her on this island based on the amount of sand that covered her body. Her under eyes were dark and baggy. She also looked like she hadn't eaten in a few days.

"Are they feeding you?" It was a rhetorical question that I knew she wasn't going to answer.

Every part of me wanted to hug her and apologize for being stubborn. The desire to cry in her arms like a little girl and feel safe overcame me. I hadn't felt safe since my fight with the Venefica. Mom needed to make everything okay. I needed my mother.

Mom spit out the gag, and fear covered her face.

"There's another one," said Mom. The fear in her voice was unmistakable. She didn't think I could handle this witch.

Every alarm bell in my body rang as a strong wind surrounded the island. The flames in the fire extinguished, leaving me in the moonlight. The Ignis must have crawled away when I was with Mom because I didn't see her glow anymore, either. My intuition screamed so many words at me that I needed to know, but I couldn't discern what I needed to hear. I covered my temples with my hands to silence it, but nothing came out clearly.

"What is she?" I stood up to face my newest enemy.

"A Ventus!"

I had no idea what witch that was. When I was reading through the encyclopedia, I never made it to the Vs other than researching the Venefica. I only planned on seeing a Mare and an Ignis, not whatever this was. I swallowed hard as I took her in.

The Ventus was ghostly white with long white hair. The thing that disturbed me most about her appearance was her black eyes. She wore a black cloak that floated at the edges as she made her own natural breeze. She was the one who prevented me from killing the Ignis. The Ventus had been watching me the entire time. My intuition finally got one word out, "*Wind*," as the breeze grew around me. It didn't make me feel better. Evil surrounded her, and she struck more fear in me than the Mare and Ignis combined.

"Guess you weren't expecting me," said the Ventus, low, allowing the wind to carry the whisper toward me.

"Not really." I reached for my mixed metal dagger in the hip holster.

My hand cried in dull pain as I held the dagger. The adrenaline hadn't worn off completely, but I was starting to notice the burn set in deeper and blister. Hopefully, some metal on this dagger would be able to kill her. Otherwise, I had little to work with.

"Don't worry. I'm not going to kill you just yet." The Ventus lifted her hands.

The wind that circled around me came under my body and threw me across the island. I landed on my back and choked on my own exhale. I rolled over, trying to gasp some air, but the wind picked me up and threw me again, closer to the water. This time I landed on my side like a rag doll. I tried to take a breath, but a sharp pain came from my ribcage. I could get past burnt hands, but I wasn't sure how many broken bones I could endure. My arm went to my rib, trying to stabilize it, and I saw the Ventus floating toward me.

"Bridgette," I said, wailing softly. I had no idea where she was, but she was the only one that would be able help me right now with Mom still tied up.

Tears flowed out of my eyes, as the Ventus lifted me up again to throw me. I sailed through the air even further than I had before. This time I landed harder on my head, making my vision blurry. I saw darkness around the edge of my sight and knew I didn't have much left in me. I released my grip on the dagger and stuck it back in the holster, so I could try to stand.

I heard Mom screaming at her to stop, but the Ventus continued toward me anyway. Through my blurred vision, I looked across the water to see the Mare retreating to the island as Tristan threw a firebomb into her back. From what I could tell, she looked burnt in some spots. Before Tristan lit the firebomb, the Mare screamed and fell into the water, trying to rinse the concoction off. Bridgette ran toward me, creating her own waves in the shallow water.

The Ventus used the wind to lift me up like a rag doll and forced me to stare into her eyes. Wind circled me, keeping my arms pressed to my side. She reached her pale hand up to my face and scratched me from my temple to my chin with one long, black, razor-sharp nail. The blood, sticky and hot, trickled down the side of my cheek. She leaned in closer to my face, so I could feel her icy breath.

"You're not much of a Captrix, are you?" The Ventus flashed a wicked smile.

I forced what bloody saliva I had from crushing my face into the ground multiple times to come to the front of my mouth and spit it directly on her face. The wind released me, and I crumpled to the ground.

I heard her groan in anger as I pushed my burnt palms into the dirt. I needed to get up. I had to get up, but everything hurt now, and I was growing weary. While I tried to crawl away, the Ventus grabbed my hair and pierced my scalp with her nails. More blood began to matte in my hair. I looked at Mom and saw her thrashing, trying to get the ropes off of her hands and ankles, but each time she picked at them, they only seemed to tighten more. Blood ran down her hands as the ropes cut into her wrists.

The Ventus lifted me by my hair, and I reached up to break her grip, but the pain in my side stopped me. She reached with her other hand and dug deep into my arm with her nails, creating deep cuts from my shoulder to my elbow. Blood immediately started pouring from the wounds. My body was in so much pain now, my brain couldn't pick one to focus on.

"Are you done fighting yet," said the Ventus.

"Let her go," said Bridgette. Her voice came out loud and full of venom.

Instantly, Bridgette's force threw the Ventus into the water. The Ventus dropped me, and I was stuck on the ground again. She snatched some of my hair with her, but this time, that pain didn't outweigh all the other pain in my body for me to take much notice. The air was full of Bridgette's anger. It hung in the air like a thick cloud, keeping me pinned to the ground.

I looked at Bridgette and saw her moving her hands to keep the Ventus underwater. The Ventus trashed in the water and fought past Bridgette's magic. A massive tornado formed on the sand next to my mother. I resisted the weight holding me down and stood up to run toward Mom.

"We have to go. I can't hold her down much longer." Bridgette tried to calm her anger. She sensed it in the air too.

The tornado moved toward me, creating a wall between my mother and me. I thought I heard Mom say, "Go," but I couldn't make it out over the howling wind. As I approached the wall, it blew me away. I worked hard to keep from falling on the ground again.

"I can't leave her here," I said. I hated that it came out more like a whimper.

The tornado gained speed and picked up all sorts of debris as it headed for us. Soon it would be Bridgette and me, trapped in the cyclone.

"We have to." Bridgette grabbed my wrist and began

dragging me into the water, away from Mom.

I struggled against her, trying to find a way around the tornado. I didn't want to fail Mom again. Leaving her here would mean defeat. The Ventus rose from the water and went behind her tornado to push it closer to us.

"Atalanta! We have to go," said Bridgette, screaming into my ear.

"No, I can't!"

"Yes, you can. Forgive me."

Bridgette snapped her fingers, and I froze. Her telekinesis held all the cells in my body perfectly still. I looked around with my eyes, but I was now a prisoner in my body. Bridgette pulled me into the water and floated me on my back to the other shore. I stared up at the moon and stars, fighting against frozen pain. I couldn't believe she had done this.

Tristan's hands touched my shoulders as he pulled me onto the sand at the other side of the swamp. Bridgette snapped her fingers, breaking the hold on my body so Tristan could pick me up. The moment she freed me, I twisted and received the searing pain in my side. I moaned, feeling every ounce of pain. I looked across to the island to see that the witches covered it in a tornado wall, preventing us from seeing anything. Debris floated in the wall, making an impenetrable fence. We wouldn't be able to go back.

The Mare stood on the edge, looking haggard, but still took control of the water. I didn't see any of the others, so I assumed they were hiding behind the wind. The Mare wanted me to come back to try again, and I was ready to fight her too, but Bridgette froze me again as if she knew what was on my mind. My frozen face leaned into Tristan's shirt, and I breathed his smell in along with the swamp water and firebomb spices. I tried to thrash, to get out of his arms and break the spell, but I remained still. Knowing there wasn't a way to break out of Bridgette's spell, I closed my eyes and took shallow breaths to avoid the pain in my ribs.

CHAPTER THIRTEEN

Bridgette unfroze me when we got to the car, but I said nothing. I sat on her seats, not caring if I got blood on them, but the blood on my arm and face dried and felt crusty. My clothes were damp from the water, causing a slight chill on my skin. I leaned my head on the headrest and closed my eyes, trying to forget the pain that radiated through my body. Tristan reached from the backseat to give me a reassuring touch on the shoulder. I thought about shrugging it off because I was angry at him too, but shrugging would require too much effort.

The drive back to the cottage was silent and tiring. Everyone suffered in the battle. Bruises surrounded Bridgette's neck along with miscellaneous scratches from the Mare. Her clothes were soaked, and I saw her shiver from the car's air conditioner. Tristan had bruises and fried hair too. He must have been close to one of the firebombs when he lit them. He also had wet clothes, but out of our wounds, he didn't look that bad. I, however, looked worse for wear. Bloody scratches down my face and arms made me a sight for sore eyes. My burnt palms blistered, creating little water sacks. The pain in my side hadn't subsided, so I assumed I had a broken rib.

The broken rib was the worst part. Every time I tried to take a deep breath it hurt, so I couldn't make dramatic sighs to show Bridgette and Tristan how angry I was. It left me to sit silent-fuming, which is the worst kind of fuming because it builds and never gets a chance to boil over. What was the point of being angry at someone if you couldn't let them know in a passive-aggressive manner?

When we reached the house, Tristan demanded to carry me inside. I hobbled away from him. No matter what part of me wanted to be carried by him, my pride was too bruised right now to be vulnerable. I winced with every step, immediately regretting my decision, but I eventually made it to the door a few moments after Bridgette and Tristan. Bridgette unlocked the door and did a quick sweep for uninvited guests. She found none and motioned us inside.

"You'll need to take a shower to wash out those wounds," Bridgette said matter-of-factly.

The sun started to rise outside, and I knew my sleep pattern would never be the same again. Then, I remembered my rib was broken or cracked. The idea of lifting my arms up alone to feel that pain was too much. I would rather go to bed bloody and dirty.

"I can't lift my arms up." I stared at Bridgette's feet.

"I'll help you. Go into the bathroom. I've got to get Tristan started on making some ointments."

She still wouldn't make eye contact with me, but I also avoided her eyes as well. I didn't know if she was angry at me for fighting with her or if she felt guilty for dragging me away. Either way, I didn't like the tension that filled the air between us.

I made my way to the bathroom and shut the door behind me. I heard Bridgette's muffled instructions to Tristan on potion bases to start. He replied to her, but I couldn't make out what he was saying. I gave up on my eavesdropping and assumed Bridgette would be a minute, so I took a moment to glance at myself in the mirror. A gasp escaped me as I tried to hold in the shock.

Blood matted my blonde hair, and it was damp at the end from the swamp water. I didn't care too much about it because I understood it would wash out, even if the micro cuts on my scalp continued to hurt. However, my face terrified me. The deep scratches the Ventus gave me looked awful in the fluorescent light. I looked like I had been in three catfights and had not won a single one. I leaned in closer to look at the scratch on my face. It didn't seem too deep except for the line on my temple. I touched it and knew it would probably scar in that spot. My arm had shallow marks that would turn into scabs. I could live with that. However, these other scratches weren't going to be a badge of honor if they scarred. They were going to be a forever reminder of my ignorance and failure. I realized that was why she had done it. The Ventus was determined to make sure that I remembered she was more powerful than I would ever be. Every time I gained a twinge of confidence in being a Captrix, something was always there to take me back to square one. This was evidence of another reason I was never meant to do this.

Bridgette opened the door and exhaled a deep breath. I had the sense she wanted to say something but wasn't sure how to start this conversation.

"I just need help taking off the top. I think I can manage my pants and boots," I said.

Bridgette untied my leather corset gently, and it fell into my arms. The pain flooded into me as the support that was keeping my rib in a good place came undone. I let out a whimper before I could catch it. Bridgette looked away and swallowed hard. She sniffled, holding back her tears.

"I'm sorry," Bridgette said softly.

I handed her the corset, and she made a pile on the floor with it. She reached her hands around me to remove my singed undershirt. My shirt didn't make it onto the floor. She threw it into the trash can instead.

"You made me leave her." I tried to choke down my anger. The pain was making me more irritable, but I had to let her know how I felt.

"I didn't have a choice. You were getting beaten up. She told us to go."

I squatted down to untie my boots. Silence filled the air again, catching up with his old friend, tension. Bridgette stood there for a moment, waiting for my response, but I didn't have one to give. In a way, I recognized she was right, but my anger wasn't going to let me see that yet. Giving up, Bridgette turned and walked out the door to leave me to shower.

After my shower, I put on a pajama set Bridgette brought into the bathroom for me. I heard her enter again, but I ignored her while she set the change of clothes on the toilet seat lid. This set was loose gray silk and floated over my cuts and bruises. It glided on my skin and felt luxurious, almost making me forget I had wounds all over my body. The set was simple to put on since the shirt was lined with buttons. Thankfully, no reaching over my head. It was a courteous thought for Bridgette to bring me something like this to put on.

The pain in my side persisted, but I got used to taking shallow breaths. The burns on my hands made it difficult for me to touch things. Every time I touched a hard surface like a doorknob, I felt the liquid in my blisters ooze. The stinging was also barely bearable, and I couldn't wait to slather on Bridgette's purple burn salve. Luckily, the kitchen wasn't too far away from the bathroom, so I wouldn't get too winded from the walk.

When I stepped into the kitchen, Bridgette stirred something on the stove. I scanned the room for Tristan, but he was nowhere to be found. I walked to the open shelving with all of Bridgette's salves and found the purple one. I grabbed it off the shelf and winced at the cool metal touching my hand. I walked it over to the table and sat down, unscrewing the lid as I went. Grabbing a glob of salve on my fingers, I began rubbing it into my hands like hand lotion. The pain was as intense as the original burn to begin with but dulled, as the salve worked in my hands to repair the skin. I recapped the salve and continued rubbing it deeper into my hands.

"Where's Tristan," I said. At first, I thought he was missing, but now I was concerned that he actually left.

Bridgette didn't turn from her pot on the stove and continued to stir the concoction.

"He ran out to call Morgana. I suggested he give her an

update." Bridgette clanged her wooden spoon on the side of the pot to clean it.

My anxiety subsided. He managed to see me fail and get beat up, but didn't leave. He shocked me since he didn't run at the first opportunity, but I was glad he was still around. The sun had completely risen now, and morning poured through the kitchen window. Exhaustion consumed me, but I also felt like I wouldn't sleep. However, my body betrayed me, and I let out a yawn. A cup of coffee sounded delicious at this moment.

"I know you're tired, but I made you some oatmeal. I added some stuff in there which should help your ribs heal." Bridgette brought a steaming bowl over to the table.

I took it from her and ate a spoonful. It tasted like apple and cinnamon oatmeal but had an earthy or nutty tone at the end I couldn't put my finger on. I figured this must be the extra stuff added to help me heal.

"What's in it," I said.

"Ground pumpkin seed and nuts. With the right intention, it will heal bones," said Bridgette.

Suddenly, the earthy flavor made more sense. I ate another spoonful. This time the taste didn't overwhelm me as I got used to the flavor.

"So, how do you feel?" Bridgette paced the kitchen.

I wanted her to sit down. I didn't like how uneasy she seemed. Bridgette was normally calm. This was something else.

"Like a rag doll that has been thrown around too many times." I took another bite of oatmeal. "How about you?"

"I've been better, but it will heal."

I clanged my spoon in the bowl of oatmeal, finishing the

last bite. I didn't feel any different at all, just a little full. Instead of fixing my hunger, I expected to instant heal, but the pain in my side only dulled itself a little. Looking up at Bridgette, I tried to catch her eye, so we could have a meaningful conversation. I wanted to ask her more about how this oatmeal would work, but she kept her distance from me and made sure I didn't see her face for very long. The tension in the room thickened, and I knew I had to address it instead of inquiring about oatmeal.

"We both know this isn't what we want to talk about." I stared into the empty bowl.

I was angry and hurt, so it was time for Bridgette to hear it. I wished I had the confidence to look her in the eye when I started this argument.

"I didn't have a choice, Atalanta," said Bridgette, putting on a loving mom-like voice.

I tried to study her in the face, but she still averted her eyes from me, even though she crafted the right tone. I wasn't falling for it this time.

"Yes, you did! You made me leave my mom there! God knows what those witches are doing to her now." I couldn't control my anger anymore.

"That Ventus was going to kill you! You were in over your head."

"I wished she finished the job, so I didn't have to live like this!" I bit my lower lip to hold back tears until it bled into my mouth. I wasn't going to cry this time and be weak.

"You don't mean that."

I pushed myself back from the table and looked at her. Bridgette faced the window over the sink. Her entire body was rigid with anger.

"And what if I do? It was my job to save her, and you stopped me."

"I did what I had to do to keep you alive. She told us to leave her there." Bridgette's words came out like a hiss.

"If that's the truth, why won't you even look at me?"

Bridgette balled her fists up and groaned in frustration. Bottles and jars from the shelf began crashing down. Dust covered the floor as valuable herbs and spices landed on the ground, wafting an intense fragrance into the air. Salves became solids free of their jars and rolled across the floor, leaving a residue as they went. The shelf shook as if an earthquake was happening to it. I rose from the table, moving away from the shelf before it tumbled over.

"Bridgette," I said, yelling to get her attention.

Bridgette looked at the shelf and released her hands from their fists, realizing what she had done. The shelf stopped shaking when she let go. I stared at the debris on the floor in disbelief. She finally turned to face me, and I could see lines that weren't there before appearing. Strands of her brown hair were turning black. Her eyes started to darken, hiding the beautiful silver flecks that were normally there. She mouthed, "I'm sorry," as she began to convulse.

She didn't have control. I had to do something.

"Am I interrupting?" Tristen walked into the kitchen.

Before I could reach out to her, Bridgette ran out of the opening, throwing Tristan to the side. He crashed against the doorjamb and cringed when the wood met his elbow. Tristan rubbed his elbow to ease the pain and steadied himself.

"I'm going to take that as a yes," said Tristan. His face broke out into a grimace as he rubbed the tender spot.

The next thing I heard was the front door slam, and Bridgette's screams from the front yard. I propelled myself into action and cupped my hand to my side to run. The ache was way more manageable now, but this would still hurt. Tristan, forgetting about his elbow, stretched his arm across the door frame, blocking my path.

"I have to go after her." I motioned with my left arm for him to move, but he remained still.

"You can't right now."

Another scream erupted from the yard, increasing my desperation. Something was very wrong with Bridgette. I had to get to her before it was too late.

"Why not?" I tried to get around him.

Tristan grabbed my spare hand and held it tight. I looked into his eyes, ready to fight him. How dare he hold me back right now? He just listened to Bridgette scream. Even if I was furious with Bridgette right now, he wasn't going to stop me from helping a friend when she sounded like that. I ripped my hand away from him and tried to duck under his arm. Tristan blocked me again, catching me gently at the waist. I would have to let go of my supportive hand to fight him off.

"You don't understand. She's changing," said Tristan.

I froze.

CHAPTER FOURTEEN

Tristan dropped his hand from my waist, but I remained in the doorway, frozen.

The dust from the potion ingredients had settled on the floor, making the air easier to breathe. Shards of glass covered the kitchen floor, but I somehow avoided getting them into my bare feet when I moved.

My head hurt thinking about what Tristan said. Bridgette was changing. I knew he was right. We talked about it before relating to Morgana, but I wanted to remain in safe denial.

Bridgette fell silent outside, but my intuition told me something was very wrong. This couldn't be a good type of silence. This was the silence before a raging storm. My body tingled with indecision. Fear crept up my spine, and I could sense my subconscious keeping my memories suppressed.

"What do you mean she's changing," I said.

Tristan grabbed my hand again, and I allowed him to hold it. It felt reassuring, but also appeared possessive. He had no intention of letting me leave this house.

"You know exactly what I'm talking about." Tristan stared at me like I was stupid. I wasn't fond of the look, but I held my tongue.

"What do you mean?" Venom leaked into my words.

"She's done too much evil witchcraft. She's morphing into a Venefica."

With my failure at the battle and losing Mom again, I completely forgot what Bridgette was giving up. She risked everything to help me save my mother. Even her own soul was at risk each time she battled witch creatures with me. Now all the sacrifice had finally gotten to her.

The ignorance I attempted to maintain faded. My subconscious let go of the memories it was trying to keep me safe from, and they all flooded in at once. The Venefica rushed at me, chanting Latin. My red blood bubbled on the surface of my skin. My soul bunny looked for a place to run.

My hands turned clammy, and my vision blurred. I could sense the panic rising in my chest to combine with the fear raging inside.

In my mind, the Venefica transformed into Bridgette right before my eyes. Her brown hair changed to black, and she was smiling at me with black soulless eyes. She drew in a deep breath and pulled my soul from my body and devoured it. I laid on the floor, an empty shell of who I once was before she ripped out my heart.

"No, not yet. She's just got to regain her balance, or she will be." Tristan read my fear.

"How do you know?" The dampness on my palms grew.

I planned my escape, trying to remember where all my stuff was, even though I had no idea how I was going to carry my mother's chest. But I had to get out of here. I didn't have what I needed to face another Venefica, and I wasn't willing to lose another piece of my soul.

Tristan dropped his hand from mine and wiped my sweat onto his pants leg. He didn't seem grossed out, but embarrassment entangled itself within all the emotions I was dealing with. My hand felt cold without his warmth. I dropped my other hand from my rib, taking a shallow breath once I removed the hand. The pain was barely there now. The oatmeal was working.

"It's happened to my mother before. Just wait. She'll come back," said Tristan.

I shook my head, and Tristan grabbed both of my hands even though they were still clammy.

"Don't worry. It's going to be fine."

"But everything isn't fine." I bit my lower lip again. The voice in my head continued to tell me something was very wrong. She wasn't going to come back on her own. Bridgette needed my help. But I didn't know how.

Tristan drew me in for a hug and held me loosely to avoid my ribs. I buried my face into his shoulder and inhaled him. He smelt like pine trees and soap. It was a clean, yet homey scent, but intoxicating, nonetheless.

"I promise I won't let her hurt you," said Tristan in my ear, as he rubbed my back.

I stayed there for a moment longer, feeling the warm buzz between us, and drew back from him. If there wasn't a life-or-death situation unfolding outside right now, I would nestle myself here all day. That luxury wasn't afforded to me right now, though. I had to find a way to help Bridgette.

I nodded, acknowledging his promise, and walked to the living room. I needed to read, so I could figure out what was going on. It was the only way to discern a solution to this problem. If I read, it would keep me distracted from my fear for a moment. I hoped in the chest there was a book to tell me more about this transformation and how I could stop it from a distance.

I entered the living room and walked over to the chest. Tristan didn't follow. I heard him sweeping the mess in the kitchen. The sound of glass scratching against the floor mixing with the herbs and potions. I felt so bad. Bridgette's lapse of control ruined so much of her spell work and intentions. I knew it would hurt her even more when she realized what she had done.

I leaned down and ran my hand over the rough wood of the chest. I turned the key I left in the lock and opened it. I rummaged through, shifting knives and books to the side until a book caught my eye.

At the bottom of the chest was a mini-sized book with an orange textured cover. At first glance, it looked like a small Bible that missionaries gave out with the New Testament. However, upon further inspection, I noticed the gold lettering on the cover said, Witches and Their Transformations instead of what was normally there, Psalms and the New Testament. It was clever for my ancestors to disguise this book as a Bible. No witch creature was going to go near that as far as I knew.

I cracked the book open and scanned the table of contents for Domums and Veneficas but didn't find either term used. I frowned, disappointed, but gave another look. There was a chapter on the human witch, so I counted on that being what I was looking for. I took note of the page number and began thumbing through the book. The thin, papery pages made a crackling noise as I flipped to the middle of the book. I smoothed them down gently and began reading.

The Human Witch

Introduction

The Human Witch is a docile witch that has more in common with humans than any other witch creature. She specializes in the healing arts by using concoctions she creates in her kitchen from items in her garden. The Human Witch can use spell work, but possesses the powers of telekinesis. She is generally harmless unless she transforms.

Transformation

The Human Witch can become evil through a transformation. Whenever she is engaged in combat, it will force a Human Witch to use evil telekinesis that is linked to their emotions. When her powers are used for evil instead of good, she will undergo a transformation into a Venefica. Veneficas are transformed Human Witches whose telekinesis powers have become soul-sucking magic.

I looked up from the book. This made sense to me. I knew Bridgette used her powers a lot lately with the initial run-in with Morgana and the failed hunt. Her having telekinesis still didn't explain why she was able to freeze me and drag me away. I continued to read on.

The book went on to say that Human Witches also had impressive control over their spell work. Whispers of Latin instantly allowed them to do anything they wanted. This power only grew with the transformation.

The writer described the Venefica transformation as a painful process. The pure spirit of the Human Witch would expel itself out, creating wrinkles and changing hair color. It also wrote that the entire body would feel physical pain as if it was being punched repeatedly. Eventually, this pain would cause a thirst for a soul. If the Human Witch extracted a soul and ate it, the transformation to a Venefica would be complete. From there on out, the Venefica would have a never-ending craving for souls and spend her life searching for them.

The screams I heard weren't screams of anger, they were blood-curdling screams of pain. I could only imagine the pain Bridgette must be going through. She desperately tried to control her emotions and not eat Tristan's or my soul, and it must be excruciating for her. I scanned the entry for a way to stop the Venefica transformation but found nothing. None of my ancestors saw a transformation stop before. Or they killed the witch creature before she stopped. There was a small passage, though, on how a Domum could prevent herself from transforming forever by doing a ritual, but it required a lot of different witch creatures' collaboration and a person already missing a piece of their soul. According to the book, it had never been successfully done, so I skimmed it being I didn't have a friendly group of witch creatures to call on.

I sighed in frustration, closing the tiny book. Tristan walked into the living room, so I slipped the orange book back into the chest and closed it.

"You said Morgana almost transformed before," I said.

"Yeah, it happened once." Tristan rested in the doorway.

"How did she come back?"

"I can't remember."

"Please, Tristan. Think."

"I'm not sure. She said she was able to get her emotions back under control. She thought about me and didn't want to hurt me. I would have been one of the first people she came after if she became a Venefica."

A lightbulb lit up in my head. It was a terrible idea, but nothing else came to me. I knew I had to go find Bridgette before the emotion was too much for her. I understood I hadn't made her keeping things under control any easier with my yelling, so I needed to find a way to make it up so I wouldn't lose her too. She wouldn't want to hurt me. I just hoped she wasn't so angry that my soul became delectable. Fear stirred in me, but I shoved it down. If I didn't do something, the consequences would be worse.

"I'm going to find her." I walked to the bathroom.

I grabbed my mixed metal dagger sheath out of my pants laid in the corner. My rib felt almost healed, and I moved now with no problem. I took a second to look in the mirror and saw my scratches had also almost healed except one small place on my temple. Tristan was there when I turned around to exit the bathroom.

"You can't do that. She doesn't have it under control right now," said Tristan.

"I know that. But I think I'm the reason she's not keeping it together." I adjusted my dagger sheath to sit on the elastic band of the silk pajamas.

"She could kill you. Suck your soul right out." Tristan held his arm out to make a wall between me and the bathroom door.

"Maybe so, but I owe it to her to try and help."

I ducked under his arm, holding the sheath to make sure it wouldn't slip off the silk. Tristan grabbed my shoulder, firmer than I would like. Electricity surged in my shoulder like I was being touched with a live wire.

"Ow!" I forcefully shrugged him off of me. The pain rang for a second, but subsided when Tristan let go.

"I can't protect you if you walk out the door." Tristan ignored the spark.

I heard the anger and desperation in his voice. I realized he wanted me to stay, so he could keep his promise, but this was something I had to do. He needed to understand that. He wouldn't keep me from trying to help Bridgette.

"You couldn't protect me from her anyway if she comes to suck our souls out," I said, a bit of venom seeping out into my words.

I wasn't sure where the venom came from, but at that moment, I ached for my mother, who had saved me before. I ached for her advice and experience. She would know exactly how to fix this.

I turned away from Tristan and walked down the hallway.

He called my name as I opened the front door. I ignored him as I stepped out to a clear sky morning, wondering if I would ever get to apologize.

CHAPTER FIFTEEN

I walked across the yard searching for any sign of Bridgette. There weren't any tracks to be found, but her car remained in the driveway. I realized wherever she went, she traveled on foot. Terror welled in my chest. Even though I wanted to find Bridgette and save her, I wasn't sure what exactly I would find. If she was already a Venefica, I would have to kill her. If she was still transforming, I needed to find a way to stop her transformation. I also knew I had little soul left to give if she attacked me.

I walked toward the back of the house to a thicket of trees when I heard Bridgette's agonizing scream again. Instead of sounding painful, these screams sounded intentional, like a battle cry. The screams reached my ears, and the high pitch caused my hands to leap to my temples. I sensed a migraine coming on. Bridgette screamed again, in a tone so high that I tried to rub the pressure building inside my brain. It felt like the screams were trying to squeeze my brain from the inside. I gave up on rubbing my temples and covered my ears. Through the pressure, I heard my intuition trying to tell me to run, but it couldn't give me a direction. It probably meant for me to run back to the cottage, but I ran toward Bridgette's screams instead, keeping my ears covered. She stopped screaming as I got closer to the trees. I removed my hands from my ears and scanned the tree line, slowing down to a walk.

I saw Bridgette at the tree line, crouched down with her head between her knees, moaning in pain. It was what I would expect from someone motion sick, ready to vomit. However, she remained still, moaning. I wanted to run to her and check if she was okay, but I kept walking until there was about five feet of distance between us.

"Bridgette," I whispered, trying to mentally prepare myself for the worst.

My fingers grazed the dagger sheath hanging off the elastic of my pajama shorts. I was now ready to pull it out at a moment's notice.

Her back stiffened at the sound of my voice, and she peered over her shoulder at me. Bridgette stood up to face me, giving me a full look at her. I took a few steps back when I took in her ghastly appearance.

Her brown waves that began changing colors in the kitchen had almost completely transformed to black with only a few chunks of wavy hair remaining brown. Black waves framed Bridgette's face and her right eye appeared black. Her left eye was still brown, but the silver flecks I was used to had turned to black. It looked like ink was clouding over her eye, making a black cataract. Deep wrinkles formed, giving her creases on her forehead as she looked at me in suspicion. I watched her rapidly age in front of my eyes. Bridgette gave me an evil smile, and my stomach flipped.

"You coming out here made this so much easier for me." Bridgette sniffed the air.

I backed away a few more steps, creating more distance between us. My fingers wrapped around the holt of the dagger. Bridgette took note of the dagger and licked her lips. She gave me a bewildered look.

"You didn't tell me you had a piece missing," said Bridgette in a disappointed tone. She sounded like someone dissatisfied with their restaurant meal. If this was a normal situation, she would send me back to the kitchen.

"This isn't you, Bridgette."

"Who am I then?"

"You're my friend." I pulled the dagger out of the sheath and held it in front of me in defense.

I really wished I had my penny right now, but I left it in the bathroom when I changed clothes earlier. I needed the extra luck. Some extra copper wouldn't hurt, either. Stabbing her with the dagger would hurt her because of the copper blended in the metal, but I was also afraid it would kill her. I didn't know how deadly copper was to a transforming Venefica, and I didn't want to kill Bridgette anyway. All that mattered was if she thought I could.

I steeled myself and walked forward with false confidence.

"Would a friend boil your blood?" Bridgette called my bluff as she advanced toward me.

She chanted something in Latin, but I already knew what

was coming. Red blotches covered my arms as all of my blood surfaced on my skin. Some blood immediately dried, leaving me covered in a crust. My blood leaked out of my facial pores and poured down my neck as my body temperature rose. I blinked red out of my eyes as my vision hazed.

All the brown patches of Bridgette's hair turned to black as she continued chanting, building the strength of her spell. The satin pajamas turned darker as the blood stained them.

"My mother trusted you to protect me." I closed the distance between us and stabbed at her with the dagger. She dodged my attack.

Bridgette lifted her hand and slung my body toward the trees. I landed on my bad side and howled in pain as my barely healed rib snapped again. My hand flew to my side, covering itself in sticky blood. The dagger flew out of my reach, but I felt too weak to crawl toward it. Going a round with a Ventus and a transforming Venefica was a bit more than my body could take in one day.

"Bridgette, you're hurting me." I tried to lift myself off the ground. I hoped if I kept using her name, she would remember her human side. It didn't seem to be working for me, though.

"I know." Bridgette broke her Latin chant. She was only a foot away from me now.

"This isn't who you are. You have to stop."

She hesitated for a moment, shaking her head as if she was trying to shake my voice out of her head. Bridgette yawned, stretching her mouth and throat, so she could gulp down what the Venefica left of my soul. Fear caught in my throat, but I tried for one more plea.

"I know you were just trying to protect me. I didn't

understand how much you were sacrificing to help me. I'm so sorry," I said through a sob.

She twitched, but began blinking rapidly. Through my darkening eyesight, I could see more black covering her left eye. There was barely any brown iris left. She was almost too far gone and taking my soul would send her over the edge. Then, she would go inside and take Tristan's soul. It would be all my fault because I didn't stop her. I would be a failed Captrix once again, leaving Mom to fend for herself instead of saving her like I promised.

Bridgette took a deep breath, and I felt the pieces of my broken soul throb in pain inside me. My mouth opened wide involuntarily, and a small rabbit wisp escaped out of my mouth. The wisp looked at me in fear as it tried to figure out a way to run, like I had seen before. More tears mixed with the blood on my face.

"Bridgette, please don't. That's all I have left." I resigned myself to my fate.

Her eyes met mine, and Bridgette finally saw me. My rabbit ran back into my mouth and nestled itself in my fractured heart. Immediately, Bridgette's eyes cleared and turned back to normal, silver flecks and all. Almost all the wrinkles disappeared from her face, and the new black hair fell in a pile on the ground as Bridgette's scalp filled in with shiny brown hair.

"Oh God. What have I done," said Bridgette, as she began sobbing too.

She ran to me and leaned down on the ground beside me. Bridgette lifted my body halfway up and forced me into a tight hug. A sharp pain pierced my side, but the sheer relief that she and I were okay allowed me to ignore it. Our tears mixed together as her cheek touched mine. Bridgette got wet blood on her cheek from my face and tried to wipe it away with her shirtsleeve. I leaned back as she still held me in her arms and looked her face over to make sure she was back to normal. She appeared fine except for crow's feet lines that etched themselves deep in the corners of Bridgette's eyes. She looked visibly older now. A casualty of an almost transformation.

Bridgette helped me stand to my feet after I picked up my dagger, and we began trudging back to the cottage. I purposely slowed us down due to my side body pain, but also because I wasn't ready to deal with Tristan yet. I knew he had to be fuming because I threw myself into danger when he demanded me not to. How could he not expect me to try to help her? Why didn't he come with me? Wouldn't that allow him to protect me better? Nothing in this situation between him and me made any sense. I was too tired now to even try to make it make sense.

"You didn't tell me," said Bridgette.

"What do you mean," I said, playing dumb. I leaned on her more as I took shallower breaths.

"That Venefica took a piece of your soul before Artemis saved you. I could smell it." Bridgette's face clouded over with disgust.

I didn't know if she was more disgusted because I was missing a piece of my soul or because she smelled it in her almost transformation. I hoped for the latter.

"It's not a big deal."

Bridgette stopped in her tracks and pulled me to a stop too. I winced a bit from the force and placed my hand on my side for more support. She gave me an apologetic look.

"It's a huge deal, Atalanta. You're missing a piece of your soul. There are irreversible consequences," said Bridgette, putting on her mother voice.

"Like?"

"When you lose a piece of your soul, you actually lose a piece of yourself."

"What do you mean lose a piece of yourself?" I tried to squash the panic welling in my stomach.

"From what I've heard, it's different for everyone. Some lose their ability to feel emotion or use logic properly. Some even lose their faith forever."

Swallowing hard, I pondered what Bridgette said. I didn't feel any different, except the overwhelming sense that something was missing. Definitely still emotional, and I thought I reasoned well, so it couldn't be either of those. I wasn't a hardcore spiritual person to begin with, so losing my faith wouldn't be terrible. I hoped maybe that was the piece that was missing, and I hadn't noticed yet.

"Do you know what's missing," said Bridgette.

"No. I just know something is. I've felt different since that hunt." I turned back toward the direction of the cottage.

Bridgette took it as a cue the conversation was over, so we began walking to the cottage again. This time I walked by myself instead of leaning on her. I didn't want Tristan to realize how badly Bridgette hurt me. Not that my faking being fine would do much since my own blood covered me.

"We'll figure it out. Don't worry," said Bridgette, as the cottage came into view.

I nodded at her. Figuring out what was wrong with my soul right now wasn't at the top of my list. I needed another shower to clean my blood off and a nap to get my head back straight. Also, another batch of Bridgette's bone healing oatmeal would be great. I couldn't figure out my next move to find my mother if I was a sleep-deprived mess in constant pain.

Before we got to the door, Tristan came out onto the porch with his arms crossed. He looked like a disapproving father staring at his daughter coming home late for curfew. Or that's what I assumed a father would look like. I had never met mine. Shock took over his face as he observed all the blood and my hand pressed to my side. The disapproval morphed into fear. Then, he forced himself back to the disapproving glance.

Bridgette immediately became annoyed with his look.

"I am way too old and more experienced for you to be looking at me like that," said Bridgette curtly. She walked up the steps to the porch and faced him.

Tristan's eyes narrowed at her. "Maybe this look isn't for you." He remained calm, unfazed by her.

"Then, who is it for?"

Tristan's eyes looked over to me and met mine. I saw the anger on the surface with a cloud of concern looming in the back of his eyes. I blinked a few times and said nothing. What could I really say in this instance? I didn't want to deal with this right now after almost dying again.

"She is the only reason I'm not here sucking your soul out right now. You should be grateful," said Bridgette, bewildered by his attitude.

"And I told her not to go," said Tristan.

A fuel of rage came across Bridgette's face. I'm not sure where it came from or why, but suddenly, her eyes turned dark again. I grabbed her hand and grasped it tightly to remind her I was there. Bridgette noticed my touch and shook the rage off her face. She wet her lips to say something but decided against it. Then, she stalked past Tristan and entered the cottage, leaving me alone to deal with him.

I walked up to Tristan, my own rage coming to the surface. How could he risk picking a fight with Bridgette right now, knowing she was barely stable? He claimed he had seen his own mother almost transform before, so he knew what would set the transformation off. Either he was being stupid, or he was trying to make her change.

"You're being an idiot," I said to him, allowing my anger to come full force through my words.

"How am I being the idiot here, Atalanta? You're the one who went running to the woods to calm a transforming Venefica after fighting three elemental witches!"

"And you're the one trying to set her off when I just stopped her from sucking out my soul!"

Tristan's face softened, and he reached out for my hand. I snatched it away before he grabbed it and put my hands in front of me in a pushing motion.

"You're not my father, or even my boyfriend, so you don't get to tell me what to do. Hell, I don't even know you well enough to be dealing with this right now." I walked past him.

"You and I both know something is going on between us. You can feel it," said Tristan to my back.

With my hand on the doorknob, I twisted my body around to look at him. He looked at me with lust in his eyes, which was surprising since I was covered in blood, but his smug voice ruined it. He was right about the feeling I had in his presence. It wasn't natural. Lust filled me anytime I let my mind wander to him. My curiosity over him even allowed him to join me in this quest to find my mom. But I wasn't going to let this mysterious need for him allow him to walk all over me.

"Just because I can feel something, doesn't mean I'm going to let you control my life," I said, as calm as I could manage, trying to quiet the anger in my voice.

"I wasn't trying—"

"If you don't like that, then you know where the tree line is. No one is forcing you to be here." It came out exactly like I wanted it to, but the moment it left my mouth, I prayed he wouldn't leave.

His mouth hung open wide. Too late to backtrack, I walked inside and headed to the bathroom before he could say anything else.

CHAPTER SIXTEEN

After I finished taking another shower, I walked to the kitchen to see Bridgette at the stove once again. She was stirring something in a pot, so I peeked over her shoulder to look at what she was making. Bridgette looked over her shoulder at me and put on a warm, but tired smile.

"What are you making this time?" I tried to decide if I wanted to tell her she looked tired.

"A bone healing broth. It's a lot like the oatmeal I made earlier, but not as strong." Bridgette furrowed her brow in concentration and closed her eyes.

I let the moment hang in the air as I watched her. Fear crept up in me before I squashed it. Was she transforming again? I forced my throat to relax, so I could speak.

"Is everything okay?"

"Yes. Sorry." Bridgette opened her eyes. "I'm trying to infuse my intention, and I can't concentrate."

"You don't have to worry about me. Really, I'm okay." The rib pain had waned after my shower, so I was hoping it wasn't as injured as it was before.

"No, I did this to you. I'm going to fix it. You just need a boost."

Bridgette clicked the burner off and reached for a cup out of the cabinet. She ladled the broth into the cup and handed me the steaming liquid. I looked down at the broth, taking a whiff. It smelled like burnt rubber tires, dirt, and chicken broth. My face contorted, and I tried to fix it, but the liquid caused me to look at Bridgette in desperation.

"It's not going to taste very good, but I promise it will make you good as new." Bridgette gave me a shrug.

I shook my head at her and hoped this concoction would taste better than it smelled. I pinched my nose and titled my head back. Then, I took the cup of broth and drowned myself with it, gulping like a frat boy shotgunning a beer. The sour, dirty flavor enveloped my mouth, and I gagged. I begged myself to keep the drink down. After a minute, I felt brave enough to let go of my nose and breathe.

"You didn't have to be that dramatic," Bridgette giggled.

It made me feel better to hear her laugh. It allowed me to imagine the event outside never took place. At this moment, we were just friends in a kitchen, laughing about a bad recipe. The world seemed quiet and still.

"Not exactly your finest work, taste wise." I stifled my own laugh. "Thanks, though."

Bridgette grabbed a glass bowl and a lid from her cabinet

and poured the leftover bone broth into it. She left it on the counter to cool more and put the pot into the sink with the rest of the dirty dishes from earlier. I considered offering to wash up, but a wave of exhaustion hit me.

"I think I'm going to lie down for a while," said Bridgette.

"Me too. I need some time to heal," I said.

Then, I realized Tristan was missing from the setting. I looked around the kitchen as if he was going to magically appear, but as expected, he did not.

"Where's—"

"I'm not sure. He's still outside, I think."

I nodded, considering going after him. However, I told him he could leave if he wanted to. I was going to stand by that. There was no sense in continuing to drag him through all of this because it was only going to get worse. I resigned myself to taking a nap instead and walked to the living room behind Bridgette.

§

When I finally fell asleep after laying down on the couch, I dreamed about when I was seventeen.

That night it poured rain, and I enjoyed listening to the soothing sound as it tapped on the roof and windows. The TV glowed on the other side of the living room with the volume turned down to a whisper. I remained in my blanket cocoon on the couch with a large textbook from our homeschool library.

I propped the thick textbook into my lap as I read about American history. I had already finished my American history studies a few months ago, but I decided to read it again, much to Mom's dismay. Even though she cared about my traditional education, at this point in my life, my Captrix education was supposed to take priority. Mom wanted me to read more books on Captrix history since I only finished the first two volumes out of four. I refused to step into the secret study where the books were kept since my grandma died months earlier. Not only because I couldn't bear to be in there, but also because I decided I was done with this path.

I overheard Mom and Grandpa say that my refusal to learn was a phase, but I knew when I turned eighteen, I would do my first hunt to gain my rights as a Captrix and then I would be long gone. It took little studying to kill one low-level witch creature. One dead witch creature was all I needed and then I would be free to hop on a bus to California. But I had to complete my first hunt to be recognized. Without completing my first hunt, I would have to stay under as my mother's charge. I understood she would never let me go as long as she had control.

Normally, Grandpa stayed home with me, especially on a rainy night like this, but he decided he wanted to walk to the corner store for some ice cream. It wasn't an out of the ordinary request, but I didn't want him to go tonight. I had a bad feeling something was going to happen. I insisted for him to not go, but he went out in the rain anyway.

After I finished reading about the beginning of the Civil War for the second time, I checked my phone and realized it had been over an hour since Grandpa left. Way too much time for a quick run to the corner store. I called his cell phone, but voicemail answered it. Something wasn't right. I decided to go out and look for him, even if I wasn't supposed to leave the house. What type of granddaughter would I be if I left him out there alone?

I closed the book and set it on the couch. I unraveled myself from my blanket cocoon and made my way to the door for boots and a raincoat. With my raincoat on, I exited out the front door and turned left to go toward the corner store. I pulled my hood up to stay dry and to give myself some anonymity. I had no idea what could be lurking on the streets, looking for a future Captrix. After walking two blocks in the downpour, I noticed a body-like shape on the sidewalk. Leaning over it was a petite body shape wearing a black hooded cape. Icy air breezed past me, even though it was a summer night.

I ran toward the body, and the female wearing the cape vanished. As I approached, I took in the figure. A man wearing light wash jeans, rain boots, and a windbreaker collapsed in the street. An opened umbrella laid discarded to the left of the gray-haired man. I leaned down closer to get a glimpse of the stranger's face and realized this person wasn't a stranger at all. My grandpa was on the ground, barely breathing. A paper sack laid soaked to the right of him, and his tub of rocky road ice cream had rolled into the street. I crouched down and tried to lift him up. A sob caught into my throat.

"We have to get you to a hospital." I tried to stifle a sob.

His breaths were shallow and grew weaker by the second. I noticed his face had a gray tinge, and his lips were a soft blue. He was too cold, and it didn't make any sense in this Georgia heat.

"Mortia," said Grandpa, using what little air he had left to get the words out.

The sob I had been holding in wrecked my body. I read about Mortias in the history books before I stopped studying. Mortias were witches that dealt with temperature, but whenever

Captrixes began thinning out witch creatures a hundred years before, the temperature witches were renamed and put on special assignments. Now, the witch creature assassins killed with the cold or heat. Witches assigned them to murder Captrixes and Captrix family members over the century before they could kill witch creatures.

Grandpa's body was as cold as ice when I touched him, and the rain continued pelting harder around us, not allowing his body to warm. I knew it was too late, but I kept trying to lift him up anyway when she appeared. Long gray hair slipped out past her black hood as she tilted her head to get a closer look at me.

The Mortia looked strangely human. It took me aback, but she was also deathly pale. Her lips were blue, but in contrast, her cheeks were flushed as if she had run a marathon. Her eyes were a cloudy greyish black, but it was difficult to tell in the darkness.

Glancing back down at Grandpa, I wiped the rain from his face, trying to dry him off, even though the rain wasn't letting up. I should run away from the Mortia, but I didn't care. I had to save him somehow, but I felt helpless, watching him slowly freeze to death. I didn't know how to save him.

His death would be on my hands. Mom would never forgive me. I didn't think I would forgive myself. With my grandpa dying in my arms, I realized I didn't want to live anymore. I couldn't face the consequences of this night. Maybe the Mortia would answer my desperation and kill me quickly.

"I didn't know you existed," said the Mortia in a low whisper. "I guess I will have to kill you too."

Before I could respond to her, Grandpa took his last breath in my arms and went completely limp. My sob became a crying howl, but the Mortia didn't react. Then, she vanished in front of me. After what seemed like hours, I heard her appear behind me. Icy breath blew on the back of my neck.

"Shhhh." The Mortia breathed ice up into my ear. "It will be all over soon."

My ear froze and pulsed with pain from instant frostbite.

"Back away from her," said Mom.

I closed my eyes, thinking I was hearing things, and prepared myself for the rest of the icing of my body. I waited for a few moments, but nothing happened. Then, I heard a tussle behind me and the Mortia screaming in pain.

"Damn it!" Mom lost the Mortia into the night.

She sheathed her bloody dagger, visibly annoyed her kill got away. Mom looked at me.

"What are you doing—" said Mom, stopping when she realized I was holding Grandpa in my lap.

"You should have just let her kill me." I continued sobbing.

I leaned my head on Grandpa's chest, begging him to come back to life, but his soul didn't respond to me. The rain began soaking through my raincoat, causing a chill to run up my spine. Surprisingly, the water and humid air defrosted my ear, causing more pain to pulse from it.

"You don't mean that. Come on, we have to get you and him inside." Mom canvassed the open area with her eyes.

"No, I do mean it," I said. "I'm so sick of this."

"Sick of what?" Mom tried to lift me up.

"Sick of being left alone. Everyone always leaves me. My father, Grandma, Grandpa."

I fought her, but she kept pulling until I rose to my feet

for her. I stood alone while Mom gathered the umbrella and ice cream. She threw it into an outdoor trash can at the end of the driveway Grandpa died at. When she was satisfied with the cleanup, Mom motioned for me to pick up Grandpa's legs, so we could tote his body back to the house.

"I'm still here."

She turned her face away from me, so I couldn't read it. I assumed she didn't care anyway.

"You'll be gone next." My raincoat hood fell behind my head as I lifted Grandpa's feet.

I heard Mom sniffle, and her body began shaking with no noise. She shook her head until she stilled and began walking. I wondered if what I said actually hurt her but remained quiet.

We walked in silence back to the house, getting soaked by the rain.

CHAPTER SEVENTEEN

THE SOUND OF TRISTAN'S voice stirred me from my sleep. Grief filled my entire body until I felt like I was drowning in it, and I didn't want to get off this couch. It had been a while since I thought of the night my grandpa died, and it was more raw now as I assumed I was making the same mistakes trying to save Mom.

You saved Bridgette today, though, I told myself.

Even with the small glimmer of success, the grief pulled me back down. I needed more sleep. Tristan murmured again, so close I could listen. It prevented me from falling asleep and avoiding the world. I hoped he would walk away and talk somewhere else.

"The transformation is incomplete." I heard Tristan's steps pace across the wooden floors.

I groaned as I endured the soreness covering my entire body. The bone broth boost had worked, and it eased my rib pain. However, I still sensed all the bruises from being thrown around like a rag doll by the Ventus and Bridgette. Tristan's voice softened at the sound of my groan, but I unfortunately still made out what he said.

"I think what you gave me is wearing off. She's fighting with me now," said Tristan, his voice low.

Why would he be telling someone we were fighting? Was he talking to Morgana? And what was the stuff wearing off?

I opened my eyes and leaned up, cringing at my sore muscles. When I turned to look at Tristan, he froze in front of Bridgette's chair and ended his phone call. He looked nervous, but gave me a soft smile. I honestly couldn't believe he was still here. Especially after I told him to leave.

"Is everything okay," I said, choosing to tread lightly with my words. I didn't want him to know I was eavesdropping on his phone conversation.

"Depends on what you're talking about?" Tristan wiped away his sheepish grin.

He gave me an icy gaze, and I reached up to touch my ear, just to make sure it wasn't frozen like in my dream. I felt a warm ear and waited for Tristan to elaborate. He remained silent, so I took a deep breath and pursed my lips. As I moved to dangle my legs off of the couch, I motioned for him to continue. He sat down in Bridgette's recliner.

"Bridgette has recovered. She took a nap for a little while, but I think she's in the kitchen right now," said Tristan. "I just got off the phone with my mom to check in. Says she hasn't seen any weird witches come in. She recommended I tell Bridgette to take it easy."

I nodded. He stood up and walked closer to the couch, so he was above me. I took it as a power move. I didn't like it, but I was trying to not be combative, so I let him have it. He must have been amused since I had to look up to him. At least now I was sure he had been talking to Morgana. The conversation still bugged me, though. I made a mental note to try to ask Bridgette about it when I got the chance.

"And as far as our creative discussion earlier." Tristan crossed his arms and stood up straighter.

I rolled my eyes. Creative discussion was one way to put it. "You mean our fight?"

Tristan stared at me for a few seconds, took a deep breath, and uncrossed his arms.

"I'm sorry for getting mad at you for going after Bridgette. I just didn't want you to get hurt anymore."

I pondered his apology and decided it was genuine. I released the tension from my body and gave him a weak smile. When I didn't gawk at him, I knew what was coming next, the buzz. Noticing my softened demeanor, Tristan came over to the couch and sat down. He grabbed my hand gently and intertwined our fingers. I didn't get a shock of electricity, the buzz, this time. I only felt the warmth of his hand. It was nice. Any suspicions I had left faded.

"I don't want to control you. I wanted to try and protect you." Tristan grazed the side of my hand with his thumb.

"You don't even know me." I stared down at the wooden floor.

Tristan delicately grabbed my chin with his hand and lifted my face to look at him. I couldn't turn away from his intense eyes, so I stayed there.

"I do know you. You're smart, brave, and kind. But you're right. I do want to know what's in here."

He reached his free hand and touched my chest over where my heart would be. I had to remind myself to breathe. I continued looking deeply into Tristan's eyes and moved my gaze to his lips. He looked at me in the same way and pulled me closer. The smell of pine trees and soap hit me.

I wanted to know what it would be like for him to hold me. I wanted him to know my heart. And most of all, I wanted to kiss him.

Tristan leaned down and came an inch away from my lips. I felt the electricity come back, and it was buzzing between our mouths, wanting to draw us together like magnets. I closed my eyes, determined to close the distance between us.

"Atalanta, I have something I think you should see," said Bridgette, entering the living room.

I pushed away from Tristan before our lips could meet. I tried to slow my heart rate down and look natural, but it was too late. Bridgette had already seen. She blinked a few times, regaining her composure, spun around, and walked back to the kitchen without saying a word. My face flushed with embarrassment.

"Be right there," I said, calling after her. Then, I noticed Bridgette had left me some clothes on the coffee table.

Tristan's disappointment was obvious on his face, but I shrugged.

"I should go see what she wants."

Tristan nodded despite his disappointment and sighed. I stood up, dropped his hand, and grabbed the jeans and white t-shirt off the coffee table to change. After putting on the clothes,

I went into the kitchen.

When I entered the kitchen, Bridgette was stooped over a table full of books showing various symbols. I peered a little closer and recognized them as diagrams for witch creature rituals. Bridgette looked calmer and well rested now, but I could tell there was still Venefica tension hiding in her body. I walked up to her and gave her a soft hug, trying to avoid my messed-up side out of habit. When I realized it didn't hurt anymore, I held her tighter, and she returned the hug. Bridgette softened some more, easing the tension in her body.

"Sorry if I interrupted anything back there."

"It was nothing," I said, trying to squash the awkwardness. "What are we looking at here?"

I thumbed the pages of a few books, but everything looked foreign to me. I never read much on rituals. Bridgette took the cue and steered the conversation away from my and Tristan's romantic encounter.

"I compiled a few of my books and your books to see if I could figure out why certain witches would work together. I think I might have figured it out." Bridgette lifted one of the oldest books that was open and handed it to me.

I recognized it as one from my new collection out of the chest from the cover, but I hadn't opened it yet. On the page were fire, water, air, and earth signs in a circle. A small triangle was in the middle. No one translated the text on the margins, but I caught the Latin words: transformation, evil, and leader. I studied Latin as my foreign language for high school to further my Captrix studies. I wasn't great at it, but I remembered enough to know I was looking at something strange.

"What type of ritual is this?"

"One that I've never heard of." Bridgette furrowed her brows in concentration.

I looked at her quizzically and squinted my eyes at the page again. I thumbed the old and thin pages with extra care around this strange ritual to check if there was anything similar to it in the book that was translated. None of the pages had notes like I saw in Mom's other books.

"I can't really make it out, but there are no other rituals like it," said Bridgette.

"There's also no other ritual in the book with that type of elemental combination. I can tell that it's some sort of transformation spell," I said.

"Exactly. So, I drew up some more of my witch books and found some notes on witch leaders."

I motioned for her to continue as Tristan appeared in the doorway. He leaned up against the doorjamb and remained silent.

"Witch leaders aren't elected. Only certain types of witches can lead without going full creature-like." Bridgette took the ritual book from me.

"There hasn't been a witch leader in centuries after Captrixes killed the last one. The witches can't figure out a way to band together." I, at least, knew that was true from reading the first two volumes of Captrix history.

One reason Captrixes were so important was because they wouldn't allow the witches to realign themselves. By keeping witch creatures on edge through hunting, the witches couldn't help but turn to their more animalistic tendencies. When they were in this state of mind, they weren't worried about taking over the world or starting a new hysteria. They strictly focused on survival.

"Because they don't have a leader," said Bridgette.

"Only Domums can be leaders. They are the only one with the rationale to do it," said Tristan.

Bridgette cut her eyes at him. I wasn't sure if she was furious with him for stealing her thunder or if she was still angry from before. Tristan stood up taller and met her gaze. I gave them both a once-over and shook my head.

"That's impossible. Domums can't lead. They will transform to Venefica from using too much power. We all know how that goes." I winced the moment the words left my mouth.

I didn't mean to bring up Bridgette's transformation in such an obvious manner, but it was clear that was how it came across. Bridgette's lips went into a thin line in shame and frustration, but she recovered.

"That's where this ritual comes in," said Bridgette.

Tristan left the doorway and peered over our shoulders to see the ritual.

"I'm not sure exactly how it works, but according to my notes, four different elemental witch creatures can perform a ceremony that protects a Domum from transforming forever. That would make her a true leader." Bridgette pointed at the symbols and made a circle on the page with her fingertip.

"And you think that this ritual here is the one to do it?" My eyes widened.

Bridgette nodded. Tristan leaned in closer to the page and pointed at the triangle in the center of the circle.

"I've seen that before. It stands for a human."

I swallowed hard. A human featured in a ritual like this couldn't be good. There was only one reason the ritual would feature a human—sacrifice or as a food source. If witch creatures were trying to create a leader, they wouldn't be having a feast.

"But I've never seen the triangle broken like that," said Tristan, finishing his thought.

I took the book from Bridgette and looked at it again. I held the book closer to my face and stared. At the very bottom of the triangle, the line skipped for a moment. It was impossible to see with the naked eye at first.

"Maybe the ink has faded. This book is really old." I peered at the pages harder, expecting the broken line to fix itself.

"I've never seen any broken symbols on purpose like that," said Bridgette.

What would a broken triangle mean for a human if it really was on purpose? Broken spirit, bones, death? It could be a multitude of things. There was no way of knowing without having someone translate the rest of the Latin to see if there were any other clues.

"I'm sure it's nothing. Probably faded pages." Tristan shrugged.

"So, it's safe to assume that if this is the ritual they are working on, my mom is the triangle," I said, trying to hold back my worry.

"That would be a safe assumption." Bridgette's voice cracked, as she laid the book down on the table.

She closed the other books on the table, but left the ritual book open to haunt me. Bridgette's eyes seemed clouded, like they were lost somewhere far from here.

"Bridgette," I said, knocking her out of her trance, "do we

have any time ideas for this?"

Bridgette blinked quickly and regained her consciousness. She shook her head. "Not yet. I was about to start working on it."

"I've got it. You look like you could use a break."

"No, I can help some more."

"I insist. You've already given us a good lead." I guided her toward the hallway.

"Okay then. I'll go sit down for a minute."

Once she left the kitchen, Tristan and I sat down at the table. I gathered the books and moved them into categories. One pile was rituals. The other two piles had books on witch society and history. I felt confident that I would be able to figure out the time if I hunkered down with my intuition. Captrix intuition had never led me astray yet, even if I was still learning all that it did.

"Can I help?" Tristan placed a few books into the rituals pile.

For a moment, I had forgotten he was there in all of my thoughts. But when I looked at him, it reminded me of the warm moment on the couch earlier. How our lips almost touched. I knew I could finish it right now if I wanted.

I let my mind swim in the idea of kissing Tristan, putting my fingers in his hair and inhaling that delicious pine tree scent. His lips would be soft and slightly damp. When we finally kissed, that buzz I had been tortured with since he first touched me would electrify and finally simmer down to tolerable warmth. For that one moment, with our lips moving in sync, all would be right in the world. There would be no witch creatures or rituals.

But the moment I let myself go, an alarm went off in my head and reminded me that the triangle we just stared at could be my dead mother soon. All my dreams of romance were crushed.

I took a deep breath and slid the witch history books to him, careful to avoid physical contact. I was already lit up enough without starting another wave of thought. If I let myself go again, I wasn't sure if I would be able to stop this time without letting myself indulge in kissing him.

"See if you can find anything about witch leaders. We need to figure out what we're dealing with. I'll start looking for a time." I pulled the ritual stack toward me.

Tristan opened the first book and skimmed his table of contents. I watched as he selected his first topic and delicately flipped the pages before I began my own research. In order to figure out a time frame, I decided I would start with transformation rituals. If I found a common time scenario in these rituals, I believed I could apply that knowledge to our mystery ritual. It would still probably be approximate, but it would be better than nothing.

A lot of rituals seemed to take place around noon when the sun was highest in the sky. These sun rituals seemed harmless enough. Witches could convert common household items to food. They could change dirt from dry to damp. They were definitely commonplace things, probably things Bridgette even did. However, the more sinister the actions became, the closer to nightfall the ritual had to be performed. My stomach churned at transformations of animals turned into killing machines. A household cat could turn into an evil scratching demon with a small incantation and blood. Sticks could be changed into tiny snakes, among other ghastly things like human limbs and matted hair. It was enough to make me paranoid about all the random things my mother had protected me from when I was younger.

The evening rituals must have visibly shaken me because Tristan scooted closer to me and grabbed my hand. I felt the beginning of the buzz.

"Are you okay," said Tristan.

"I'm fine. Did you find anything?"

Before things got away from me, I snatched my hand away and held it in my lap. I stared down at the words, begging Tristan to ignore my actions and talk business.

"How do you do that?"

I looked up and saw in his eyes the same anger he had when I left him to go after Bridgette.

"How do I do what?"

"Act like you feel something for me and then turn it off."

"What are you talking about? I'm just trying to figure this out." I motioned toward the book page. "I think I've almost got something."

He shook his head at me. I sensed his anger seething off of him. I knew snatching my hand away came across as cruel, but I felt more in control now than since we met. No shock of electricity every time we touched. It seemed like I could control myself instead of wanting to be all over him. I enjoyed having more focus. Focus and intuition was what I needed right now. Not a boyfriend.

My intuition started screaming when I came to that conclusion. Thoughts of something being wrong flooded my brain.

"Someone is lying to you."

My stomach got queasy, wondering if the message could be about Tristan. After my intuition finished those screams, it turned on for my research, even though before it had been silent.

To think of it, my intuition fell silent a lot around Tristan. The realization settled in my mind, but I batted it away to listen to what my intuition was telling me about my research.

"Back of the book," said my intuition, so I flipped my book to its back page. On this page was a ritual to transform a human into a witch that had to be performed during the witching hour on a full moon. It wasn't exactly what I was looking for. It was actually nothing like the ritual we thought we were looking at, but it still required a variety of powers to complete. This particular ritual didn't require an earth element, only air, water, and fire. The triangle was without a doubt complete in the picture. There was no brokenness in the line to be found.

I wasn't sure how this could be what I was looking for, but my intuition wouldn't let me tear away from this page. I grabbed the old book with the leader transformation ritual and compared the images. To my surprise, the placement of the elemental witch creatures remained the same. They both showed a tight circle of witches around a triangle. The only difference other than the broken triangle was the addition of another witch in the first ritual.

I stood up and took the books with me to the living room. Tristan remained in the kitchen and looked at me with irritation when I left. I found Bridgette in the living room, sitting in her recliner by the window. She was tilted back with her eyes closed, but the moment I walked in, she snapped to attention.

"Did you find anything?" Bridgette slid to the edge of the seat, trying to not be too excited.

I walked to the coffee table and laid the books out in

front of her, careful to avoid the few leftover blessed water vials from the swamp hunt.

"I'm not really sure. But my intuition thinks so," I said. "These rituals are almost the same. Look at the witch placement."

Bridgette nodded. She ran her fingers across the human transformation, observing each witch placement. Then, she glanced over to the leader transformation ritual.

"That's interesting. Seems like they are performed around the same time too," said Bridgette.

"Could they do both at the same time?"

"I hope not. The human to witch transformation never goes well for a Captrix. Unless that's how they plan to get their sacrifice for the leader," said Bridgette.

"What do you mean it doesn't go well," I said.

"Wow. You really don't know anything, do you," said Tristan, entering the living room.

His words seethed with irritation, stinging me to the core. I couldn't believe he said that. He knew how much that would hurt me. I avoided looking for him at the door. Instead, I turned to Bridgette with pleading eyes, begging for her to continue.

"Most humans don't survive the change. Captrixes never survive the change. I think it's something to do with your intuition and make-up," said Bridgette.

I thought hard about the two rituals and tried to fit them together like puzzle pieces in my head. Why would a witch creature want to turn a Captrix, knowing she will die and use that sacrifice to make a witch leader? There were plenty of easier ways to kill Captrixes than trying to transform them into witch creatures.

"It doesn't make a lot of sense, but what if they are using the witch ritual, knowing it will kill my mom to use her for the sacrifice," I said.

Bridgette furrowed her brow. She obviously didn't believe my theory, but had no other evidence to use against it.

"It makes sense in a way. They would be trying to turn a Captrix into the things they hunt. Seems like a revenge plot to me." Tristan's face remained expressionless.

I didn't like the matter-of-fact tone he used. I stared at him hard, wishing I could set him on fire like an Ignis.

"Do I need to remind you that my mother is their play toy for these rituals?"

Since I had rejected him in the kitchen, Tristan seemed like a different person. I wondered if I had gone too far. If he kept this up for too much longer, I needed to figure out a way to get away from him.

"I'll run with this theory for the sake of time." Bridgette stared at the pages like they would give her a different answer. "Both of these rituals need to happen on a full moon."

"That's in two days." Tristan took a seat on the sofa.

"I guess we better get ready then." I looked down at the books again, begging them to give me a better answer.

I had a feeling these two days were going to be the longest two days of my life.

CHAPTER EIGHTEEN

I LEFT THE BOOKS with Bridgette for her to study them closer. Tristan still stood in the living room opening, brooding. I desperately needed some air. Grabbing a spare blessed water vial off the coffee table, I slipped it into my pocket and walked out of the living room, cutting my eyes at Tristan as I passed. I gave him the dirtiest look possible because I needed him to understand I was angry. For extra effect, in case he didn't know how I felt, I slammed the front door.

I didn't plan on going far, but I desired a moment to think where I wasn't being watched. Realizing your mother was going to be turned into a witch creature in order to be sacrificed, so a Domum could lead all the witches, was a tough pill to swallow. I didn't want Bridgette or Tristan to see me swallow it. On top of learning about Mom's fate, Tristan was being a complete terror.

I wondered what type of witch creature Mom would be. Would she immediately turn into a Venefica and start sucking out souls? Or would an elemental connection I didn't know about suddenly materialize? The fire in her could make her become an Ignis, and she would burn the entire world with all the pent-up anger she carried. Maybe she would lean into her huntress skills and become a Mortia. The options were endless. I imagined her face contorting as the power surged through her body, changing her chemical makeup. Then, her eyes would go black, and she would die as the thing she hunted for so many years.

If she survived, it would be my duty to kill her.

Emptiness enveloped my entire body at this realization. My duty as a daughter and a Captrix would be to kill the last family member I had left. If Mom died, I would truly be alone. The only thing I had left of her was the family trunk, some weapons, and a few books with her notes in it.

The smell of the damp night air filled my nose, and I looked up to the sky. The sun was setting, so the sky was full of orange and red streaks. I could feel the tears coming, but I tried to keep them at bay. Instead of a loud sob like I was used to doing, the tears came silently down my cheeks. I delicately wiped them away with my shirt collar.

Before I went further than the front yard, I heard Tristan calling my name.

"Atalanta! Wait!"

I regained my composure and stopped walking as Tristan ran up beside me. Little beads of sweat lined his forehead, and he was panting from his sprint. I looked over at him and raised my eyebrows.

"Where are you going," said Tristan, catching his breath.

"I don't know. I just needed a moment to think."

I sighed and looked back up at the sky. I was waiting on a message to be written with the clouds to tell me what I should do, but none came.

"I'm sorry about earlier. I was just mad."

"A poor excuse is better than none." I continued to look at the sky, determined to ignore Tristan's presence.

Tristan rolled his eyes at me and took a deep breath.

"Being mad wasn't an excuse for how I acted. I'm sorry."

"You really hurt my feelings with your comments."

"I know." Tristan's voice was soft and had a tinge of regret.

"You can't say stuff like that to me again. I mean it."

Tristan's eyes widened as he realized how serious I was. I didn't want him to believe he could walk all over me and I would be fine with it. I needed to set a firm boundary now.

"I won't say stuff like that again. I promise," said Tristan.

I gave him a weak smile and nodded to let him know his apology was accepted. He took it as an invitation to grab my hand, and I let him. Tristan's hands were warm and felt safe. We walked closer to the woods, holding hands. I stopped right before the end of the house, not wanting to go back to Bridgette's transformation spot.

"You're just so hard to read sometimes."

"So are you," I whispered.

"I don't know if you like me or not. Or what we're even doing here. You're hot one minute, and the next minute, you're snatching yourself away."

I stared at the wood line where Bridgette tried to suck out

my soul earlier. I imagined a wispy rabbit bouncing around the ground. A piece of my soul left out there for me to catch. The piece I had lost, ready for me to bring it back home. Blinking, I saw nothing was there but trees.

Tristan squeezed my hand to make sure he had my attention.

"I just have a lot on my plate right now with my mom. And trying to be a Captrix when I've avoided it for years. It's hard to even think about this," I pointed at him and then back to myself, "when I'm constantly getting beaten up or having to figure out how to kill witch creatures."

My words tumbled out like vomit with no way to make them stop. I realized I said them too fast when I noticed Tristan stared at me blankly. There was a moment of silence between us while he processed my word vomit.

"You're right. I've been so caught up in this that I forgot why I was here in the first place."

"Not to mention, touching you is painful, and I don't know why." Relief flooded my body. I was happy to finally admit that something weird was happening between us. "This is one of the only times I've been able to touch you without being shocked or wanting to jump your bones. I don't like feeling out of control like that."

"Jump my bones, eh?" Tristan let out a laugh that I couldn't help but smile at.

"I'm serious. And now sometimes when I get close to you, my intuition screams at me that there's something wrong."

I thought I would get a more visceral reaction from him when I told him my Captrix superpower was telling me to stay away from him, but Tristan remained calm. He pulled me into a deep, warm hug.

My safe place was here. It had to be. After so much running, hiding, and killing, this had to be one of the good things the universe gave me in this life. With all of my family gone, I needed a person to lean on. I needed a person to make me feel safe again. Hiding my face in his chest, I held on for dear life. I heard my intuition upset in the back of my mind, but I told it to can it. This moment was mine to be had alone.

Tristan whispered, "Shh, shh," into my hair and rubbed my back. When I came up for air, he looked at me with love in his eyes.

"We'll figure this out and save your mom. We'll do it together," said Tristan.

"No more stupid anger." I gave him my sternest look.

Apparently, it wasn't scary because he broke out into a chuckle like I was a cute puppy.

"No more stupid anger."

Tristan closed his eyes and took a deep breath. His smile disappeared, replaced by a serious expression. He loosened his grip on our hug but kept my hand in his.

"I need to tell you something."

I didn't want this moment to end. The moment was too perfect, and it felt good. I was afraid that what he had to say would ruin everything.

"It can wait." I pulled him back into our hug.

Tristan hesitated at first but, eventually, allowed it. He sighed and let whatever was on his mind drift away. I gave him my biggest smile and doe eyes. Then, he chuckled again, giving me a grin. Tristan leaned back and moved his hand to my face, cupping my chin and tilting my head up toward his. This was it. I knew it in my entire body: we were about to kiss. He leaned down and touched his warm lips to mine.

I waited for the fireworks to come but got absolutely nothing. It was like taking a burning match and dropping it into a pool of water. All the passion and lust I held for him was immediately doused.

"No, no," I said.

It came out as a panicked scream. I grabbed the back of his hair and kissed him again. Nothing. I covered his lips in pecks until he broke away from me, confused. Again, I got nothing.

The kiss sucked all the warmth and safety I experienced out of me. When I looked at him, all I felt was cold and empty. Bridgette said I would figure out what part of my soul was missing soon. Staring at Tristan, I realized the Venefica ate my ability to love him romantically. She broke me in the worst kind of way.

"What's wrong?" Tristan grabbed my shoulder and looked me in the eye.

I was too far away to really see him. Everything about me turned cold, and I felt like a monster.

"I'm broken," I said, almost too low for him to hear.

He shook me a few times, trying to get me to return to him.

"What do you mean you're broken?" Tristan's tone was coated in worry and pain.

"My soul."

Before Tristan responded, rustling sounds came from the woods. Out of the shadows came Morgana and the Ventus I fought in the swamp. My intuition screamed, *Trap.* Morgana and the Ventus were closing in, but I understood if I ran back to the house, they would find Bridgette. If Tristan was betraying me like I thought he was, she would be my only hope. I couldn't lead them to her. I froze with indecision.

"Tell her to come to me," said Morgana.

I stared at Tristan and looked at him with confusion, raising my eyebrows. I was ready to give him a tongue lashing about how he didn't control me but remained silent.

"I can't," said Tristan.

I thought I heard a tinge of remorse in his voice, but I didn't know if it was for me or Morgana.

"Why not?" Morgana motioned at the Ventus, who promptly took control.

The Ventus lifted me up with her powers and squeezed my neck with invisible hands. I choked out breaths of air.

"She doesn't love me," said Tristan.

"The love potion didn't work?" Morgana pondered the idea. "Interesting."

Love potion? This explained everything that had happened between Tristan and me. The buzzing. The uncontrollable lust. My inhibited intuition around him. Every feeling I had was a side-effect of a love potion. As it wore off, I must have gained some of my brain back, which is why I snatched away from him. But what about the one wonderful moment before our kiss? Was that love potion talking?

I looked at Tristan with disgust and kicked my legs, trying to break free from the Ventus.

"What is going on?" I struggled to get the words out with the pressure on my neck.

Morgana turned her attention toward me and smiled. "I

gave Tristan a love potion, so you would fall in love with him. I needed an inside man, and it was the perfect scenario. I saw how you looked at him in the alley and thought it would be an easy match." Morgana patted Tristan on the back.

Instead of looking proud of himself, revulsion covered Tristan's face. I choked out a laugh that removed the smile from her face.

"What's so funny?" Morgana motioned at the Ventus again.

The Ventus rolled her black eyes and loosened the grip on my neck, so I could speak better.

"Joke's on you. I can't fall in love."

"That answers the potion question then."

Hysterical laughter spilled out of my body as the stress of everything became too much. My fake boyfriend's mom was evil and tried to force me to fall in love, only for me to find that I can't fall in love. I found it hilarious. The only person that made me feel safe for a moment turned out to be a lying traitor. If only Mom could see me now.

They all stared at me in disbelief. To make a point, the Ventus slammed me on the ground. The pain didn't stop my laughter, though. Tristan leaned down beside me and tried to help me up.

"I'm sorry," whispered Tristan.

I allowed him to stand me up as I tried to stop laughing. The hysteria passed, but I needed to continue making a scene, so I could try to work out a plan. I had the vial of blessed water in my pocket. I knew it wouldn't do anything against Morgana. The blessed water also wouldn't kill the Ventus, but it would make her uncomfortable. A plan formed in my mind, but I needed to get a message to Bridgette without them realizing.

I'm sure Tristan made Morgana aware of the delicate state she was in by feeding her information, so I needed to keep them away from her as long as possible.

"I can't do this anymore, Ma. I can't let you hurt her," said Tristan.

"Don't tell me you're in love with her." Morgana frowned.

Her frown turned into seething anger. I heard her yelling about potion side-effects but ignored it. I tried to remember something Mom had told me about our intuition. Strong Captrixes could use it to send messages to people as long as there was a strong connection. I hoped my connection with Bridgette was strong enough, but I didn't know if I developed my nature enough to do it.

I focused all of my energy on Bridgette. In my mind's eye, I saw her resting in her chair, waiting for Tristan and me to return. We had been gone a while, so she checked her watch for the time.

"It's not the love potion," said Tristan. "I really feel something for her."

Instead of listening more to their conversation, I concentrated harder on Bridgette. One chance was all I had to get this right. I thought I could send one word, but I needed to choose my word wisely. I required a word that would not make her run outside to me like I knew she would want to. Saying "help" wasn't an option. With my mind's eye, I pushed the word *"run"* toward Bridgette sitting in the recliner as hard as possible. I didn't believe it was working, but suddenly, I witnessed Bridgette jump off the couch and gasp.

"Run" kept flooding out of my mind into hers. It was too much for Bridgette because her hands flew up to her temples

and she moaned, but I couldn't stop. My intuition took over and sent her flashing mental pictures of Morgana and the Ventus. *"Run"* continued to scream out of my head, causing Bridgette to crumble to the floor.

Before I broke the connection on my own, the Ventus picked me up and threw me toward the woods. When I hit the ground, air flew out of my body, and I coughed. As I gasped for air, Tristan ran over to me, followed by Morgana. The Ventus strolled like she didn't have a care in the world. She knew she had the upper hand.

"What are you doing," said Tristan, screaming at the Ventus.

"She was doing something. I could feel it."

Morgana shrugged at Tristan, which flew him into a rage. He rushed at the Ventus, rearing back to punch her. She easily avoided him and lifted him up in the air, using invisible hands to strangle his throat. Morgana yelled at her, telling her to drop her son.

This was my chance to escape.

I stood up and rummaged in my pocket for the vile of blessed water. I uncapped it and splashed it all over the Ventus. Her skin smoked where the water touched it, causing her to scream. Tristan fell to the ground immediately into a crumpled pile. I broke out into a sprint across the yard, toward the dirt road where I first entered Bridgette's cottage. If I made it through Bridgette's glimmer, I would be able to hide out down the road before the witches would be able to find me. I heard the screams and the tussle behind me, but I continued to run as fast as I could.

When I saw the glitter of the glimmer in my sights, a gust of wind tripped me. I tried to crawl back up, but the Ventus's invisible hands dragged me back to her. My entire body rubbed across the ground at a crazy speed. Sticks and yard debris scratched my face and arms, causing shallow gashes to form. I couldn't control my urge to scream, so it came pouring out. I prayed Bridgette was far away, so she wouldn't have to listen to it. I didn't want to cause her anymore pain.

I finally reached the wood line where Morgana, Tristan, and the Ventus remained. Morgana flipped me over, forcing me to gaze upon all of their faces. I looked at Tristan, pleading for his help. He froze with indecision, not sure what to do. His inability to choose to help me hurt worse than the gashes covering my body.

I squirmed, trying to get up again, but the Ventus forced wind on top of me, keeping me pinned to the ground. I focused on the stars, trying to think of an alternative plan. Before a new one came to me, I saw a rock coming at my skull. Then, everything went black.

CHAPTER NINETEEN

I woke to the smell of humid swamp. The air felt so thick like a hot, wet washcloth laid over my face. The moisture caused sweat beads to mix with the dried blood on my head. Old scratchy wood planks rested under my body, so I moved my hands gently to avoid splinters. The planks were damp, filled with the same humidity from the air. When I opened my eyes, I noticed dawn breaking through a small open window containing no glass.

I placed my hand to my forehead, touching the knot left by the rock. I winced at the pain, but didn't find it dripping with blood, so I took that as a plus. The rest of my body was a bit sore from all the scrapes, but other than that, I was good. Physically, at least.

After taking a moment to check out my surroundings, I

realized I woke up in some sort of wooden shack. The boards were old and a gray, weathered color. The window opening was sawed into the side and finished with a ledge but never encased with glass. The shack itself seemed on the smaller side, but it still had enough room for a few cots or sleeping bags, so I wondered if it was used for camping once. I gazed out the open window again, trying to determine if I could discern the time. Since the sun peeked over the horizon, I assumed it was between six thirty and seven AM. I slept for around twelve hours. Today had to be the day of the full moon for the rituals. And I sat in an old shack with no weapons and no friends.

Tristan's betrayal still perplexed me. I honestly thought we had a connection before the love potion thing. I felt safe with him. He seemed to not judge me for my lack of skill, even when I was hard on myself. I even dreamed he might have feelings for me. Boy, was I wrong. Tristan tried healing me only to betray me to Morgana, who was probably going to kill my mother.

I leaned up from my lying position to find they chained my leg to the wooden shack wall. I cursed under my breath and yanked on the chain. For such an old wall, the chain didn't even pull away from it. It remained so secure that I figured it had to be enchanted. I let out an enormous sigh of frustration, trying to figure out a plan. Before I could tap into my intuition, I heard rustling noises coming from the other end of the shack.

"Atalanta? Is that you," said a familiar voice that sounded like my mother.

"Mom?" My eyes darted to the other side of the shack and searched for the location of the voice.

"Yes, it's me."

Mom's voice sounded drained, like she hadn't slept in days. It hurt me to listen to her like this.

"Are you okay," I said.

I heard more sounds of movement and fixated my eyes on the corner of the shack. Into the beam of morning light, Mom crawled on her stomach toward me. Her chain stopped when she got within arm's reach. A cruel distance.

I gasped at the sight of her. Her left eye was swollen, and her entire body was covered in purplish bruises. I could tell she had been fighting because her nails contained random bits of blood and what looked like bits of skin underneath them.

After spending so much time planning to escape my heritage and my mother, I wanted nothing more than to crawl into her arms and for her to hold me like a little girl. I wanted to whisper to her all of my problems and for her to fix them like she always had, even when I didn't appreciate it. In her most vulnerable state, Artemis Capp was simply my mother. She wasn't the best Captrix who ever lived who tried to force me to be like her.

"I'm okay, sweetie. I promise. Now, tell me what has happened to you." Mom remained on her stomach, but leaned up to hold her head in her hands.

I told her the story of meeting Bridgette, causing a smile to break across her weary face. I continued with meeting Tristan and feeling the powerful connection with him. She knew about the swamp battle, so I didn't need to go into too much detail there.

She looked horrified when I told her about Bridgette's almost transformation, so I didn't want to tell her about my soul just yet. I concluded my tale with my capture and Tristan's betrayal.

"What did they do to you?" I didn't really want to know, but I had to. She looked awful.

"Just bits of torture. For some reason, they haven't killed me yet. I'm being saved."

"They are going to use you for a ritual."

"Tell me what you know."

"We looked into various witch rituals trying to figure out what was going on. Two seemed to match the types of witches she was working with—a witch transformation and an ascension ritual."

Mom nodded, soaking in every word.

"I think they are going to do the witch transformation ritual first to kill you. Your death will be the sacrifice for Morgana's ascension to leader."

"Can you draw the ritual diagrams for me?" Mom pressed her lips together hard in concentration. Then, she reached into her pocket and pulled out a sliver of coal she found on her side of the shack.

My eyes widened. She never asked something like that of me before with such a serious tone. Instead of suffering like a student being forced to recall information, I felt like an equal. It seemed she actually thought I was competent enough to do this.

Mom slid the coal across the floor to me. The fragment tumbled over the wood floor before reaching my hand. Bits of coal fragments had fallen off on its travels, but there was still enough for me to draw. I drew the first ritual, placing all the elemental witches in their proper place, and drew the completed triangle in the center of the diagram. I reached my arm as far right as possible and drew in the second ritual. When outlining the triangle, I made sure to the triangle remained perfect on the sides with the bottom line being separated by a skip that couldn't have been more than a few centimeters. One little break in the line haunted me.

"Bridgette thought it was a misprint or ink weathering, but I figured I would draw it this way for you in case it really meant something." I gestured toward the broken triangle.

Mom looked at it closely and followed the broken part of the line with her finger. For what seemed like an eternity, she studied the diagram in silence. I got antsy and picked at the coal with my fingernails, waiting for her response.

"I've never seen anything quite like this, but I don't believe it stands for a transformed witch. Triangles always stand for humans. If what you're saying is right, then this can't represent me for the second ritual," said Mom.

"That doesn't make any sense. They would have to do two different rituals for no reason. The end goal is for Morgana to ascend."

"I need to think about it some more. Why don't you tell me about what happened with this Tristan person?"

I hesitated to tell her about the love potion. How I had been duped to fall in love in order to be captured. Most of all, I didn't want to tell her I was missing a piece of my soul. I knew it would cause all of her confidence in me to crumble, and I would be stuck back at square one. She was going to find out one way or another, though, so I would rather tell her now than her find out on her own.

I began my story by talking about how I went back to the house with Bridgette and chased Tristan to Morgana's store.

Then, shortly afterwards, I allowed him to help with our rescue. I tried to describe the electricity between us and the way I had felt.

"Wait, you had a buzz? What do you mean," said Mom.

"You know, uh, kinda like static electricity, but more intense."

Mom cringed, recognizing what I assumed was a telltale sign of a love potion.

"Then, he finally kissed me, and everything just died. The buzz and the passion," I said.

Before I told her why, the door at the front of the shack opened. Mom and I quickly used our bodies to rub away the coal drawings I had made. I tucked the coal in my pocket and scooted further away from Mom, back toward my wall. Morgana entered the shack with the Ignis in tow. The Ignis herself looked at me with utter hatred. I figured she would light me on fire now since the last time we had fought, I almost killed her. She clearly held a grudge from our last encounter. I began to mentally prepare myself for the burning, but Morgana held her hand up to calm her. The Ignis shrank back into the background.

"I love a pleasant family reunion." A disturbing smile took over Morgana's face, stretching up to the corner of her eyes.

Mom and I remained silent and avoided looking at her. Mom took a deep breath, and I assumed she was trying to keep me calm, so I followed suit.

"I'm here about Tristan. What did you do to him," said Morgana.

In a blink of an eye, she was so close to my face I felt her hot breath on my skin. The fake smile disappeared and replaced itself with a scowl. Her eyes bore their anger deep into my soul. I tried to remain calm, but the longer she was in my face, the more uncomfortable I became.

"I didn't do anything," I said, confused by what she was talking about.

Tristan betrayed me and refused to help me when I needed him the most. What could I have possibly done to him?

"Liar!" Morgana reared back and slapped me across the face.

The contact was so hard, it caused my face to turn. Mom lunged at Morgana, reaching after her with her hands. Mom screamed so many angry things I couldn't discern them all. The Ignis stepped in quickly, grabbing Mom's forearms and pushed her backwards. The smell of burnt skin and hair filled my nose as Mom and the Ignis tussled on the floor. At first, it looked like Mom had the upper hand, but she became the loser as more of her skin blistered with burns. With nothing to put the Ignis out with, it was a hard battle to win.

"I didn't do anything. I swear!" The line came out in my pathetic, high-pitched voice.

I wanted Mom to stop being burnt. I hated the smell and the screams of pain.

"Please, stop," I said, trying to keep myself from crying.

Morgana held up her hand, and the Ignis stopped. She stepped away from Mom and left her in a ball on the floor, covered in burns. Mom's breaths were haggard as the pain overtook her body.

"I know you did something. He ran off with Bridgette instead of coming home." Morgana bored her eyes into me, searching for an answer I didn't possess.

Shock covered my face. There was no way after allowing me to be kidnapped and finding out I couldn't love him, Tristan ran off with Bridgette. A lot must have happened after the rock collided with my head.

"I can't even love him. What could I have done," I asked.

"Yes. I keep forgetting you're broken."

Her tone had an edge to it, so I knew she was expecting me to react. But I held firm eye contact with her instead.

"Your son makes his own choices. I can't help if he's in love with me." I allowed the anger to rise out of my fear.

Morgana's face contorted with fury again. She pointed, and the Ignis rushed upon me. A massive grin spread across the Ignis's face. This was the moment she had been waiting for. Her hands glowed a light orange as she touched my chest.

The pain wasn't immediate. It felt like my pain receptors turned themselves off in advance because they knew what was coming. But when it finally hit, I screamed. The smell of my burnt skin mingled with Mom's in the shack. Swelling began immediately, causing blisters to blossom all over my chest. When the Ignis was satisfied with how deep her burn was, she backed away to make sure Mom wasn't trying to get up. Morgana, satisfied with my punishment, backed away from me, smirking.

"It's going to be so fun sacrificing you." Morgana glanced over at Mom.

She turned on her heels and marched out of the shack with the Ignis. I immediately laid down as close to Mom as possible, trying to forget my burned skin. The Ignis was so close to my face that I would have been permanently disfigured if she went any higher. I looked over at Mom to take inventory of her condition. Luckily, she only had one major burn on both of her arms. The rest looked to be superficial and would heal within a few days. If we had a few days.

"What did she mean when she said you're broken?" Mom turned her head toward me and looked at me with sorrow.

I knew this question was coming, but I still wasn't prepared for the truth. If I told her the truth, it would change everything. However, keeping it from her now, even if I wanted to, proved impossible.

"I'm missing a piece of my soul. The Venefica at the warehouse ate a piece before you saved me," I said.

"That's impossible!" Mom's voice shrieked with disbelief. Even though I'm sure moving hurt her, she forced herself to lean up.

"I watched my soul. A rabbit came out of me, and she devoured it. She was pulling a second piece out when you got there." I continued lying on my back.

I turned my head to look at her, hoping it would convince her I was telling her the truth. I had never seen her cry before, but her guilty tears began to drift down her face. They were silent, stoic tears. Nothing like the loud, snotty cries I normally had.

"That's why I can't love Tristan. My side effect is I can't love him romantically like that," I said. "But something tells me I'm supposed to be with him. I guess that's just the love potion talking, huh?"

"You're supposed to love him." More tears streamed down her face. "The thing is with love potions, it can only amplify what is already fate. Sure, it can make you feel lustful or strange. Maybe even have a little shock every now and them. But the electricity you described to me isn't from a normal love potion. With that much electricity between you two, you're soulmates."

Her statement took me aback. Tristan and I soulmates? Everything I knew about him was a lie. He betrayed me to witches. He tried to control me when he had the chance, and I hated it. But he also apparently ran off with Bridgette for me, if I was to believe what Morgana was saying.

"I don't know if I'm ready to accept that," I said.

Mom nodded. "I'm so sorry she took away your love from you. I didn't get there in time." She wiped her tears away with dirty hands.

"It's not your fault."

Mom laid back down on her back, trying to avoid her burn spots. I figured she had to be processing the idea I was missing my soul. The longer she sat there, though, the sleepier she got, until her eyes closed.

I was also exhausted from the Morgana encounter, but I didn't want to fall asleep. I needed to find a way for us to get out of here. Even though the sun was now high in the sky, I recognized it was only a matter of time before it would be the witching hour. But with no resources other than a lump of coal in my pocket, I wasn't sure what I could do.

Scooting back toward the wall, I laid up against the piece where my chain was attached. I looked at the plate where the chain was bolted into the wall and tried to find a crack or any sign of wear. I fiddled with the chain for a moment, trying to not be too loud. This chain appeared recently installed onto this plate. There was no way it would come off, especially if Morgana spelled the plate to remain fixed to the wall.

The only way this chain was coming off this wall was if I took the old board from the shack with it. I stroked the rough wood with the palm of my hand, searching for a loose nail. I carefully avoided splinters until I found what I was looking for. A large wood nail lifted from the board. The nail felt loose enough to be able to wedge something underneath to get it off. I pulled the piece of coal from my pocket and tried to use it to pry the nail loose. The nail barely moved as the coal chipped away.

"Dang it," I said to myself.

I looked down at the chain length and wondered if I could get that under the nail. I sighed heavily, realizing how aggravating this was going to be. Laying onto my back, I pushed my butt up against the wall. I grabbed a chain link with my right hand and lifted my legs into the air to stretch out the chain. This put the chain link and my hand right next to the nail. I closed my eyes, tightened my core muscles, and let my intuition help me loosen the nail by prying it with the chain link. After a few minutes of work, the rusty nail fell to the floor.

I picked up the nail and used it to help pry another nail on the board. This one took a lot longer, but eventually, it came loose as well. Now, I could get my hands under the board and try to rip it off the wall. I hoped witches didn't think about finding studs for their magical chains and that it would come off with the board. I lifted the board as much as my strength would allow and pulled hard. A crack rang through the shack, and the board with the chain flew behind me. I looked at the wall and saw the board broke right after the chain plate, leaving the other half on the wall.

"What are you doing?" Mom stirred from her sleep and looked at me.

"We're getting out of here."

I stood up and dragged my half board behind me to where Mom's chain was in the shack. She stared at me while I worked on her board the same as mine. The board they bolted her chain on was more secure, so it took way longer than mine. After an hour of constantly prying and lifting, the board was loose. I pulled it off the wall the same as mine until it cracked in half. The board fell to the floor, holding her chain.

I picked up my board and chain as best I could and walked over to the small window to look out to the swamp. The sun looked like it was late afternoon. I scanned the landscape but didn't see any witch creatures or Morgana in sight. I began to get the feeling that this was too easy.

"Do they have any sort of schedule here?"

"Not that I've been able to tell. More active at night. That's when they've been coming in here," said Mom.

She still laid on the floor, but I didn't want to make her get up until I knew exactly how we were going to get out. Getting loose was one thing. Leaving a shack undetected, surrounded by various elemental witch creatures, was a whole other situation.

I walked to the shack's front door and paused. It sounded like an alarm rang in my head when I stood next to the door. I closed my eyes and listened to my intuition. My mind had an overwhelming sense that someone was right outside the door.

"There's someone outside the door," I whispered.

"I feel it too."

The only other option was the window unless I wanted to waste time prying off every board in the shack. I walked back over to the window and peeked over the edge. The drop looked manageable, and the window seemed big enough for us to squeeze through. It was still a tight fit, though, which would be excruciating on our burnt skin. I didn't see us having any other choice. Time was running out.

"We're going to have to—" I said.

"Go out the window," said Mom, echoing my thoughts.

She winced, already knowing this wasn't going to be a good time. With all the burns the Ignis left on her, it would be impossible for her to avoid having her wounds rub against the wooden windowpane. Mom stood up slowly, grabbed her chain and board off the floor, and walked toward me.

"You go first, so I can help you." I moved to the side of the window.

Mom nodded and lowered her chain and half board out the window to touch the ground. I held her hand as she began shimmying backwards through the window. Mom let out a small yelp of pain when her arms rubbed against the sides of the window, but still managed to get out and land softly on the ground. We paused, waiting to determine if anyone heard us. A breath passed by, and we remained alone.

I followed suit, lowering my chain and board out the window, and shimmied backwards out the window. Carefully avoiding my chest, I pivoted out on my stomach instead. I gave one last push away from the shack window and landed on the ground.

We stood breathless, next to the shack, again waiting to see if anyone came for us. There was no movement from the front of the shack, so we made a break for it. Mom and I ran toward the left to a thicket of trees, finally free of our wooden prison.

CHAPTER TWENTY

We rushed through the trees until Mom stopped. She doubled over, panting, and threw her board and chain to the ground. I forgot how hard it must be to run for your life after being a prisoner for almost a week. Even though I was full of energy, there was no way Mom could keep up at this pace.

Mom's board landed with a thud, causing the chain to rattle. The sound echoed through the woods, making me nervous. I needed to figure out a way to get these chains off, but I was afraid if I messed with them directly, something bad would happen. I took slow, deep breaths, trying to calm my mind as I took in the scenery.

We remained in the swamp, but in this place, the ground wasn't incredibly soft, which benefited us. No water meant the Mare wouldn't be able to track us. But this also meant we were way more inland than I thought. There was no way we were close to the original island they took Mom to. I sighed, realizing I had no sense of direction. Hell, I didn't even know which way was north. I needed a lot of intuition to get out of these woods undetected.

Even if we made it out, I didn't know where we would find resources to leave town. All of my things got left at Bridgette's cottage, and the cottage would be one of the first places Morgana would look for me. We were just going to rough it until we were miles away from this forsaken place. I set out to take us somewhere new, like I planned before. No more witch hunting. No more Captrix responsibilities. All I wanted was a new life with my mother safe.

Closing my eyes, I tried to tap into my intuition, but it remained silent. I thought hard about safety and asked questions about where I should go, but nothing appeared in my mind. I shook my head in frustration. If my intuition chose not to help, I would get us out of here myself.

"Come on. We have to go," I said.

I gently touched Mom's back, letting my plank dangle to the ground. Her breathing slowed, but she appeared tired. I tried to guide her forward, further away from the camp, but she shrugged me off after only walking a few steps. Her face filled with indecision, and I could tell she was deep in reflection.

"We can't go." Mom stood up taller. She visibly shook off all the pain from her burns and torture.

"Yes, we can. It's almost sunset." I pulled her with me, careful to avoid her forearms.

A switch flipped over in every part of Mom's body. My eyes widened as she changed in front of me. Gone was the pained, worried mother I interacted with in the shack. She stood up tall and steeled her face. I was no longer looking at my mom. I was now looking at Artemis, one of the greatest Captrixes to ever live. My heart sank.

"We will go back there and eradicate all of them. We can't let them gain a new witch leader," said Mom. Her tone was fierce, like a general providing battle instructions.

"They won't if we aren't there." I found myself desperate for her to shake off the facade. I wanted her to return to being my mom. "We don't even have any weapons!"

"They will just find someone else that fits the profile. Captrixes don't let that happen." Mom made herself straighten up as much as possible. Even though I hated it, she looked regal. "Our bodies and knowledge are the only weapons we need."

"It's not our problem if we get out now. Another Captrix will take care of this. Everything isn't always our problem."

I could feel time slipping away. At this point, the witches may have realized we escaped. I'm sure they were preparing their search. If we didn't get moving, we would be sitting ducks soon.

"What is your intuition telling you?" I hoped it was on my side.

Mom stood still for a moment and looked up to the sky as if she was listening to something in her head. I tried to tap into my intuition, but it remained silent.

"It's saying we need to do something."

"That something is to get out of here! Mom, we don't have time to argue."

"Captrixes don't run away from their duty."

Anger simmered inside my body. How dare she bring up

our family duty when she was about to be turned into a witch and sacrificed? How could she force us to be tortured and die for nothing? Why was this our fight?

"Our duty? It's our duty to die? To watch everyone we love die," I said, fuming. My voice became shrill with anger. "It's our duty to not have a life?"

"It's our duty to save people from witch creatures. That is what we train for. That is what we live for. If no one else does it, they will take this entire world over. Do you really want that on your hands?"

"You can't save the world when you're dead."

I put my hands on her shoulders, careful to avoid any burns. I tried to calm my fury, but it still simmered inside me.

"Mom, please." I begged her to see reason.

"You still haven't accepted who you are or your duty. You are a Captrix. This is what we do." Mom placed one of her hands on mine. "I have to try and stop this. Even if it kills me."

Her voice became her calm, Artemis voice. She was going to make herself into a sacrifice for nothing but her pride. All to say that Artemis did what she was born to do, rather than give up on this family heritage and save herself. I didn't understand why she was doing this to me.

"I won't die for a family duty I don't even understand." I pushed her hand off mine, let go of her shoulders, and shook my head.

I picked up my chain plank and walked forward, away from her. I expected Mom to follow me to change my mind, but she remained frozen in her spot. When I peeked over my shoulder, I saw the look of disappointment on her face. I walked a few more steps away until I barely saw her. My steely resolve dissolved into a yearning for my mother. As much as I hated it, I couldn't let her do her plan on her own. I was just going to have to work harder to change her mind.

My intuition kicked in, telling me to turn back. I shook my head, surprised it was finally talking to me. My hunch was correct. There was no way I could leave my mom alone. I sighed with disbelief in myself and turned around. Fear tightened my stomach, and I broke out into a run. Behind Mom stood Morgana, showing a sly smile. Morgana planted herself on the plank of wood still connected to Mom's wrist, holding her down. In her other hand was a pair of new shackles. Mom struggled against Morgana, trying to pull her plank from under Morgana's foot.

"Get away from her," I said, screaming as I ran.

At the sound of my voice, Mom gave up trying to pull her plank out from under Morgana's foot. She reared her head back and did a strange headbutt move that landed in Morgana's groin area. The hit was enough to make Morgana topple over onto the ground. Mom tackled her, scratching and beating on her. Morgana tried to push her off of her with no success and let out a scream. Mom flew up into the air, a victim of Morgana's telekinesis, and landed a few feet in front of me with a thud. Morgana stood up and walked toward Mom with her clenched fists.

I ran faster, so I could reach Mom before her. I didn't have any weapons, but my board would make a good crack against Morgana's face. In fact, I would enjoy smacking her across the face after our last encounter. I reared the plank back and prepared to hit as I stopped in front of them.

"I wouldn't do that if I were you," whispered someone

in my ear.

Their breath was cold, and they breathed a trickle of ice down my neck. My hand immediately touched the cold spot on my neck and tried to wipe the chill away. Mom's eyes widened as she shook off her confident, Captrix persona from before. She scrambled off the ground and reached for me as Morgana grabbed her arm.

Only one witch creature would make her act like that. I turned to look at my side and saw the same Mortia that killed my grandpa years before. She looked exactly the same in her black cloak. Her face hadn't aged, and she was clearly not dead. She was alive and peering at me with her black eyes. The Mortia grinned when I made eye contact with her.

I turned away and met Morgana's eyes with a steely glare. Her eyes were tinged with black in the corner from her power usage.

"You won't kill her. You need her for your ritual," I said. Morgana could bluff all she wanted, but I already knew her plan. Not to mention after her telekinesis, there was nothing she could do to Mom or me. Otherwise, she would run the risk of fully transforming.

"An on-the-verge-of-death body works just the same for a witch transformation." Morgana blinked rapidly, trying to clear the black from her eyes. "And I hear being almost killed by a Mortia multiple times in a row is extremely painful."

The Mortia breathed out a wind of cold air. I observed Mom's left hand turn from a light tan to a pale blue. The Mortia covered her in frostbite. Mom didn't make a sound, but I saw on her face that the pain wasn't pleasant. I looked away from her. I couldn't watch this.

"I can do that to each part of her body and chill her heart over and over. Then, warm her back up," whispered the Mortia in my ear.

She breathed out hot air that shimmered in the sun and warmed Mom's arm back up. Steam drifted off Mom's arm as her face tensed more.

"We have a few hours before the first ritual can start," said Morgana.

"Plenty of time." The Mortia twisted her hands in the air and conjured one tiny snowflake to make her point.

I lowered the wood plank. It wouldn't be enough to take out Morgana and the Mortia. Because of Mom wanting to be the hero, they captured us again. This time I knew there wouldn't be a chance for a simple escape like we had before. We were too close to the ritual times now.

Before I thought of something to do, the Mortia pulled two potion bottles out of her cloak pocket and passed them to Morgana. Inside the glass vials laid a pale green liquid that imitated the color of snot. Before I studied them any longer, the Mortia held her hand over my heart, sending a chill through my entire body. My vision clouded.

"Drink the vial, or we kill her right now," said Morgana to Mom.

Morgana held the vial in front of Mom's face and looked back at me. I felt the cold spread through my entire body. Little streams of ice prickled in my veins as my blood froze, and I gasped. My whole body froze solid, and my eyelids fluttered. I couldn't even move. Suddenly, sleep seemed like a great idea to distract myself from the cold.

"Give it to me." Mom tried to forcibly grab the vile out of Morgana's hands.

Morgana cruelly held the vial out of Mom's reach. The cold covered more of my body, and I could observe actual frost on my skin. The chill now froze my eyes open, not allowing me to blink.

"Give it to me," said Mom, screaming. She reached for the vial again.

Morgana grinned, uncorking the vial, and handed it to her. Through frozen eyes, I saw Mom guzzle down the green liquid. She fell to the ground like a sack of potatoes. I tried to reach for her, but my body didn't move.

The Mortia changed the temperature coming from her hand on my chest, and I warmed back up. Ice melted from my veins, and I could move my limbs again. Before I assessed my freedom, the Mortia forced my mouth open and froze my jaw into place. I clawed at her, but it did nothing except make her laugh at me more. Morgana uncorked the other vial and poured the snot green potion directly down my throat. It tasted metallic and herbally. As soon as it hit the back of my throat, I wanted to vomit, but my face stayed stuck. I had no choice, but to swallow it or choke. The Mortia thawed my jaw, and I closed my mouth to swallow.

In seconds, I fell to the ground next to my mother.

CHAPTER TWENTY ONE

I OPENED MY EYES to meet a dark, starless sky. The full moon lit the cool ground around me as I inhaled the scent of smoke. Nausea took over my body, so I immediately rolled over to my hands and knees before I choked. I puked the snot green liquid Morgana forced down my throat. The metallic taste of the potion mixed with my stomach acid made my stomach churn even more. I hurled a few more times until nothing came out anymore. I craved water, but my body only rewarded me with thick saliva and a pool of green beside me.

Alone in the dark, I found myself somewhere deep in the woods. I wasn't sure if this was the same place where Morgana and the Mortia captured us, but I knew I wasn't anywhere near the witch camp. To my surprise, they left me unshackled and abandoned. My chain plank was nowhere in sight as far I saw.

I could run if I wanted to, but I had no sense of time anymore. I may be too late to save Mom, or I possibly have enough time. This felt like another sick game.

I stood up and looked around for any way to figure out where I was. But in the dark, every tree in the swamp closed in upon itself. It seemed like the trees surrounded me in a black fence. No wonder I wasn't left with shackles. This forest was enough of a prison to keep me trapped and wandering aimlessly forever.

The smell of smoke drifted into my nose again. A fire had to be off in the distance for me to inhale smoke like this. I scanned the landscape again until I saw it. One small flicker of light hiding in the trees before me. This had to be where the witches were organizing. It would be the perfect place to perform the ritual and celebrate their success.

I desired to run away so badly, but I couldn't leave Mom without trying one more time to save her. I didn't care if the witches organized and murdered everyone else. I just wanted her to be safe. Every Captrix in my entire family line would roll in their graves if they heard me say that. Captrixes always put everyone before themselves, and it had gotten them killed for centuries. I didn't want to be one of them. I wanted my mom back. But if she went back this time, after I saved her again, there would be nothing else I could do.

I began to walk toward the flickering light. Roots and vines pulled at my clothes as I walked through the trees, but I kept trudging forward. The stink of smoke grew stronger as the light got bigger, so I knew I headed in the right direction. Luckily, the scent of smoke stopped making my stomach churn as my nausea subsided. To my dismay, it was impossible for me to be silent walking in the dark woods. I constantly cracked small limbs and stomped the ground when I stumbled.

It reminded me of how a few days before Tristan made the exact same sounds I made now. Then, Bridgette and I gave him dirty looks for giving away our position. I smiled at the memory and wished I was still trying to convince Bridgette not to strangle him. Things were so much simpler than they were now.

I didn't know where she hid right now, but I hoped Bridgette was safe. I missed her and our little team. For a time, when we were together, I felt invincible. Like I could almost do this Captrix thing. Bridgette had almost convinced me this may be my purpose in life, even if I fought it. If I wasn't meant to do this, how did I realize how to save her?

Even though I hated him and couldn't love him, I missed Tristan too. I wanted nothing more than to wrap myself in his arms and inhale the pine tree smell that lived on him. He had made me feel so safe and wanted. I almost missed the buzzing electricity between us. I shook my head, trying to get Tristan out of my brain. No point in thinking about him. He was a traitor who was possibly my soulmate. My soulmate that I didn't have the ability to even love if I wanted to because I was broken.

The crackling sound of a fire came into my hearing range, and I assumed I was close. My intuition hummed with pent up energy. I felt anxious and jittery, like I was going to be around too many people. My intuition had never done this to me before, so I assumed this was how it reacted to a large group of witches. As I crept closer to the gathering, my arm hairs stood up and chills covered my body. My intuition clearly didn't think this was a good idea.

I could make out a small clearing in the middle of the woods. The trees circled around it in a perfect circle. Witches I never saw before crowded the edges of the trees as they became spectators for the spectacle. In the middle of the clearing, the fire that had led me here crackled. Next to the fire stood the elemental witches I was used to seeing.

The Mare stood the furthest away from the warmth and looked uncomfortable. Basking in the heat rays, the Ignis looked as if she siphoned energy off of it. The Ventus remained alone, messing around with objects on a table placed a few feet away from the fire by creating gusts of air. I scanned the clearing for Mom or Morgana, but found neither one of them.

I moved closer and heard the murmurs of witches carrying on conversations with each other. They seemed so human-like now, gossiping about the night's events. But when I focused on them, I noticed each quirk they had, proving they were more creature-like. Mares dripped with water puddling at their feet. Little ice patches lined the ground around Mortias. There were tons of other witch species I didn't recognize, causing tree roots to grow or animals to gather. Veneficas caused a light tension in their corner as they tried to keep it together, and I prayed they wouldn't smell my broken soul. The entire clearing appeared chaotic with all of these powers coming together.

The witches continued talking, and I realized they separated themselves into small factions. None of them would look at or converse with other types. Even though it was obvious they weren't completely human, it was a scary thought that beings I saw as creatures had more intelligence than I gave them credit for. It would be easy for them to take over the world in a state like this if they could get organized. They were missing a uniting force. They were missing someone like Morgana to bring them together.

"Sisters! It is time for us to gather together," said Morgana in the distance.

She appeared with Mom in tow at the end of the clearing. Morgana walked with confidence and radiated leader vibes. All the witches watched her in awe. I was in shock. This woman really could lead them if she had this type of power before they even made a sacrifice. Morgana was just naturally commanding.

"Tonight, we will come together and rise to a new dawn." Morgana dragged Mom closer to the fire with a chain.

Cheers erupted into the forest. I moved as close as possible to see things, in order to try to hatch a plan. Creeping behind a bush, I tried to think. I had no idea what to do, and my head was swimming with anxiety. Running out there now would be suicide. I didn't know if Mom expected me to make that type of sacrifice. She would have a better chance of containing these witches if I was the one to die with her knowledge and skills. I never wanted this anyway. But a conscious decision to die was hard for me to swallow.

Morgana and Mom made it to the table next to the fire. Morgana motioned for her to get onto the table, but Mom refused. She swung her shackled hands and hit Morgana across the face. Morgana reached up and touched her face gently. I could tell she was trying to hold in the anger, but a patch of hair turned white as the objects on the table the Ventus was playing with, floated into the air. The Venefica inside of her tried to take over.

All the other elemental witch creatures around the fire that had been helping ran to Morgana's side. They threw Mom on the table and chained her to it. Mom thrashed and tried to get away, but there wasn't any use now. The elemental witches took their posts in the circle exactly like the drawing I drew for Mom earlier. The floating objects crashed back down to the table, so I squinted to make them out but only saw the gleam of a knife.

Morgana stood to the side, trying to calm herself down to prevent the transformation from continuing. After a few beats of silence, her hair returned to brown. She plastered a fake smile on and addressed the witches.

"It is time to begin the transformation of this Captrix," said Morgana.

Cheers rang out through the crowd again.

"Think of how many witch sisters have been murdered by her hand."

Mumbles of hatred and anger spilled out now. A chant of, "Kill her," began. I couldn't wait any longer to make a move. I took a deep breath, trying to push down my nervous energy. My intuition screamed at me not to do what I was about to do so much that a pressure headache built in my head. I had no choice. I had to try to do something.

"Over my dead body," I said to the crowd.

I stood up from behind the bush serving as my hiding place. Gasps and questions overtook all the witches. Some lurched for me, but stopped moving when Morgana raised her hand.

"How nice of you to join us, Atalanta." Morgana held her hand high as a stop sign for all the witches.

I walked toward the ritual fire with my head held high. The only thing I could try to do would be to make the witches disperse. I thought I might be able to do that by making

Morgana complete her transformation.

"How nice of you to invite me," I said. "Unfortunately, it doesn't look like my date is here."

Morgana's eyes flared with anger.

"I was really looking forward to seeing him again, but I guess he isn't here." I added a shrug for effect.

A blood-curdling yell came out of her. Suddenly, strips of white hair grew all over her head, causing her brown hair to fall out. Her eyes still maintained their color as black began tinting the edges. The witches in the circle grew restless, like they didn't belong here. Morgana's leader aura was melting away. For once, my plan was actually working.

Mom turned to me and mouthed run. Before I reacted, a cloaked witch creature with a hood grabbed me from behind. I struggled against them, but the witch clasped me tightly. The hooded black cloak shielded me from them, so I couldn't see who or what they were.

"Having someone else do your dirty work like always, huh," I said. "You could never attack me alone. You're weak, Morgana, and every witch here is going to know it."

Black crowded in Morgana's eyes. Murmurs erupted across the witch factions as they took what I said to heart.

"Enough," said Morgana. Her voice came out gruff, tainted with rage. "Hush her up, witch sister."

The cloaked witch placed their hand over my mouth and cinched it down. I tried to bite their hand, but they forced it down harder, so I wasn't able to move my mouth anymore.

"Begin the ritual now!" Morgana gave the cloaked witch a thank you nod.

I shook my head, trying to break free. The elemental witches began saying incantations in their designated spot. The longer they spoke the words, the more uncomfortable Mom became. Her body began writhing on the table. There tossing and turning made her look like she was having a seizure.

"No," I said, my voice muffled by the hand. I wasn't strong anymore, so it came out like a sad whimper.

Mom's back arched, making her lift her entire body toward the moon. The elemental witch creatures held their hands up to the sky, producing their medium out of their hand. A small tornado turned in the Ventus's hand. A fireball glowed in the Ignis's hand. A spout of water came from the Mare. They spoke more incantations, and their elements grew stronger. All at once, they pointed them at Mom and covered her in fire, water, and air. Morgana took a place in front of her and threw dirt on top and said a Latin sentence I couldn't make out. Then, she backed away from the table.

Mom screamed. In that moment, it felt like she stole all the oxygen in the air to fill her lungs. Her skin boiled, making ripples as if something moved through her veins. She was transforming into a witch creature, but her body wasn't handling it well. Her hair fell out in patches as Mom pushed her body closer to the moon. Then, the air became ice cold.

My breath leaked through the fingers of the witch creature into foggy clouds. Dew froze on the ground in small icicles. The group of Ignises rubbed their arms but didn't dare to move closer to the circle. All the other witches watched in amazement, like they looked at nothing quite like this before. I wanted to close my eyes and turn away, but I fixated on the image before me.

Mom's skin stopped bubbling and began covering itself in the ice, turning her lips a pale blue. Then, her arched body fell flat back onto the table. She was still and quiet for a moment. Little snowflakes fell out of an invisible cloud above her.

"Is she a Mortia," said a witch in the crowd.

No answers came to answer the question. All the witches' mouths dropped, not believing a Captrix had survived the transformation. Morgana approached Mom, admiring the work that was almost complete. Mom looked confused, but also in pain.

"See, the thing is, Atalanta, this ritual was never about her." Morgana grabbed the knife from the table I spotted earlier. The blade glistened in the moonlight.

"It was you. It's always been about you."

I didn't understand what she was talking about. I tried to bite the hand over my mouth again but couldn't move my lips. The figure leaned in closer, and I sniffed them. The familiar smell of pine trees drifted into my nose. Tristan's hand was over my mouth. He was the one holding me back, betraying me again.

"I needed someone broken to rise. This was a way to see how much more I could break you," said Morgana.

Mom looked at me and began to say something, but Morgana took the knife in her hand and sliced Mom's throat. Blood poured out of her neck immediately, making a sticky, red pool on the table. I blinked quickly, trying to blur the vision from my eyes.

"We have to go now," whispered Tristan into my ear.

I squirmed in his arms again, trying to get free, but he wrapped his arms around me and threw me over his shoulder like a potato sack. Tristan broke out into a sprint in a direction I hadn't been yet. I heard Morgana yelling in the background, obviously not happy I was being carried away. He ran with me for what seemed like forever until he finally stopped. He doubled over, panting, and tried to catch his breath.

"What are you doing? You made me leave her," I said.

"I'm trying—" said Tristan, drawing in a deep breath, "—to save you."

Before I said anything else, my intuition came over me. My mom told me my intuition would let me know when someone I cared about died, but she never told me how it would feel. My heart raced, and I gasped for air as if I was the one who couldn't breathe anymore. I closed my eyes and involuntarily transported myself above Mom's body like I did to message Bridgette before.

I could see everything that Tristan carried me away from. Mom's blood now flooded the table. The snowflake cloud dissipated as Mom's new powers grew weaker. Chaos surrounded us as witch creatures tore out of the clearing to find me, the true sacrifice. I reached out and tried to touch her hand, so she would realize I was there. Then, my mother stopped breathing.

I felt her die.

CHAPTER TWENTY TWO

"Atalanta?" Tristan waved his hands in front of my face, trying to get me to come back.

I stood there frozen, staring off into the distance. I still couldn't breathe. The overwhelming feeling of emptiness consumed me. I had just watched Mom die inside my mind and experienced the breath leave her body. It was unlike anything I ever had to endure. It was even worse than having a piece of my soul devoured.

Tristan shook my shoulders, trying to get me to speak. I still had no words.

"Can you walk?" Tristan took my hand, and I let him. It was warm and familiar.

I nodded, not taking my eyes off my mark in the distance. In my twisted mind, I thought that if I kept staring there, I would see Mom come out of the clearing. She would be alive and fine, bringing me steak and orange juice along with a lecture on my studies to say how I wasn't trying to even be a Captrix. Then, Mom would lament about me trying to leave after my hunt. If I apologized enough, she would wrap me in her arms in the tightest hug.

Nothing moved on the tree line.

Tears poured out of me as Tristan dragged me along in the woods. My body rocked with sobs, so I covered my mouth with my other hand to stifle the sound. Tristan wouldn't look at me, keeping his eyes wherever he was taking me. When I studied his face, it wasn't full of concentration. He looked pained, like he was trying to keep everything together.

There were so many things I wanted to yell at him, but I remained silent. I wanted to curse him. This was all his fault. He let me be captured by his mother and stopped me from saving my mother.

Images burned into my mind again. The wooden table soaked with blood. The perfect gash across my mom's neck. The chains holding her to the table.

I shook uncontrollably. My head spun, and waves of nausea took me over. I froze in place in my fear. I let go of Tristan's hand and sat down in the middle of the forest, allowing the dampness of the cool ground to soak my pants. I crouched into a tiny ball and put my head in between my legs.

Tristan didn't try to get me up. I listened to his footsteps as he walked away. At this point, I didn't care if he left me in this forest. A few minutes later, I heard his footsteps along with another set. Muffled conversation filtered toward my ear.

Next thing I knew, someone enclosed me in a tight hug.

Bridgette's hair touched my face, and it swept itself down between my knees. Feeling her and knowing she was safe caused another wave of sobs to wreck my body. She held me tighter for what seemed like hours and leaned back as my hard cries slowed down.

"Talk to me," said Bridgette, as she rubbed my back.

I leaned up to look into her brown eyes and swam in the silver flecks for a moment while I tried to find my voice. I still shook with wet cheeks, but Bridgette put her hands on my side to steady me.

"She's dead, Bridgette. I watched," I said, getting choked on the words. "I watched her die."

Bridgette turned back to look at Tristan, then back to me. "Artemis?"

I nodded while I held back another sobbing session. I saw tears well in Bridgette's eyes too, but she held them back to speak.

"Can you tell me what happened?"

"They did the transformation. She turned into a Mortia and survived." I trembled even more. "Morgana slit her throat."

At the sound of his mother's name, Tristan grimaced. He turned away from me with the anger tensing all over him.

"They never wanted her. They wanted me."

Bridgette gave me a questioning glance.

"I'm the broken triangle." I forced it out, so I could be silent once again.

Bridgette stood up and walked over to Tristan. Tristan paced a little path in the ground, but when she approached him, he stopped.

"Did you know this?" Bridgette looked at him with disbelief.

"I swear I didn't know why Mom—" Hesitation filled

Tristan's voice. "—Morgana wanted her. I put the pieces together after they took her."

Bridgette stared through him in a way that made me even more queasy. At least I knew I wasn't the only one Tristan was keeping secrets from. She came back over to me and held out her hands.

"Let's get you up. My car is at the edge of the woods."

She helped me off the ground, and we walked back to the car. Tristan trailed behind us, lost in thought. All I wanted was to get to the car and get a drink of water. Processing what happened to me wasn't high on my to-do list. When we reached the car, Bridgette reached in and gave me a bottle of lukewarm water. I took it gladly and guzzled it down. She tried to offer me a granola bar, but I refused. Even though I hadn't eaten all day, the idea of putting something in my stomach made me even more nauseated than I already was.

"Can you give me a minute?" Bridgette sat down in the driver's seat of the car.

I nodded and walked to the back of the car. When I got a few steps away, I heard Bridgette release the grief of losing her best friend to the steering wheel.

Tristan rested on the bumper with his face still tangled in knots. I stood in front of him with my arms crossed and gave him a once over. His shaggy black hair looked greasy instead of having the fluff it normally had. The color of his skin appeared pale with deep under eye circles. His dark blue skinny jeans were naturally distressed from running in the forest tonight, and his gray t-shirt was covered in dirt stains. The carefree ambiance he had before shattered and filled itself with brooding anger.

He looked up at me and held my gaze. I wasn't able to look into his eyes without remembering the last time I stared into them so deeply. All I felt was my soul ache for its missing piece. And the anger I endured because of his betrayal.

"Atalanta, I—" said Tristan.

I held up a finger to cut him off and swallowed. My mouth was moist enough to make words now, but I wasn't sure if I could get them out without causing another panic attack. I had to try, though.

"How could you drag me away from her," I said.

His eyes widened at the directness of my question.

"You were going to get yourself killed. I couldn't let you be their next sacrifice," said Tristan.

"I'm so sick of everyone making decisions for me. You, Bridgette, Morgana." The panic was welling up in me again. "My mother."

I continued to hold eye contact with him, determined to make him uncomfortable.

"I never wanted any of this. I just wanted to leave town and have my own life. Then, the only thing I wanted was to save my mother." My panic transformed into a venom. "You ruined that for me."

Tristan broke the gaze, but I couldn't stand it anymore. I walked to him and started punching his arms and chest with all I had. With each punch, I released more and more anger I held inside of me. It felt good to let it all out. Tristan winced in pain on some punches but let me keep going.

"I'm so sick of having to watch everyone die," I said.

He grabbed my arms and held them to stop my punching.

"I can never apologize enough for what I did to you with the love potion and giving you to Morgana." Tristan drew in a deep breath. "Hell, I can't even forgive myself for what I did. But I'm trying to make it right."

I wiggled back and forth until he let my arms go.

"I'm not sorry for taking you away. They were going to kill you. I couldn't let that happen."

"Why not?"

"Because you're the only person standing between Morgana and witches taking over the world."

I heard the car door open and slam. Bridgette walked up beside us.

"He's right, you know." Bridgette quickly dried her face with her shirtsleeve.

I looked at Bridgette, pleading for her not to agree. I didn't want this. Any of it.

Bridgette motioned at Tristan to move, so he obliged. She popped open the trunk and in the compartment was my mother's chest. The same one Bridgette has presented me with before the swamp. They tilted it open, so I could see the huntress outfit perfectly clean. It was ready to be worn again. Next to the huntress outfit was Mom's mixed metal dagger. I felt it calling to me, but I looked away.

"You're the only one who can stop Morgana. If you don't, she will just make another broken girl and take over anyway," said Tristan. "I know her."

Bridgette reached out to me and held my shoulders. "It's what Artemis would want. To keep people safe." Bridgette rubbed my arms, trying to soothe me. "It's what Captrixes do.

This is what they fight for."

"I can't do this," I said. "I'm not her. I'm not like any Captrix."

I broke from Bridgette's grip and ran away from the car back into the woods toward where I sat down earlier. I heard their calls behind me, but I couldn't do it. Who did they think I was?

When I assumed I was far enough away from them to breathe, I stopped. The trees encased me, and I got lost in them. Lost in them like I had always seemed throughout my entire life. I couldn't remember a time I actually felt like I knew what I was doing.

When I tried studying Captrix knowledge, I never understood what I was reading. I didn't know what to do when my grandparents died. I didn't know what to do when Mom wasn't around. Hell, I didn't even understand how to kill witch creatures properly, proven by a Venefica devouring a piece of my soul.

Even though I gained some knowledge over the past few days, it didn't mean I would be a good Captrix. I still was the lazy, complacent runner I had always been. Except now, I couldn't even love someone.

I leaned against a tree trunk and closed my eyes.

I didn't want this. I didn't want to be a Captrix. I just wanted my world to be safe. It seemed like my family heritage was sacrifice after sacrifice to save others. Why were we never allowed to be winners in our own destiny?

I heard a voice in my head that sounded faintly like my mom. The robotic woman's voice my intuition normally came across as had changed. Hearing a voice like my mother's was more comforting and sounded right.

"Then, why don't you change it," said the voice.

I shrugged my shoulders. After all, I had been through, I was having even more side conversations in my head. More evidence that I wasn't cut out for this.

"What if I'm not cut out for this?" I said to the voice aloud.

"*You can do anything. No one is asking you to make a decision today, but you have to stop Morgana,*" said the voice.

"I don't know."

"*You've been so afraid of failing, that you have forgotten who you are.*"

I slid down the tree, feeling the bark scratch my back on the way down. "I don't even know who I am."

"*You know exactly who you are. You've been avoiding it your entire life. Think, Atalanta.*"

Who was I?

I was Atalanta Capp, Artemis's daughter. I came from a long line of Captrixes, witch huntresses, who saved the world from witch creatures. We were huntresses that never left each other behind. Then, it donned on me. Everything I had ever done was against my intrinsic nature.

My fear of failure and death had caused me to leave my mother behind so many times. I was going to leave her when I skipped town. I left her in the forest when she refused to come with me. Now, I tried to leave her body to rot in a clearing surrounded by the creatures she defended the world from.

I couldn't leave her in that clearing alone. Everything about it felt intrinsically wrong for me. I was the only Captrix here who possessed the intuition and had the supplies to survive a gathering of witch creatures. I was the only one able to save my mom from her resting place and give her a proper burial.

I refused to leave her behind this time. I would figure out the rest of the Captrix stuff later.

"Am I really doing this," I said to the voice in my head.

"*Yes, you are,*" said the voice.

CHAPTER TWENTY THREE

I walked back to Bridgette and Tristan slowly. Not because I wasn't ready to go back to the clearing, but because I didn't want to have to see their faces of disappointment. I had run off and let them down when it was my time to shine. Who knew if they would be there waiting for me?

But when I reached the car, they were there. Bridgette sat in the driver's seat with the car door open. Her head laid in her hands like she wasn't sure what she should do. Tristan remained where I left him, leaning on the back of the car. His eyes remained closed as if he was taking a nap, but I knew better.

The moment I left the woods and walked out into the opening, Tristan's eyes flew open and looked at me. He gave me a sly grin like he had when I met him in Morgana's shop for the first time. Even though I didn't feel the same butterflies I had that day, his grin was contagious. I smiled back at him and shook my head.

"Bridgette!" Tristan yelled to the front of the car. "She's back."

Bridgette ran out of the driver's seat and sprinted toward me. She grabbed a hold of me in a tight hug and began checking me for fresh wounds. Once she was content nothing hurt me, she let me go and gave me a stern look.

"Thank God," said Bridgette. "You're never allowed to do that again."

I pulled her into another hug and clung for a moment. I needed her to recognize how much she meant to me. That I wasn't running from her.

"I'm sorry. Never again," I said.

"Do I get a hug too," said Tristan.

I was flabbergasted. He walked toward me, and I broke my hug with Bridgette. I couldn't believe after punching him and yelling at him, he still wanted a hug. After everything he had done to me, did I want a hug from him? I didn't know why, but I did.

Tristan batted his eyes at me like a seductress trying to capture her prey. I couldn't help but laugh. I rolled my eyes at him. He raised his eyebrows, and I nodded yes.

His hug was warm, and I sensed the love he had for me radiating out of his body. His pine tree smell was fainter than normal, overcome by all the swamp scents and mud on his clothes. After all we'd been through, he still felt like my safe place, even if I was angry at him. I let him go before the hug continued on too long.

I wished I didn't have to leave his arms to murder his mother. That was going to suck.

Bridgette popped the trunk again. My chest was still where it was earlier, undisturbed, waiting for me to open it. I reached in and pulled it out to set it on the ground. Crouching, I opened the lid. My huntress outfit called out to me like a swan song, and I was ready to be the Captrix that outfit deserved, for tonight at least. I held it up to me and shooed Tristan away.

He walked to the front of the car, rested on the hood, and forced his eyes to stare at the trees. I paused for a few seconds, making sure Tristan wasn't going to turn around to look. When he didn't move, I stripped my disgusting clothes off and threw them into a pile on the ground. I pulled on my huntress outfit like I had before, but this time it seemed right. Like it belonged. I strapped on my knife sheath and placed my dagger into it.

Immediately, it felt like the world cleared. My senses heightened, and I heard every movement in the forest. Animals shifting in their beds. Bugs flying by. Witches returning to the clearing. I sensed Tristan leave the front of the car to come back. It was like my intuition was in overdrive.

I turned to Bridgette, and she read the shock on my face. Tristan arrived next to her with his eyebrows raised in curiosity.

"What's wrong," said Bridgette.

"I know everything," I said. "I feel everything."

"Artemis said when you accept your heritage, your intuition deepens." Bridgette smiled. "Must be what is happening to you."

The thought of accepting my heritage echoed through my mind. Did I finally do that after all this time? Clearly my senses guessed so. I leaned into my intuition deeper and suddenly realized I could do something extraordinary.

"Tristan." I smiled wide. "I want you to try and punch me."

"What," said Tristan. The confusion was evident on his face.

"Just try it, okay?" I took a fighter's stance and held up my fists.

Tristan mimicked my pose, shaking his head. He clearly didn't think this was a good idea, but if I was right about my intuition, this was going to be a cakewalk. I focused all of my energy on the impending fight. When Tristan reached back and swung to hit me, my intuition told me exactly when to dodge. It's like I just knew how and when he was going to hit me. I dodged his punch and caught his wrist in midair. I gave it a small twist to make him uncomfortable.

"Alright, alright!" Tristan tried to pull his wrist from me, but I let it go before he tugged too hard.

"I knew exactly how he was going to hit me." I faced Bridgette and giggled with pleasure. "Now I'll know how the witches attack before they realize."

Finally, after all this time, I felt like a real Captrix. I possessed the skill that made them so lethal to witch creatures.

"Perfect. But we will still need to come up with a strategy," said Bridgette.

I looked down into my chest to determine what other supplies we had to work with. My crossbow and quiver sat to the side among all the research books. I pulled them out of the chest and sat them on the ground. Plundering through the chest, I noticed a few vials of blessed water and some firebombs. These would come in handy for a few witches, but an entire congregation would use these up quickly. Not to mention, I wasn't one hundred percent sure of all the different types of witches we were facing. Making a strategy for this type of fight would not be simple. I dug to the bottom of the chest, making sure nothing else was in there to use, and saw my penny laying at the bottom. Bridgette had been thoughtful enough to put my treasured item in there for me, and her thoughtfulness pulled on my heartstrings. I quickly tucked the penny into my pocket and felt a wave of calm. Not only would I be taking my friends into battle with me, but now I walked with my family in my pocket. I wanted to thank Bridgette, but I knew it could make me too emotional, so I focused on the task at hand.

"I think the key to winning would be to kill Morgana as soon as possible." I tried to not stare at Tristan, so my uneasy eyes looked to Bridgette. "Without her, there's nothing for the rest of the witches to fight for."

Bridgette nodded. She avoided Tristan's eyes as well. It appeared callous to talk about murdering his mother in front of him. I experienced what it felt like to lose a mother now and received the pang of grief deep inside of me. But it was the only way to win this fight.

"I know she's become a terrible person, but I can't do it." Tristan fidgeted with his hands and stared at a spot on the ground. It pained me to look at him.

"It has to be you, Atalanta," said Bridgette.

She avoided eye contact with me now. I knew Bridgette was right, but the idea of killing someone's mother hurt what I had left of my soul. I wanted to protest, but Tristan couldn't do it. If Bridgette did it, she would turn into a Venefica. But more than anything, I was afraid if I did it, I would become like Morgana. A mother killer—a murderer.

Morgana killed my mother, though. That was enough to

stoke a rage inside me only tamed by revenge. If anyone else was going to die tonight, it had to be her.

"This is what we're going to do." I grabbed a stick off the ground and drew out the clearing in the dirt.

I drew a square where the sacrificial table sat and left the opening at the other edge where Morgana had appeared. I drew some circles to show different sects of witches. Tristan and Bridgette watched me draw, intrigued by the picture I was sketching.

"We will have to cover both entrances to the clearing." I said, motioning with my stick. "Bridgette and I will enter the front. Tristan, you will cover the back entrance."

They both nodded at me. Tristan's discomfort continued to grow. However, I knew if Morgana tried to exit from the back and Tristan was there, she would stop. It would be like setting a small trap.

"Before, the witches separated themselves into their different factions. I'm going to assume they are still going to be like that." I waved the stick over the circles. "So, we're going to attack each group one at a time until chaos happens. We can throw the various bombs we have into the groups to cut down on some of them."

Bridgette nodded again. Tristan shifted his weight onto a different foot. I hoped he wouldn't back out on me in the last minute. I was used to him being so sure of himself. His confidence evaporated the moment we mentioned Morgana.

"I'm going to do my best to work through the witches as quickly as possible, so I can get to Morgana. After she is dead, I'll recover Mom's body and we'll leave," I said.

I looked up to them to determine if they understood the plan.

They both looked at me with solemn stares. I knew this would not be easy based on the look on their faces. But we had to try.

"Let's get suited up then," I said.

"I've got some more gear in the trunk," said Bridgette to Tristan.

CHAPTER TWENTY FOUR

Bridgette and Tristan put on their gear quickly, and we gathered like the motley crew we were. Tristan still looked exactly the same, but he had wiped away some of the dirt off of his pants and added a strap across his chest. Instead of this strap holding bullets, this one contained little holsters for various vials filled with blessed water and firebombs. Bridgette created them the moment after Morgana kidnapped me. She had prepared to come rescue me, but now these vials were ready for battle.

Bridgette changed from her normal flowy house dress into a pair of slim fit skinny jeans and a black tee shirt. She also put up her wavy hair into a bun on the back of her head. She looked like a regular person, ready to hit up the local grocery store. If a person going to the grocery store wore a strap across their chest filled with potions and had skin that glittered in the moonlight.

Bridgette strapped a dagger to the side of her leg for an emergency.

My hand immediately went to my hair. It was dirty and matted beyond belief. I stroked it a few times to remove a few tangles with no luck. I cringed at the pulls to my tender head and looked at Bridgette with pleading eyes. She reached in her pocket, knowing what I desired, and handed me a black ponytail holder. I took it and put my hair into a matching bun like Bridgette's hair.

I couldn't wear a front strap like they did. I recognized I needed to be more agile, so I chose a belt with holsters for vials. Even though I had only seen my mom wear the belt a handful of times, it fit perfectly with my huntress outfit. I filled it with a few blessed water vials and one firebomb since the rest of the bombs had gone to Bridgette and Tristan.

"I have one more thing for you," said Bridgette.

Her face was full of sadness and worry, but I wasn't sure what to make of it. Out of the backseat of the car, she pulled out a long copper spear. She hit it down on the ground, and the spear retracted to half length.

"If anything happens to me and I change…" Bridgette closed her mouth for a beat and sighed. "I want you to use this on me."

Dread covered my entire body. It was one thing to kill Morgana. It was another to kill Bridgette. She was the only mother figure I had left, my mentor. My mouth went dry.

"I don't know if I can do that," I said.

Bridgette placed the spear in my hand and wrapped my fingers around it. Tristan looked at the ground like he was going to vomit.

"You need to." A light haze of water covered Bridgette's

eyes, but she refused to let the tears slide out. "I've had a taste of you. If I change this time, I won't stop."

She looked ashamed of herself, but there was nothing I could say or do. I didn't want to lie to her and tell her everything would be okay when we were about to run into a nest of witch creatures. Suddenly, the stakes rose even higher. Before, I was only worried about myself dying or killing Morgana. I never took the time to stop and realize what Bridgette and Tristan were risking as well.

"You two don't have to do this. I don't want to put you in any more danger than I already have," I said.

Tristan and Bridgette both looked at each other and back to me.

"We're in this together," said Tristan. "I'm not leaving you this time."

I nodded. They both seemed firm in their decision, so I didn't want to waste time trying to change their minds. I put the retracted spear in my pants pocket and prayed to never use it.

"We ready to go then?" I wanted to give them one last chance to back out.

Tristan gave me a dorky, half-hearted thumbs up that caused Bridgette to roll her eyes. Bridgette just nodded, and we made our way back toward the woods.

Tristan had a brief idea of where he was going since this was the way he came to save me from Morgana before. With his navigation skills and my intuition leading the way, we easily covered ground across the land. I waited to see a fire rising or a smell of smoke, but nothing came.

"Can you believe they put the fire out that fast," I said.

"I'm perplexed about that too," said Bridgette.

"Do you think they're not regrouping," said Tristan.

I pondered that idea. Everything in my body told me that couldn't be the case. My intuition buzzed with the sense that witches were still in the area. This time, though, they didn't appear like a unit. It was a different feeling than before. They were scattered, but still working together. Confusion enveloped me.

"No, they're hunting me. I think they've broken into their factions. This isn't going to be the battle we planned for," I said. "They aren't congregating in one spot like I thought."

Instead of facing them all in the clearing at once, we would fight groups of them as we went. It would be like facing hidden ninjas in the forest. Of course, we knew of some to expect, but what about all the unknown creatures? I had no idea how to kill them from a distance, and I had never taken the life of something so close.

"They're scattering like normal instead of working together. This is actually good news. It's better to face them in small batches than all at once," said Bridgette.

I nodded, but I still worried about our plan crumbling. If we were fighting like this, there wouldn't be a way to send Tristan off to cut Morgana off in the clearing. For all I knew, she was scattered around the forest or gone completely. If I could tap into Bridgette's mind with my intuition, could I tap into Morgana's too? If I looked for her in my mind's eye, would she realize I was there?

The thought settled into my brain as we covered more ground in the swamp, however I decided it was a bad idea as the soft glow of the moonlight led us through the wooded terrain. I thought we were getting close to where the gathering was, but my senses didn't tingle with the feeling of witches. The silence was overwhelming. Nothing like the noise I felt before.

A branch snapped behind us. My internal alarms screamed. Bridgette and Tristan didn't react, ignorant of the danger that had just arrived behind us. I pulled my dagger from my sheath and turned around to see her.

The Ignis, who burned me more times than I would like to admit, stood there glowering. Behind her stood five other Ignises holding fireballs in their hands. They were all completely naked. Their flames had incinerated their clothes at some point before they doused their flames to sneak around the swamp. Her short red hair remained distressed on the top of her head, tangled with leaves and branches she chose not to dodge on her hunt. She gave me a light smile, but her eyes burned with hatred.

I sheathed the dagger back into my hip holster and began reaching for my crossbow on my back. Before we left, I loaded it with one blessed water bolt, and I knew exactly where I planned on shooting it. The Ignis turned around to her clan and nodded. The witches burst into flames, becoming colossal figures of fire. They burned so brightly that I had to squint my eyes to try and make out their human shape. Bridgette slipped her fingers under one of the blessed water vials on her chest and pulled it off. She threw it hard at the clan, but her grip slipped, and the water crashed on the ground right at the clan's feet.

A few droplets landed on the Ignis's feet, and she yelled in anger. Then, the figures of fire began hurling fireballs at us. Tristan, Bridgette, and I scattered to dodge the balls. I finished pulling out my crossbow and held it close but pointed it down to the ground. A fireball sailed over my head and crashed behind the tree, lighting the moss on fire. Panic consumed me as I realized that this much fire would call every witch to our location. Witch creatures would surround us instead of us surrounding them.

Another fireball came toward my face, but I ducked. Tristan and Bridgette threw water vials at the rest of the clan. The other Ignises' screams filled the air as some of the water made contact. They made progress, but I could still see flames licking their feet. Tracker fireballs started their work on the both of them. The leader Ignis kept stalking toward me, her hand ready with another fireball. There was too much going on in my head to think. I had to calm down, or I would kill myself with panic.

I almost killed her before I had my fancy intuition. Why was I panicking right now, knowing what I could do? I took in a deep breath and calmed myself. When my fear subsided, I heard the voice of my intuition coming to the surface of my mind.

The Ignis was only a few feet away from me, boring her eyes into my soul. I needed to shoot her now, but my intuition told me to hold my ground. I glanced down at my crossbow, eyeing the blessed water bolt I had loaded in it. There looked to be no sign of it jamming, so I didn't know why my intuition wanted me to wait when she was getting so close. I knew this time the Ignis wouldn't be interested in using fireballs, she would want to touch me and burn me alive like in the shack earlier. The idea of having my face burned off didn't sit well with me.

She was so close now that I saw a better outline of her human form instead of just a raging figure of fire. I aimed the crossbow toward her heart and held my finger on the trigger, waiting for a sign. At the sight of the crossbow, the Ignis broke out into a sprint toward me. *Anytime now*, I thought, begging for my intuition to tell me it was time. When the Ignis was an arm's length away, I was told to shoot.

The arrow sailed perfectly into her chest, right into her heart. Upon contact, the Ignis's eyes grew large, and she fell backwards onto the ground like a sack of potatoes. In shock, her hands grasped at the bolt, trying to pull it out, but the bolt was lodged so well, it wouldn't budge. The droplets of blessed water dripped from the bolt into the heart. Her heart spread the water throughout her body, and she extinguished. I stood there slack jawed, staring at a naked corpse that caused me so much pain. I couldn't believe it, but I just killed my first witch creature.

Bridgette's screams pulled me out of my reverie. The fireball that had been laid at her feet was burning up to her kneecaps and there wasn't a way to douse it. It would keep trailing her unless I killed the Ignis that cast the fireball on her. I loaded another bolt and scanned the woods to see if I could find her. The figure of fire stood across from Bridgette. I assumed she admired her work because she stood there with her arms crossed. I ran toward them, holding my crossbow out to aim, waiting for my intuition signal. When the Ignis realized I was coming, she conjured a fireball into her hand. I shot her before she could cast it. I didn't quite hit her in the heart, so she extinguished slower, but the chest shot still took her out. Upon seeing another one of their clan members dead, the remaining Ignises retreated further into the swamp.

I ran over to Bridgette and doused the flames at her feet with one of the blessed water vials from my belt. The flames died instantly with the small amount of water. I looked over at Tristan and observed that he already doused his flames. He didn't look burnt at all, as if they purposely avoided maiming him. Bridgette on the other hand had clearly been the target of the onslaught apart from me.

"Are you okay," I said to Bridgette and Tristan.

Bridgette glanced down at her legs to see the damage. It blistered like my chest, but luckily it hadn't been a long burn. Tristan looked at his own self, and I glanced at the slight singe on the edge of his pants.

"Just blistered a bit. I'll be fine," said Bridgette.

Her pants had burned up to her knee, so she was now wearing funny burnt off bermuda shorts. The fire melted her shoes onto her feet, but there would be no way to get them off right now.

"I think they're avoiding killing me." Tristan's tone was embarrassed, as if he felt he was being let off easy.

"You're probably right." I motioned to his clothes. "You're nowhere near as burnt. They weren't throwing the tracking fireballs at you."

Tristan shook his head and sighed. He looked like he had words on the tip of his tongue, but he swallowed them back and steeled his face. I gave a weak smile to reassure him, but it fell flat since I didn't know what to do to coddle him. I figured it would be pleasant to not be forced to burn or be killed. But I guess I was wrong in this instance.

"We're going to have to keep moving fast. That probably attracted a lot of attention," I said.

Bridgette winced, and I wanted to die right there. Navigating the rest of the swamp at the speed we needed to go was going to be painful for her. I didn't see any other options. I started to speak, but Bridgette cut me off.

"I'm fine. Let's move." Bridgette gritted her teeth.

With that, we began speed walking through the forest, not caring what noise we made. Our position was already compromised, so our only choice was to get to the clearing as fast as possible. There wasn't any way to sneak attack. We walked for another ten minutes, and I noticed the clearing ahead of us. But I also felt something was around us, and it wasn't right.

I froze, trying to tap into my senses and figure out what exactly I sensed. I held out my arm to stop Bridgette and Tristan. They froze in place and listened to the swamp around them. Confusion clouded both of their faces, but I shook my head and pointed to my temple. Their faces cleared as they understood this was something only I could identify. I closed my eyes and dug deeper into my brain, trying to hear my intuition. Images of stretching tree roots encompassed my mind with flashes of roots coming up from the ground grabbing at flesh.

I opened my eyes and gasped. I accepted whatever I just saw was closing in on us. My entire body tingled, experiencing the danger. Tristan and Bridgette stared at me with waiting eyes, but I didn't even know how to tell them what was coming.

"Uh, tree roots coming out of the ground. Grabbing at us," I said.

As soon as it came out my mouth, a tree root rushed behind me out of the ground. I grabbed my dagger out of its sheath and stabbed the tree root before it grabbed my ankle. The tree root reared back in what I assumed was pain and retracted. The roots began sprouting everywhere, grabbing at us. One root grabbed

Tristan's ankle and pulled him down. The plant dragged him toward the meadow. I ran after him, tripping over a root. These things had a mind of their own. I crawled, trying to get myself back up, stabbing at whatever roots grappled at my hands.

"Atalanta," said Tristan. His voice grew more distant, but I still made out a small peek of him.

Bridgette fought her own roots using her knife, but I could tell she was wearing thin.

"Bridgette!" I needed to capture her attention.

I pulled the only firebomb I had from my belt and looked at her with pleading eyes, hoping she understood. I threw the bomb toward Tristan and the evil root. Bridgette held out her hand and caught it in midair with her telekinesis. Then, she launched it directly at the root, dragging Tristan away. The bomb exploded on the root, barely missing Tristan's ankle, and engulfed the root in flames. I squinted my eyes to see Tristan breaking free and running back toward us. This time he pulled out some more firebombs, ready to throw at a moment's notice.

I continued to stab at the roots climbing at me, but I was getting so tired. They seemed to change their focus to me instead of dispersing themselves among our entire group, as if they wanted to wear me down. Through my stabbing, I felt a cool breeze rustle through the trees, knowing who was coming. The roots stopped and receded back into the ground.

The Ventus came through the trees, her black eyes boring into me. She wore the same sickening grin as she always did that I had grown to hate. She gave me a small wave, immediately sending me onto my butt. I cursed, trying to figure out what I was going to do. Knowing her, the Ventus was about to toss me all around this swamp like a rag doll. The idea of possibly breaking my ribs again wasn't appealing to me this time. Not that it had ever been appealing.

I stood up to see another witch creature following behind the Ventus. She looked like a normal human. It was honestly scary how average she looked. Her brown dress swallowed her body like she was wearing an overgrown burlap sack. The only thing that gave her away was the leaves that lined her forearms like petals. The witch pulled her brown hair back into a small bun behind her head.

Roots. This is where the roots came from.

As soon as the thought entered my mind, the root witch stretched her fingers out, and all the roots that had rescinded back into the swamp's soil sprang forth to action again. Instead of focusing on me this time, all the roots turned their attention to Bridgette. She stabbed at them once again, but there were so many that she couldn't keep up. Tristan was almost back from being dragged away, but the roots paid him no attention. My brain fogged, consumed with too much stimuli.

My intuition screamed. Distraction. Everything was a distraction.

Before I reset my eyes on the Ventus, I sailed through air, tossed by a sudden wind. I landed hard enough to knock the breath from me, but not hard enough to break a rib. The Ventus lifted me again, holding me in the air, tightening an invisible grip around my throat. My windpipe struggled to breathe in air as I watched the other witch creature stalk closer toward Bridgette. I couldn't find Tristan, though. I flailed my limbs, trying to shake loose from the Ventus's grip, but all it caused was uncontrollable laughter from her. She lowered me down until she forced me to meet her eyes like I had before.

She opened her mouth to taunt me, but I saw the glimmer of a blade come around her neck and slice it clean across. Hands clutched to her neck, the Ventus involuntarily released me from her grip. Blood spewed from the gash, covering my face. Behind, Tristan backed away, awestruck by what he had done. I pulled out my dagger and tackled the Ventus. I mounted myself on top of her and stabbed her repeatedly in the chest and the heart. Blood went everywhere as I kept stabbing.

A stab for all my pain. A stab for my ribs. A stab for all the taunting. A stab for my mother. My fury wouldn't let me stop even after she stopped wriggling under me. I kept stabbing at the corpse until Tristan's hand grabbed my shoulder, forcing me to stop.

"She's dead, Atalanta. Look," said Tristan.

I finally really looked at her. The Ventus's black eyes stared frozen into the sky. She was covered in gashes and her own blood, leaving a completely lifeless, mutilated corpse from my overkill.

A bomb exploded behind us, and I realized Bridgette must have used a firebomb on the root witch because all the roots went back to their trees. Tristan helped me up, and I tried to steel my visible shakiness. My face and body were covered in blood, but luckily, the dark leather didn't reveal the visible red stains. I expected Bridgette to gasp at me, but she just handed me a handkerchief from her pocket. I used it to wipe the Ventus's blood from my face and my dagger.

"Can you try not to do that if we find Ma—Morgana," said Tristan.

I never thought how horrific it must have been for him to watch that, imagining his mother was being overkilled instead of the Ventus. It felt like the soulless monster I had been keeping locked away just reared its ugly head. If I couldn't love him, what was stopping me from becoming a crazy murderer?

"I'll try my best." I didn't want to lie, but I felt so dirty saying it like that. I didn't know how I would react if I saw Morgana.

Tristan nodded. Without a word, he turned back toward the clearing and walked away from me.

CHAPTER TWENTY FIVE

We walked the rest of the way in silence, listening for more potential battles and enduring the tension in the air. Bridgette kept flexing her hands and staring at them. I wasn't sure if she was in pain, or if she was weighing how much more death she could cause before turning, but I decided it was best for me to avoid the discussion altogether. I didn't want her to mention the copper spear again that laid snugly in a pocket on the opposite leg from my dagger.

Tristan walked in silence, staring at the horizon line as he pulled inward. He looked lost in thought, but I imagined the horror reel playing in his mind where he watched me violently murder a witch creature. He saw me covered with blood splatter that wasn't mine. I was almost positive he was reliving it in his mind, except Morgana was on the other end of the dagger.

It was similar to the horror reel that jumped into my mind if I didn't focus on my intuition or hunting witches. Morgana lifting Mom's neck and slicing her throat. Blood seeping out of the wound. That overwhelming feeling of death. Her method matched the way Tristan sliced the throat of the Ventus. My breath caught in my throat as I stifled another panic attack.

I found it difficult to think about Morgana raising Tristan. She would have taught him all the same things my mother taught me—how to ride a bike, how to read, how to kill. It humanized her in a way I didn't like. The more human she became in my mind, the harder it was for me to imagine killing her. I wouldn't just be removing a witch creature from the world to get revenge for my mother and save humanity. I would be removing my supposed soulmate's mother.

"I'm sorry," I whispered to Tristan.

Bridgette sped up her pace to give us some extra room. She was thoughtful when it felt like most others would have stayed and lingered. I checked my hand for blood. There were a few streaks, but they were dry. I scooched as close as I could to Tristan and intertwined my fingers in his. He looked surprised but didn't let go. I realized it was wrong of me to do this, but I needed this comfort right now.

"About what," said Tristan, keeping his voice low.

"About what I did. They've just hurt me so much."

Tristan gave my hand a gentle squeeze.

"I know. That's why I'm scared about what you'll do."

The words hit me hard. I didn't know what to say. I thought this was who I was meant to be, a midnight huntress, saving humanity from the witch creatures of the world. A protector, the

Captrix, who does what everyone else can't do. This was why I accepted this heritage and was letting it define me. I expected good to come from my sacrifice.

"I know it's what you have to do. I've just never seen you so violent," said Tristan.

"And you don't know if you want to see that again." I dropped Tristan's hand.

I saw the clearing a few feet in front of us. The sacrificial table glowed in the moonlight with the faint outline of my mother's body on it. I went to continue walking, but Tristan grabbed my shoulder and made me face him. Bridgette stopped in front and turned back to observe what was happening. Tristan looked at her and then looked back at me.

"Don't do that right now." Tristan held my shoulders firm. He loosened his grip a little but forced me to stay right there.

"Do what?" I looked toward the clearing, breaking our eye contact.

Tristan let one hand go from my shoulder and put it on my face. He gently turned my head back to him, forcing eye contact once again.

"Push me away because I'm trying to understand what I just saw. Especially when we're at the end like this."

I blinked and stared into his brown eyes, wanting to feel something for him. I sensed the passion he had for me radiating from his body, but I gave Tristan nothing except cold. Bridgette started looking around for any traps to take her attention away from us.

"You know I can't love you like that," I said. "My soul—"

"I'm well aware. But that or what I just saw doesn't change

the things I'm feeling for you."

"I am only going to hurt you. Nothing good will come from this."

"I know. But I'm not ready to give up." Tristan's hand stroked my face tenderly.

I noticed something churn in the pit of my stomach. The essence of butterflies, but it was like they couldn't reach my heart, leaving a pit of sadness. I wished I'd experienced how this would have felt before the warehouse, so I could at least fake the emotion for myself.

"We have to finish this first." I pointed at the clearing.

Tristan dropped his hands and released me from his grasp. Bridgette reappeared in front of us, taking the hint that our conversation was over.

"Are we ready?" Bridgette checked her supplies remaining on her person.

Tristan also took a mental inventory of his supplies. We already used so much on the first two battles, but I hoped there wouldn't be any more surprises in the clearing. I only had a blessed water vial on my belt left apart from my crossbow, my dagger, and the copper spear. Anything I did from now on wouldn't be from a distance. It would be even more up close and personal.

"As ready as we're going to be," I said. "Let's go get Mom."

The clearing was eerily silent when we stepped in. The soft breeze that flowed by before had dwindled to nothing. There wasn't a witch creature to be seen, so I led the way with Bridgette and Tristan flanking behind me. I had my senses at full attention, trying to feel anything before it snuck up on us. But everything was quiet on that front too.

We walked up to the table, and I looked at Mom's body. I swallowed hard. I never prepared to get this far, so I wasn't sure what to do now. Her dead blue eyes stared up at me, tinged with black in the corner. I reached my fingers out and forced her eyelids closed. The gash on her throat looked less horrid now, but was caked in dried blood.

Bridgette cleared her throat behind me and walked next to the table. She took in a deep breath and grabbed Mom's hand and held it. She sniffled as her nose ran along with her tears. Tristan stood solemnly behind us and rubbed our backs for a moment.

"I didn't plan on how we would get her out of here," I said.

"I can float her out of the clearing. Then, we will figure something out." Bridgette dropped Mom's hand and gave me a weak smile. "Let's go home."

Bridgette lifted her hands, and Mom's body floated in midair. She turned and began floating the body out of the clearing. Her arms tensed as they continued to hold their position, but Bridgette held them firm. Tristan followed behind her and held out his hand for me to follow along. I couldn't move, though. Something didn't seem right. Everything was too easy, and a pit grew in my stomach full of tingling. We weren't here alone. There was no way.

Cold air tickled my ear, and I felt her breath next to my cheek.

"Hello, Atalanta," whispered the Mortia.

I turned around to face her. She wore the same cloak she always had with the hood drawn up. I didn't know what to do, so I reared back and punched her in the nose. Immediately, her hand flew up to her nose, and she looked at the blood on her fingers. Confused, but also amused, the Mortia shook her head.

Groups of Mortias began appearing all over the clearing out of thin air. Their chill covered the entire swamp, and my teeth chattered. They surrounded us with at least twenty or more crowding around. With this many lethal witches in one spot, it was impossible to figure a way out.

"Bridgette," I said. "How do you kill a Mortia?"

"You don't." Bridgette sat Mom's body on the ground and took a fighting stance.

The Mortia grinned and reached out for me. I grabbed the last blessed water vial on my belt and poured it all over her before she could reach. She laughed at me again, completely unfazed and damp. I backed away out of her grasp, and she disappeared right in front of me. The other Mortias advanced on Tristan and Bridgette. I pulled my crossbow and loaded a bolt in. I aimed at one of the Mortias at Bridgette's back that was about to touch her and pulled the trigger. The bolt sailed in the air until it made contact with the witch's side. The witch howled with pain from the bolt but didn't react to the water. Bridgette kicked behind her and knocked her down.

I loaded another bolt when my Mortia appeared behind me again. This time she grabbed my shoulder, and I felt the frost leak onto my skin. It was painful, but I had no choice but to fight through it. I lifted my crossbow and rammed it backwards into her gut. If I had no idea how to kill her, I could at least kill time. She doubled over, choking on another laugh. I honestly didn't know if she didn't endure pain, or if this was how she got through it. It was getting annoying, though. My intuition told me to point it at her forehead as I finished loading the bolt. When the Mortia came up for air, I squeezed the trigger and the arrow went clean through her skull, causing her head to split open like a watermelon.

I gagged as she fell to the ground. This time she didn't move. It was absolutely disgusting, but I figured out how to kill a Mortia. I reminded myself that I only had seventeen bolts left unless I managed to pick them up as I ran. Seventeen bolts wouldn't be enough to kill all the Mortias, but maybe it would be just enough to make an escape. I loaded another bolt into the crossbow and began scanning the clearing for another target.

Bridgette was holding her own even though the Mortias kept surrounding her. She tossed them back with her telekinesis, but I could see it wearing her down. The ends of her hair were turning white. It was a telltale sign she couldn't keep this up for much longer. I ran toward Bridgette, asking for my intuition's help. When I was only a foot away, I noticed two Mortias moving next to each other, trying to reach out and touch Bridgette. I aimed at the head of one and moved to pull the trigger, but my intuition told me to wait. I waited, fingering the trigger, until it gave me the sign to pull.

The bolt sailed through the air and collided with the first Mortia's head. Then, the bolt continued sailing through into the other Mortia where it got stuck. Both of them fell to the ground, dead. I reached Bridgette standing beside her.

"I don't know how much longer I can keep this up." I loaded another bolt in the crossbow.

"I'm not feeling well," said Bridgette. The gravity of her voice told me exactly what I needed to know.

Another Mortia appeared in front of me, and I smacked her across the face with the crossbow. She fell down but wasn't amused. I placed another bolt in her head, holding in the gag. Then, I picked the bolt off the ground, tried to ignore the substances on it, and reloaded it into the crossbow.

"You need to make a break for it. Take Mom and go," I said.

"I can't leave you here," said Bridgette.

"I'll be fine. I'm Artemis Capp's daughter."

The Mortias started to realize their numbers were dwindling. I saw a few examine the Mortia that I killed first, and they were flabbergasted. I wondered if I killed their clan leader since a few dissipated and didn't reappear. With them running, there weren't so many now. We could actually win this.

The Mortias began leaving Bridgette alone and changed their focus to me. Bridgette floated Mom's body and ran out of the clearing. I prayed they would be able to make it. I turned my focus to Tristan and saw him being frozen and defrosted by a Mortia. She was doing enough to cause him pain, but not enough to kill him. I began running toward him when I stopped dead in my tracks. Morgana entered from the back of the clearing like I thought she would and began approaching us. I shook myself out of my shock and got a foot away from Tristan. All the Mortias looked at her as if they were waiting for a sign.

"Sweetheart, don't you think it's time to come home now?" Morgana held her arms outstretched, trying to bring Tristan in for a hug.

Tristan grimaced. He shook his head at her. Morgana nodded at the Mortia, and she iced Tristan into a popsicle. I walked a few more steps while Morgana was distracted and took my shot, splitting the Mortia's head open like I had done before. As she fell to the ground, Tristan returned to his normal state, rubbing his arms to get the last bit of chill off.

"He doesn't want to go with you." I placed the crossbow on my back, knowing I wouldn't get another chance to take a shot like that, and placed my hand over the copper spear delicately.

The remaining Mortias around us disappeared. Morgana, Tristan, and I were left in the clearing alone. Morgana walked until she was five feet away from us and stopped. Her eyes twitched with rage. She clasped her hands in front of her so tight her knuckles turned white. She looked at Tristan again, ignoring me.

"Tristan, it's time to go," said Morgana. Her voice was shrill with anger.

Her forehead wrinkles deepened, and I had the overwhelming sense that she was on the verge of changing. I just needed to tip her over the edge. It would be less horrific for me to kill Morgana in front of Tristan if she was a Venefica.

"I'm not leaving with you," said Tristan.

He moved closer to me. Was it possible for me to send him the message of my plan? I thought I needed to try. I didn't want him to assume I was using him for my own gain, but I couldn't dwell on that too much or I would convince myself that I was using him.

"Why?" Morgana remained in place, refusing to close the gap between us.

I saw Tristan giving her a response, but I closed my eyes to drop into my mind. I knew I needed to be gentle if I wanted to give him a message, so he wouldn't end up with head pain like Bridgette did when I sent her a message before. Blocking out all the sound around me, I settled into a dark silence. Then, I imagined myself looking over the clearing with a bird's eye view, zooming in on Tristan arguing with Morgana. I focused on him and tried to imagine giving him a soft whisper in his ear.

Can you hear me? I thought, hoping it would translate.

In my mind, I observed Tristan flinch a little. It must be working. *This might hurt.* Recognition crossed his face, and I saw him listening to a response from Morgana. I tried to let the images flow easily, but they flashed out of my mind uncontrolled. I bombarded Tristan with images of us kissing and holding hands. Images of Morgana transforming into a Venefica tumbled out, and I kept flooding his mind with my plans. I was overwhelming him too fast. I heard him scream and snapped out of my mindset. When I opened my eyes, Tristan was doubled over with his hands planted to his temples, and I felt awful. I had no idea how powerful sending messages was, and I was playing without understanding it. I felt so guilty, but I knew this would be my only chance to use it to my advantage before Morgana figured out what I was doing.

I reached out to Tristan and wrapped my arms around him, trying to help him lean up. I put on a scowl and looked at Morgana with disgust.

"What are you doing to him," I said. I used all the scorn I could muster up. I needed this to work.

Morgana took one step closer, but confusion clouded the anger on her face.

"I haven't done anything to him," said Morgana. "I wouldn't."

I helped Tristan lean back up and rubbed his temples. The affectionate touch drove Morgana wild. Her hair finally began turning black with splotches of white. I pushed Tristan's hair back.

"Are you okay?" I wanted to come across as a doting

girlfriend, but I also really wanted to know if my message had scrambled his brain.

Tristan looked me in the eye and then back at Morgana. To my surprise, he gave me a light kiss on the forehead and then pressed his forehead to mine.

"I'll be okay," said Tristan. He lowered his voice for a moment, so only I heard. "Do what you need to do."

I gave him a kiss, interlocking our lips together. Nothing came of it. It was soft and moist, like I wanted it to be. Kissing Tristan was easy and seemed like second nature. The only downside was that it felt so empty. I held it out for as long as I could until a howl came from Morgana. I broke the kiss and turned to see that her transformation was complete.

CHAPTER TWENTY SIX

MORGANA'S HAIR TURNED COMPLETELY black along with her eyes. Deep set wrinkles crowded all over her furious face. I pulled the copper spear from my pocket and expanded it.

Tristan and I separated as she started yelling things in Latin. I prepared myself for the blood boiling, but I seemed fine. Nothing happened until my entire body collapsed. I dropped the spear and stared at the clear sky while I convulsed. My eyes blinked rapidly, and I continued my uncontrollable seizure. My vision grew hazy as a small terrified wispy bunny escaped from my mouth.

The pain of my soul leaving my body as I seized was white hot and unlike anything else I had ever experienced. It wasn't like having your blood boiled, more like an overwhelming sense of dread and helplessness. My innards were being burned as she sucked my soul out of my body. I could feel every drop of

Morgana's anger. She pinned me with this strange spell, leaving me with no control over my body. My worst fear was realized. I was going to die trying to save humanity, like all my other ancestors. Worst of all, I was going to die soulless.

I tried to turn my head to the side, so I would see Tristan and tell him goodbye, but my head remained frozen, staring up at the night sky. Even though I was terrified of dying, in this moment, a stunning sense of peace consumed me. Soft sounds of my intuition whispered to me it would be alright. I trusted it like I had grown to over the past few days. I forced my eyes to stop blinking and held them closed, so I could die in my own darkness.

Morgana's scream disturbed my peace. My mouth flew open, and my bunny jumped in, re-nestling herself in my body. My body felt like jello, but it was mine again. I leaned up and watched the copper spear run through Morgana's body with Tristan on the other end. Using a bit of strength I had left, I stood up and saw Morgana die. Tristan still held the spear and stared at the body in shock. I came up behind him and forced his hands to release the spear. I drew him into a hug as sobs rocked his body. Tristan killed his own mother to save me. That was a deep love I didn't understand and didn't believe. I held him tighter and rubbed his back as his tears dampened the shoulder of my undershirt. After a few moments, Tristan released me and wiped his eyes.

I pulled the spear out of Morgana's body, praying Tristan would look away. He stayed fixated, though, regarding my every move. I retracted the spear and placed it back in my pocket. I reached for Tristan's belt and pulled off the last firebomb and blessed water vial he had left. We backed up a few steps, and

I threw the firebomb onto Morgana's body. Immediately, she incinerated, leaving behind gray dust. I poured the water vial out and kneeled down. Drying the vial with my clothes to the best of my ability, I filled it with Morgana's dust. I recapped it and handed it to Tristan. As much as I hated Morgana, I hated Tristan's pain more. He deserved something to remember his mother by. The good parts, at least.

Tristan stared at the vial for a moment and placed it in his pocket. I grabbed his hand, and we began making our way out of the godforsaken clearing. This place, this swamp, had brought everyone so much pain, suffering, and grief. I wanted to light it on fire and watch the flames engulf the entire area. I desired the fire to take all the negatives with it, to let something new grow. But I couldn't. I had to leave this place stained with blood and misery. I hurt bad for this swamp, but not as bad as I felt for Bridgette.

We found her sitting on the ground next to Mom's body just outside the clearing where we fought the Ventus. She looked haggard and tired, like she was ready to let go. Half of her hair was black, and black tinged the corner of her eyes. Upon seeing me, a visible hunger enveloped her, and she began licking her lips.

"Bridgette. It's me," I said. "We're okay. Everything is okay."

She shook her head as her eyes darkened more. Tristan got closer to her and touched her arm. I backed away a few steps, not wanting to tempt her anymore. I knew she could smell my broken soul. The rest of it must have been calling to her like a swan song.

"Remember who you are. You love Atalanta," said Tristan. "We won the battle."

"We can go home now," I said, continuing to back away.

Bridgette's eyes cleared and returned to their beautiful brown color. The wrinkles that had deepened on her face refilled with collagen. She looked like normal Bridgette again. She almost looked like the same woman that had opened her cottage to me a few days earlier, but there seemed to be a lot more behind her eyes now than there was then.

"What about Morgana," said Bridgette.

I knew why she was asking the question, but it still hung thick in the air. My mouth was dry, not sure how to tell her without hurting her feelings more. No matter what I said, it would be callous in my eyes.

"She's dead," said Tristan. His words were matter of fact, as if he read something out of a history textbook. But it was enough to give her context.

"I'm sorry." Tears spilled over Bridgette's eyes.

She stood up and hugged the both of us tightly until she leaned back and looked at us, smiling through her tears. Then, Bridgette rubbed Tristan's back, taking in the sacrifice he made to save us.

"Let's all go home now," said Bridgette.

Tristan and I nodded. We began the long process of taking Mom's body back to Bridgette's blue sedan at the other end of the swamp. When we reached the car, we delicately placed her body in the trunk. As I closed the trunk, Tristan took my hand, and we stood there for a moment in silence, watching the sun rise over the horizon, bringing in a new day.

CHAPTER TWENTY SEVEN

We buried my mother, Artemis Renee Capp, the next day on Bridgette's property. Given the severity of her death and the way she looked, I thought this was the best idea. There would be no way for me to explain the wounds to anyone without revealing this whole secret world I lived in. Even though it might have been selfish, I also liked the idea of having her close by. Bridgette made a small cross out of tree limbs she found in the woods. I carved 'ARC' into the limb, and we placed it at the head of the grave for the quiet funeral. I didn't know any of Mom's other colleagues to tell them what had happened. I assumed they would find out soon enough and would come find me. But right now, in this small grief-stricken peace, I was with the ones I cared about. I was with the ones that risked their lives for me just to see this happen.

I didn't know where I wanted to go. Running off to California didn't seem right anymore, and any desire I had to do that had died for now. I didn't have anywhere to stay, either, making me a depressed drifter without my mom. I think Bridgette could sense the change in how I felt because, the day after the funeral, she sat me down in the kitchen.

The kitchen filled with the smells of baking as Bridgette spent most of the day coming up with concoctions to heal our bodies faster. I sat at the table thumbing through the Captrix encyclopedia, seeing if there were any entries I could add when Bridgette grabbed my hand. She startled me out of my reading, and I looked at her with confusion.

"Is everything okay?" I worried she was going to tell me it was time to leave.

"You know you can stay here as long as you want, right?" Bridgette gave my hand a soft squeeze. "I understand the couch isn't much, but this is your home too now."

I nodded and let the tears of relief flow down my face. Even though I had only known Bridgette for a few days, I loved her. It was comforting to have someone that knew my mom and that I could talk to. Living with her for a little while was everything I could hope for.

"However, if you don't want to stay, that's fine too. You deserve to have the life you want, Atalanta." Bridgette gave me a sad smile.

"But what about my duty?"

"Your mother wouldn't agree with me, but I think having to save the whole world all the time is a lot to ask of an eighteen-year-old."

"But—"

Bridgette held her hand in the air to silence me.

"You don't have to make a decision now. I just want you to hear from someone that you have a choice. It's okay to change your mind."

The idea of having a choice in my destiny was mind-boggling, but I didn't feel capable of making a decision against Mom's wishes for now. I wiped my wet face with my hands and sniffled.

"I want to stay here with you for now and give this Captrix thing a shot. At least for a little while. If that's okay?"

"Of course. I would love to have you." Bridgette nodded and rose to take some pastries out of the oven.

A day after Bridgette's and my talk, Tristan decided to go home, so we went back to Morgana's herb shop. They lived in a two-bedroom apartment over the shop that Tristan grew up in. We checked the inside of the shop and saw nothing was disturbed. The herbs and potions still sat still in their jars. In the front of the shop, the various teas they sold to the public lined the shelves, ready to be distributed. Content with the look of the store, Tristan walked me to the back into the alley where metal stairs took us up to the apartment.

Tristan opened the door to the apartment and led me into the home. It was small, but cozy with tones of black, white, and brown. Morgana definitely favored a neutral color palette when it came to her home design style. On the wall where the television was hung, a fake fireplace sat with a wide mantle. Stacks of books and various knick-knacks lined the shelf, creating a lived-in design touch. Tristan scooted all the decor over and placed the vial of Morgana's ashes on the far corner of the mantle. I rubbed his back as he let out his tears. I, more than anyone, knew what he was dealing with right now. Just because his mother killed mine didn't make his feelings invalid. It just left us in a messed-up grief pool where all the wrongs our families had done to each other didn't make a right. It left us lonely, waiting for a day to dawn where we wouldn't feel so empty. I gave him a hug and held him as we both cried for the people we lost, wondering how we would manage to go on without them.

§

I held the encyclopedia close to my chest and took it with a pen outside to my mother's grave. The air was humid and muggy, like normal, but the temperature cooled to a pleasant summer sunset, so the heat was bearable. I looked at the limb cross, checking to see if the twine still held the marker together. A smidgen of the twine appeared frayed, but other than that, everything seemed intact. I planned on getting something more substantial to mark the grave soon, so I didn't have to worry about checking it every day.

I sat the Captrix encyclopedia on the grass and took a seat next to it. The yellowed grass remained already worn down into a butt sized circle, used to me sitting on it. I came out here almost every day to clear my head and to try to feel like I was moving in the right direction. It had been a few weeks since the swamp battle, and I still felt lost. I wasn't sure if I was ever going to be the Captrix my mother was, but I thought I would give it a try.

"Hey, Mom." I pulled the old book into my lap and held the pen tightly in my hand to prevent it from shaking.

Today was the day I decided to make my first entry into the Captrix encyclopedia. I pondered what I chose to add for the past few days while also starting a journal of my hunts, writing in all of my experiences over the past few weeks. The journal wasn't for me to look back on things I've done, but I considered it would be helpful for the next Captrix. I never read anything that didn't show unwavering confidence, so I thought it would be nice to show we didn't all have it figured out. I also annotated the ritual book from my collection with what a broken triangle actually meant, refusing to let anyone else make that same mistake again.

I flipped open the book to the section on Mortias. I skimmed the entry to see what it said about killing them, but there were only comments about how they were hard to kill and disappeared before you finished the job. There was no strategy for defeating them, or no one had ever thought about writing it down. Clicking the pen, I held it close to the page while holding my breath. I hesitated, feeling impostor syndrome creep in. I fought the voice in my head telling me I wasn't good enough or that I didn't want this. Right now, this was what I wanted to do, and nothing was going to stop me. I began writing my first entry into the encyclopedia.

> *To kill a Mortia, you must chop off or blow up her head. Since they apparate so quickly, I recommend using a distraction technique. Hand to hand combat doesn't really hurt them, but it is good enough to distract them for a limited time, so you can perform the final blow. My recommendation is to punch them in the stomach or the nose. When they are doubled*

over, shoot a bolt straight into their head. It will split open their head like a watermelon and be absolutely disgusting, but they will be dead.

I blew on the ink to dry it into the pages and closed the book. I smoothed the front of the cover, still wrestling with this idea that this book was mine. It was mine to care for, and now my responsibility to keep adding to the pages. But in this silence, I thought maybe for a moment my mother was proud of me. That was enough to keep me going during this time.

I heard the sound of a clunking car driving up the driveway. I looked up as Tristan slammed the car door of the old car. He gave me a wide grin and pushed his shaggy hair back out of his eyes. Tristan bought the car with the money Morgana left behind, and even though it was a white nineties Toyota Corolla, it remained his crown jewel and showed in the sparkle in his brown eyes. I stood up with the book and began closing the distance between us.

"You know, we've got a case." Tristan reached out to take the book and pen from me.

He sat the book and pen on the roof of the car and gave me a hug. I leaned back from him in wonder, but he kept his arms around me, holding me close.

"A case," I said, giving him my signature questioning look.

"I think it's a Brujadan, actually."

"Are you sure? The last Brujadan I dealt with didn't end up being one." I winced at the memory.

"I swear it. Eating all the babies' insides and everything. Worse, I think it's hiding out in that warehouse."

I groaned. Going into an abandoned warehouse, especially that one, was the last thing I really wanted to be doing that evening. However, it would be interesting since it was the first post-swamp hunt I would be doing with Tristan. We had decided to remain partners in witch hunting, while navigating our strange relationship.

"Let me go get my stuff and let Bridgette know." I grabbed the book and pen from the top of the car, then entered the cottage to put on my gear.

I sauntered inside, put on my huntress uniform, and packed it with all the supplies I needed. The supplies included plenty of copper and silver, just in case things went awry. I endured a line of questions from Bridgette, but I reassured her that Tristan and I could handle it. She followed me to the door like a parent sending their kid to prom and gave Tristan a light wave before closing the door behind me. Before I finished walking off the porch, the door flew back open.

"Forgetting something?" In Bridgette's palm glittered my lucky copper penny. She wore a smirk as she dropped the penny into my outstretched hand. "Figured you would probably need it."

"Thank you." I clutched the penny tight and slipped it into my pocket. I hoped this time I wouldn't have to shove it down any witch creature's throat. The penny and I had been through enough the past couple of weeks.

"Be careful. Call me if you need me." Bridgette gave me a serious look, then smiled at Tristan and I before going back into the house.

I walked off the porch where Tristan was still sitting on

the hood, waiting for me.

When I got close, he pulled me into a deep kiss. It was nice, but I still felt absolutely nothing. Not even a quickened heartbeat. In the back of my mind, I sensed a feeling of emptiness creeping up inside, but I pushed it back down.

"You know I don't feel anything when you do that," I said. The guilt of leading Tristan on ate at me. We agreed to try this weird relationship thing, but my broken soul remained uncooperative.

"I know," he said, grabbing my hand. He ran his thumb across the back in a calming gesture that I appreciated.

"I just don't know how this is going to work. It doesn't seem fair to you."

"I promise you two things."

I nodded back at him, eager to hear them.

"I promise I will be okay no matter how this works out. You don't have to feel guilty about what we're doing here. If it gets too hard, I'll let you know."

I swallowed hard. It amazed me how this person could read my mind like that. He recognized my deepest fears, even if I didn't verbalize them. Was this what a soulmate was really like?

"I also promise that we will figure this soul thing out. We'll go to the ends of the earth to put you back together."

I squeezed his hand. Bridgette and I had already been researching how I could get a piece of my soul back, but found no concrete evidence. From what we read, no one had ever put their soul back together, but I still wanted to remain optimistic since we decided it would be our main focus over the next few weeks to find some useful information.

I leaned up and gave Tristan a quick peck on the cheek, knowing he would appreciate it. Even if we didn't stay together like this, I felt we would end up being best friends. He was my supposed soulmate after all. Tristan let go of my hand and took a dramatic bow, pointing me to the passenger side of his chariot.

"Madame," said Tristan.

I let out a small giggle as he opened the car door for me. "My liege," I said.

Tristan held out his hand like a butler and assisted me into the car. My giggle grew louder as I couldn't hold it back anymore. Tristan made his way around the car and into the driver's side. I rolled my eyes at him as I giggled, so he wouldn't get too big of a head.

"Now, madame, let's go hunting," said Tristan.

We backed out of Bridgette's driveway and drove into the sunset in the direction of the warehouse to find a Brujadan. He drove with one hand on the steering wheel and one hand reaching across the console to hold mine. It was in this moment, this small nugget of time riding in a nineties Toyota Corolla with Tristan at my side, I hoped, somehow, everything would be okay.

ACKNOWLEDGEMENTS

Thank you so much for reading The Midnight Huntress. Without your readership, this book wouldn't be successful, which is all I've ever wanted for almost two years. To be honest, I have dreamed of becoming a published author since I was a girl writing about having magical powers in elementary school. Writing, editing, and publishing this book has been a long journey, but I wouldn't change it for the world. This book is the manifestation of one of my biggest dreams coming true.

There are so many people to thank for making this book possible, but I want to begin with my mother, Tammy. This book is dedicated to you because without you, it never would've happened. My entire life, my mom has given me paranormal books to read and fostered my love for reading this genre. She also exposed me to some of my favorite shows, *Buffy the Vampire Slayer*, *Charmed*, *Lost Girl*, among many others, that serve as nuggets of inspiration for this book. Without her, there is no telling what genre I would have written for my first book or if I would have written one at all. Also, she is one of the first people who listened to the concept for this book and didn't write me off as crazy. Instead, she nodded her head in the kitchen, told me it sounded interesting, and encouraged me to write it.

Second, I need to thank my husband, Shawn, who has been with me for every part of this book and encouraged me through two NaNoWriMos and hard editing days. Every time I second guess myself, his favorite line is "don't." He is also my best marketing tool and tells everyone about my book wherever he goes. Thank you, Shawn, for your unconditional support and your belief in me that I could do this.

A big thank you to my sister, Melanie, who not only answered in a text what happens when you shoot something in close range with a crossbow, but she beta read this book for me too. Melanie also was the first person I ever showed the first draft of the opening chapter to. She told me it sounded cool and encouraged me to stick with it. Trust me, the opening chapter to this book was way different from what you see published, so the fact that she liked it when it was rough around the edges says a lot about sisterly love.

I can't end these acknowledgements without mentioning my editor, Whitney at Whitney's Book Works, my book cover designer, Stone Ridge Books, my beta readers, and my writer friend community. Thank you all so much. Also, a special thank you to my viewers on Twitch who have seen me write and edit most of this book live.

Finally, my dogs, Kayla and Tilly, thank you for sitting with me for all my writing days and walking by to check on me and get pets when I'm at my desk. You both make living a little brighter and I can't thank God enough for choosing me to be your dog mom.

CHAPTER ONE

I STOOD IN THE dark clearing, feeling the waterlogged ground of the swamp beneath me. Trees surrounded the meadow like a cage with no exit in sight. A sharp breeze whipped through the trees and my oversized t-shirt, making my teeth rattle. I wrapped my arms around myself, chilled to the bone as my bare legs and feet froze in the night air. The full moon remained high in the sky, illuminating one particular spot in the clearing. I blinked and focused my eyes on the highlighted spot.

In front of me, a long wooden table laid in the moonlight with shackles and chains tumbling over the sides. I stared at the chains, wondering what they were for, and got the overwhelming sense I had been in this clearing before. I was supposed to know what this table meant.

I walked closer to the table, cold water squishing between

my toes, and tried to remember what I didn't know. In a blink, my mother, Artemis, appeared with her blonde pixie cut, shackled to the table, peering into my confused eyes. She wore her huntress outfit made of black leather pants, a corset, and a white undershirt, so it made little sense to me why she was on this table and not fighting witch creatures.

Then, I remembered why I had been in this clearing before. This was the place she was going to die.

"Atalanta, help me," said Mom, reaching her chained hands out to me. I broke out into a run as she pulled at the shackles in an escape attempt.

In the corner of my vision, I saw a silver pen knife floating in the air and racing toward her, faster than I could run. I panicked and quickened my pace, even though I realized there would be no way to beat the floating blade. The knife reached her first, leaving me petrified almost a foot away. The shackles pinned my mother's hands to her side as the blade touched her throat. I tried to close the distance, but couldn't move.

"No!" I tried again to close the gap, but my feet remained stuck in the ground.

The blade pierced Mom's throat and slid across, creating a huge gash. Blood began spurting out everywhere, almost reaching me. Her hands suddenly came loose from her chains, allowing her to grasp her neck as her blood flowed over her fingers, dripping red dots onto the table.

"Mom!" I fought harder to get loose. I had to save her.

She fell over onto the table, her body growing lifeless as the bleeding slowed. My feet came loose, but before I could move, a hand grabbed me from behind and pulled me backward. I screamed, needing my voice to change the outcome.

"Atalanta, wake up," said a familiar voice. They continued to pull me toward them. "You're having a bad dream."

I snapped awake, almost colliding with Bridgette's face. She leaned back just in time to avoid the collision. She held my sweaty hand and looked at me with sorrow in her eyes. I felt tears form at the corner of my eyes, a consequence of having a nightmare, and wiped them away with my free hand. Perspiration mixed with salty tears as I tried to slow my panicked breathing with deep breaths.

"I'm sorry. I didn't mean to wake you." I leaned up on my makeshift couch bed and ignored the aches overcoming my body.

I had been staying with Bridgette, my mom's best friend, ever since Mom died in the swamp battle six months ago and witch creatures turned my life upside down. With no home to go to and no family, Bridgette invited me to stay in her cottage as long as I wanted. She didn't have a spare room, so we turned her couch and part of the living room into my bedroom. Unfortunately, my "bedroom" was also next to Bridgette's room, meaning my terrible nightmares also kept her awake.

"It's okay. Were you having the nightmare again?" Bridgette rubbed my hand as she sat on the edge of the couch.

She secured her long, brown, wavy hair into a knot on the top of her head with a black elastic. Little pieces of gray frizz stuck out on the edges, showing the hairstyle had a few hours of sleep before I woke her. However, Bridgette's brown eyes with silver flecks were shadowed by her dark circles. She looked about as tired as I was. I felt guilty for keeping her up.

"It was a little bit different this time, but yeah." I squeezed her hand back. I wanted her to feel like I was okay, so maybe she would go back to sleep.

"That's the third time this week." Bridgette let go of my hand to rub her eyes. "You've been having the same dream for six months."

"I know. I'm sorry." I closed my eyes, trying to figure out something better to say.

She was wrong about it being the third time. I had endured a similar version of watching my mother die every day this week. Evidently, the past few times, I was quiet.

I tried numerous times to not end up in a dream hellscape where my mother kept dying in front of me, but every time I drifted to sleep, I was in the swamp where she died. Most of the time, I couldn't reach her before the knife due to freezing or my lack of speed. Sometimes, I spent the dream fighting witch creatures and got to her right as she took her last breath. No matter what I did or tried, she kept ending up as dead as she remained in reality.

"I didn't mean I was upset. I'm worried about you."

Bridgette looked at me with so much concern that it reminded me of how my mom used to look at me when she had the time to. Most of her life was spent in and out of the house hunting witch creatures rather than being a doting mother. Even though our relationship was strained, an ache throbbed inside of me.

I missed her. And I was the reason she was dead.

I swallowed hard to keep the tears contained.

"What time is it," I asked, trying to distract myself. I pushed my fingers through my medium length blonde hair and combed the nightmare induced tangles out.

Bridgette raised an eyebrow and handed me my phone from the coffee table, deciding to let my diversion pass. Then, she slid my feet closer to the back cushion so she could sit further in on the brown leather couch. I clicked on my phone screen and squinted at the bright light. Through squinted eyes, I read three am, as known as the witching hour. How convenient. I laid the phone down on the couch and glanced back up at Bridgette. She still watched me with concern.

"I'll be fine. I promise. You should go get a few more hours of sleep." I gave her a weak smile.

"Are you sure?" My facade didn't fool Bridgette. Even though she wasn't my mother, she could see through me better than I gave her credit for.

"I'll be fine. I might read some before I go back to sleep."

"Maybe you should text Tristan. Isn't he normally up now? With the whole flipped sleep schedule to help hunt witches?"

I stifled a laugh. The witch creature world had been quiet for the past few months, so Tristan, Bridgette, and I weren't hunting much of anything. His sleep schedule would still be flipped for me. That is, if Tristan continued staying up late for no reason.

"I'll think about it. Go get some sleep. We can talk some more in the morning," I said, gesturing toward Bridgette's bedroom.

She yawned as she tried to come up with something else to say, but after a second large yawn, Bridgette decided not to fight me anymore. She lifted herself off the couch and walked half asleep back to her bedroom.

I glanced at the phone again, trying to decide if I wanted to text Tristan. If someone asked me about a month ago, I would have immediately said yes. He was my best friend and had been there for me ever since we fought the swamp battle that killed both of our mothers. We even tried dating, even though I was missing a chunk of my soul, so I couldn't love him romantically.

I broke it off a little over a month ago because it got too complicated and decided to keep my distance for a while. We hadn't seen each other in weeks. Before, I would text him every time I dreamed this nightmare. This was the actual reason he had started staying up this late, but it seemed unfair of me to expect him to always be there.

Rubbing my eyes, I tried to convince myself I wasn't tired anymore. I knew I needed some more sleep, but I couldn't bear to watch my mother die again in my dreams tonight. Pulling my knees to my chest, I laid my tired head on them. I hated my stupid brain for forcing me to live that nightmare over and over. My eyes stayed closed for a few moments, and I felt myself drifting off back to sleep.

I jumped off the couch, jerking myself awake, and went over to my trunk next to Bridgette's fireplace. I turned the key I left in the lock and began rummaging through all of my witch creature books. Being a witch huntress required a lot of back studying that I had refused to do before one attacked me. Since taking up the duty, I decided it was time to learn as many creatures as possible. With my voice inside my head, also known as my intuition, to guide me, I had been researching a ton of creatures while hunting was slow. I touched the books and asked my intuition which one I should read. My mind's voice was silent for a second, and then said, "*Sleep.*"

I huffed and picked a book on my own. Pulling out the

Captrix encyclopedia, I decided to continue reading more entries from my ancestors about their own hunts. I returned to the couch with my book and opened it to a new letter I hadn't read before. I glanced at the Latin names of the listed witch creatures, but they all ran together due to my tired eyes. My head drooped again as I focused on a bare entry without many Captrix comments. I bolted upward, rubbed my eyes, and tried to read the first sentence. Before I could read past the beginning sentence, I felt drawn back to sleep. This time, there was no fighting it.

LOVED THIS BOOK?

Leave a review on

amazon

or

goodreads

Reviews help authors more than you know!

LOVE THE CAPTRIX WORLD AND CAN'T GET ENOUGH?

Be the first to know when the next book is coming +

Short Story From Bridgette's POV

Behind-the-Scenes Details

Book Soundtracks

Merch Discounts

And More!

SIGN UP FOR MY NEWSLETTER:

www.shelbymccraley.com/members

ABOUT THE AUTHOR

Shelby McCraley lives in coastal Georgia with her husband and two rescue dogs. When she's not writing or spending time with her family, Shelby loves watching a good fantasy movie or playing video games. Her favorite things are a good cup of coffee on a rainy morning, dog snuggles, and pasta with red sauce. Before publishing her novels, Shelby has been the author of a writing blog called *The Writing Addict* since 2017, where she shares writing tips, book recommendations, and some of her shorter works.

Get first looks of her upcoming books and behind the scenes content by subscribing to her newsletter:

shelbymccraley.com/members

instagram.com/shelbymccraley
tiktok.com/authorshelbymccraley
facebook.com/thewritingaddict